A NOBLE RESOLVE

A Regency Romance

Sara Blayne

Zebra Books
Kensington Publishing Corp.

http://www.zebrabooks.com

ZEBRA BOOKS are published by

Kensington Publishing Corp.
850 Third Avenue
New York, NY 10022

First Printing: June, 1998
10 9 8 7 6 5 4 3 2 1

Printed in the United States of America

In loving memory of W. G. Longacre.

And with love to Aunt Beverly, who has been a sympathetic listener and a dear friend.

Chapter 1

The attic room beneath the eaves basked serenely in the afternoon sun. It was a cozy room made comfortable with a blue braided rug and worn furniture. An overstuffed armchair, an oak bureau, a neat secretary, a cot made bright with a quilt, and a small round worktable with two straight-backed chairs shared the meager space with various and sundry personal items—a workbasket, still half-full of socks, a pair of nankeens, and a shirt in need of mending, all of which had long since outlived their usefulness to any of the Powell brood who had once worn them; well-worn books, the pages marked with smudges and turned-down corners and some hiding ancient treasures of pressed flowers; old journals brimming with entries made in a neat, flowing hand; watercolors, pastels, and sketch pads; a stack of much used, outdated issues of *La Belle Assemblée;* and, in one corner, a basketful of assorted feathers.

To Josephine Louise Powell, the room seemed cluttered with memories. Indeed, she fancied she could hear the murmur of voices and the echoes of giggling laughter reverberating like disembodied souls in the silence. For her the room was haunted, a perpetual reminder that all of her numerous siblings had long since grown up and removed from Greensward—scattered, like seeds borne on the wind.

Even her dearest sister Lucy, she thought, staring out the window at Lathrop Castle crouched atop the heather-covered hill. Lucy, the writer of Gothic Romances. How eager she had been to travel in order to gather research for her writing! And, now, with Napolean banished to St. Helena and the war in the Americas at an end, the Duke and Duchess of Lathrop had departed on a tour of the Continent, taking Patrick, the seven-year-old heir, and Emma and Evalina, the five-year-old twins, with them.

Aside from her mama and papa and the servants, Josephine was left to wander the now quiet halls alone, to sit in the Summer Room with her needlework and tatting, to read her beloved books or to stare out over the rolling fields of Greensward and dream of a world that had passed her by. At nineteen, she had never been farther from the family manor than the two miles to the village, and now it looked as if she never would, she thought with an unexpectedly bitter pang of regret.

"Now you are being absurd," she scolded out loud to the frowning reflection of herself in the looking glass hung on one wall. "And exceedingly selfish. It is hardly Papa's fault that he was thrown off Ajax and broke his arm. Indeed, Josephine Louise Powell, you may be sure he would much prefer he had not. He is in a great deal of discomfort, and here you are, crying over what cannot be helped. You should know by now that you will very likely spend the rest of your life doing precisely what you have always done."

Josephine experienced a surge of rebellion at such a

bleak prospect. She had long ago accepted the fact that she was of necessity restricted in her activities by a regrettably fragile constitution. She had borne her frequent bouts with illness, her proscribed existence of quiet pursuits, her enforced stay at home with an outward show of patience that hid a fierce yearning for something more. Of all the Powell brood, Josephine was the one most given to intro-spection, and in her heart she knew that she would surely die inside if she allowed herself to dwindle away into sedate spinsterhood without ever having gone anywhere or done anything at all.

She was not precisely an invalid, after all, she told herself as, hugging to her breast a pillow bearing the inscription, "A dreamer of dreams," which Lucy had stitched at thir-teen, she gazed out over the green, rolling fields of Green-sward. Except for her propensity to develop inflammations of the throat, suffer colds, and run a high fever at the least little thing, she managed to rub along well enough. In spite of all her mama's doubts, she had learned to ride a horse, had she not? And though she might not be blessed with the strength and endurance of her more robust sib-lings, she knew she had grown stronger the past few years. She had not been ill once that winter, save for a minor sniffle now and again, she reminded herself with an uncon-scious jut of her delicately molded chin, a gesture of defi-ance which gave way almost instantly to a wry grimace.

She had not, that was, until only a month past, at the first dawning of spring, when she had had the misfortune to be caught out by a sudden rain shower and as a conse-quence had taken to her bed with a wracking cough and a fever that had left her absurdly pulled.

It had, as a matter of fact, caused her to miss her come-out in London for the second Season in a row, an eventual-ity that would undoubtedly preclude her from ever making her bow in society. At twenty, after all, she would be considered perilously close to being on the shelf.

That disappointment, strangely enough, had not loomed nearly so large as that which had caused her to seek seclusion in the attic room until she should be able to face her mama with at least a semblance of her usual calm acceptance. She had never allowed herself to believe she would actually have a Season in London, let alone a husband. Indeed, the latter would be hoping for too much. A prolonged stay at Harrogate, however, was quite another proposition altogether. A few weeks at the fashionable watering hole was, in fact, precisely what the doctor had ordered for what he described as Josephine's generally low spirits. It was the first and only prescription from a doctor that had ever presented itself as something remotely agreeable, and Josephine had come immediately to look forward to it.

It was only Harrogate, she told herself. She would not even have been stepping a foot outside the bounds of Yorkshire, but it was the closest she had ever come to so much as a glimpse of what lay beyond the rolling fields of Greensward. It was a pitifully small excursion when one took into account that the twins had yet to return from the Americas, that Francie and her husband Harry had sailed to the Orient, and that Lucy and Phillip were even then touring the Continent; but it had been her adventure, her *only* adventure, and now even that had proven little more than a wisp of a dream that vanishes before the sudden dawning of reality.

Lady Bancroft could not possibly leave Greensward, not now, when the earl needed her. Indeed, Josephine would be the last person ever to ask such a thing of her mama. Nor would she herself wish to abandon her papa just when he would welcome having someone around to read to him or bring him fresh flowers from the garden or perform any of the numerous other small tasks that she could do to help lift him from the doldrums. It was utterly selfish to even think of herself at a time such as this.

Still, she could not quite stifle a sigh at the thought that she had wished very much to go someplace she had never been before—almost anyplace away from Greensward would have done equally well, since she had never been anywhere at all—simply to see new faces, smell new scents, hear new sounds, experience something out of her dreadfully ordinary world. Going to Harrogate had seemed such a small thing to ask.

That, of course, was hardly to the point, Josephine reflected, laying the hand-stitched pillow back in its place on the cot. The facts of the matter were her dearest papa *had* been thrown from a green colt; her mama would naturally wish to be at Greensward with him; and Josephine would of course remain here with her. She must simply resign herself to the inevitable: Harrogate would have to be put off indefinitely.

Having viewed the matter in all its logical ramifications, Josephine deliberately squared her shoulders. It was time she went below, to pretend that she did not mind that another door had been closed to her or that she felt old beyond her years, as if her youth had been sapped from her while she waited for something of moment to happen to her.

Enough, Josephine Louise Powell, she told herself, ashamed that she had been allowing herself to wallow in self-pity. She must naturally be grateful that her circumstances were comfortable enough to allow her the luxury of an uneventful existence. A regular reader of *Blackwood's Magazine* and the "Political Register," she was acutely aware that there were far too many souls in England struggling merely to survive in these uncertain times. Plagued by unemployment and low wages, the inevitable by-products of peace in an economy ravaged by years of war, the poor were fleeing in droves to America in search of a better life. She did not mean to be an ungrateful wretch, and yet she could not but envy them in some small way. They, at least, were willing to risk all in pursuit of a dream, no matter that desperation drove them to it. How she despised her own weakness, which kept her a virtual prisoner in her own comfortable surrounds!

But then, she reminded herself with a sardonic twist of her lovely lips, that was only another form of feeling sorry for herself, and, more than anything, she detested being viewed as an object for pity. "Poor Lady Josephine, the sickly one of the Earl of Bancroft's seven children." She had heard that one often enough in her nineteen years, as if she were no more than the runt of the litter, she thought sardonically. Her fragile constitution was humiliation enough without having to suffer the added onus of hearing it constantly pointed out to her, especially as it was often assumed her understanding was as debilitated as her physical being.

Josephine, however, was neither a child nor an idiot. Thanks to her dearest papa, who had spared no effort to engage her interest in books and learning, she was far better educated than most of her female contemporaries, not to mention a large number of those of the masculine sex. Unfortunately, she was possessed of a quixotic humor, which prompted her in the presence of those who knew her least well to don a concealing cloak of Socratic irony. While she derived no little entertainment from answering questions with questions, which to those of a less astute acumen must seem childishly simplistic, she could not but admit the practice tended to reinforce the erroneous supposition that she was lamentably feeble in the head. On the other hand, there was not a great demand for a female who was adept at employing Descarte's scientific methodology, not to mention Euclid's theories of mathematics, who was as familiar with Aristophanes and Seneca as she was with Shakespeare and Congreve, or who might as easily have parsed Latin, Greek, French, or Russian grammar as English.

If knowledge could ever be considered useless, she had been wont to reflect, then she was possessed of a surfeit of it for a woman of her station. Aside from her dearest papa and Lucy's husband Phillip, she had never found anyone with whom she could share her intellectual achievements.

As for feminine accomplishments, her mother had not stinted in teaching her those things considered appropriate to a female of refinement. She could sew and do needlework, arrange flowers, sketch with charcoal and paint with watercolors or oils, plan a seven-course meal to perfection, curtsey with grace, dance the minuet, and play the pianoforte and harp more than moderately well. She would have traded any or all of these accomplishments for sturdy limbs, a strong pair of lungs, and a daring disposition, all of which had been generously meted out to her older siblings. She, had she but known it, was left with beauty and grace, an uncommon intellect, and a heart that was as discerning as it was generous.

If Josephine was unaware of it, however, her mama was not. Of all her children, Lady Bancroft recognized in Josephine a rare creature of noble bearing, one whose spirit was as gentle as it was enduring. Josephine's power of understanding was surpassed only by her capacity for love. And there was the rub, the countess reflected soberly, as she sat, doing her needlework by the light of a single candle while she watched over the earl asleep in his bed.

Knowing her youngest daughter as well as she did,

Emmaline did not doubt that Josephine had by now had more than enough time to peruse the new, unfortunate turn of events at Greensward and to come to the conclusion that there was nothing for it but to give up any thought of leaving when her mama and papa needed her. Worse, she would have convinced herself that to even think of herself at a time like this was paramount to a betrayal of those whom she loved best in the world. She had probably even managed to persuade herself that the last thing she had ever wished to do was go away to Harrogate.

Emmaline, however, was perfectly aware that Josephine had been counting on the trip with an eagerness that had shone in her daughter's eyes, a bright glow of happiness that was not often manifested there. Josephine might wear the appearance of contentment, but Emmaline was far too discerning a parent not to recognize when one of her children was blue-deviled. Josephine had been alone and prey to loneliness for far too long. Her heart yearned for things she probably could not even define. She was a beautiful girl blossoming into womanhood. How could she not feel a growing dissatisfaction with her secluded existence?

Not for the first time Emmaline felt herself plagued with doubts. Josephine, her seventh and final offspring, had seemed threatened from her very conception. From the very beginning, Emmaline had felt a growing unease about the child she carried within her. In the end, she had been forced to take to her bed to avoid a stillbirth. Even so, the child had come prematurely. From the moment she looked down into the tiny infant's face, she had known a fierce, abiding love—and the fear that this precious life would somehow be taken from her. Her little Josephine had been so perfect and yet so delicate—like a fragile bud that must be carefully nurtured and protected from the elements!

Had she held her too close? Emmaline wondered, thinking back over the years of constant vigilance. Had she been right to deny her the things the others had taken for granted—romps in the wood along the bourne, a wetting in the sudden showers that swept over the moors, children's parties away from home, a visit to the Gypsy camp on the village outskirts at fair time? Was she wrong to have kept her home rather than risk exposing her to the rigors of a come-out in London? Had she been merely thinking of herself when, a year ago, she discarded the notion of a Small Season in Bath because Josephine had lost weight over the winter months?

The child had suffered a lifetime of disappointments, and now this. It was so dreadfully unfair.

Emmaline, stabbing the needle through the fabric, was swept with an unwonted anger at the vagaries of fate—and perhaps more than a mere twinge of annoyance at her husband, who should have known better than to bestride a green colt at his age, especially as Wiggens, the groom, had warned him the animal was dangerous. How like a man, even one normally blest with common sense, to be unable to resist putting his fate to the touch!

Emmaline yanked the thread taut and again jabbed the needle through. She was considerably shaken at the thought of how close she had come to losing him. Indeed, she was as near as she had ever come to being out of all patience with his lordship. Bancroft was all of nine-and-forty. He should be well beyond giving into the absurd impulse to prove his manhood. But then, that was, of course, what was at the heart of the matter, was it not? she thought, and suddenly let go of her anger in a long sigh of resignation.

Dropping her embroidery-filled hands into her lap, she gazed down at the still face against the pillows. Her dearest Bancroft was approaching the age when he must feel his manhood most sorely tested. After all, his son and heir, named William after his father, was a man of six-and-twenty. Nearing the prime of manhood, he stood fully two inches taller than Bancroft, as did the twins, Timothy and Thomas, who at one-and-twenty were as strong and agile as young stallions. Bancroft's brown hair, peppered with grey, had begun to recede in a widow's peak, and there were lines about the mouth and eyes that bespoke the years. Furthermore, though his body was as lean as ever she remembered it, the shoulders yet broad and the stomach pleasingly firm, she knew he had come to experience a certain ache in his joints, a stiffness when he rose from his bed in the mornings. He had come of late to feel the cold of the Yorkshire winters more keenly than in years past.

A gentle man of reason and intellect, he had yet taken a quiet pride in his athletic ability. Did he feel himself slipping into middle-age?

Lord knew, she had long since accepted the fact that she was a grandmama, and, while she could not rejoice in noting the skin at her throat had begun to demonstrate a disturbing tendency to crinkle like parchment paper or that there was a subtle heaviness that blurred the line of her jaw or that faint brown spots had begun to manifest themselves on the backs of her hands, she had consoled herself with the thought that she did not mind growing old so long as she could do so with her dearest William.

How dare he risk robbing her of that consolation! she thought, knowing, no matter how much she might be tempted to have done, she could not ask him to be less than he was, that, indeed, her fears must remain her own. She had lost her heart to him when she was a child of eight and he a slender youth of ten. She loved him far too much ever to wish to emasculate him.

Upon this thought, Emmaline became aware with a start that Bancroft's eyes were open and studying her with a fond expression.

"Do you know," he said whimsically, "bathed in the candlelight, you look just as you did when I proposed to you thirty years ago? Except, perhaps, that you are grown even lovelier, if that is possible."

Emmaline slowly released a breath. "Obviously Dr. Evans was right," she retorted, reaching quickly for his hand on top of the counterpane, "you did strike your head in the fall." With her other hand, she smoothed the hair from his brow. "Either that, or you are feverish, my lord. Does it hurt very much?"

"Like a thousand toothaches, but Dr. Evans assures me I shall survive."

Her fingers tightened in quick concern on his. "You had better," she said, the look in her eyes robbing the words of their sting. "You know how perfectly dreadful I look in black." Feeling distinctly helpless, she glanced uncertainly at his left arm, lying unnaturally stiff in its splints and bandages at his side. "He dosed you with laudanum before he left. I'm afraid it is too soon for more. Perhaps some willow bark tea?"

"Emmaline," he said, stopping her as she made as if to rise, "I shall be fine. I have been through this once before, you remember."

"Oh, indeed. And, because you have, you naturally think nothing of a broken bone now and again."

For a moment he studied her.

"You are angry with me, my dear," he observed, his lips twisted in a lop-sided grin that even after nearly forty years still had the power to utterly disarm her. "And who can blame you. It was a foolish stunt, I own. No doubt green colts were better left to younger men."

Instantly Emmaline leaned over him, her lips brushing his. "Hush," she scolded, "or I shall *know* your wits are addled. It might have happened to anyone. There is not a finer horseman at Greensward than you, and you know it."

"I know it is good to hear you say it." The fine lines at the corners of his eyes crinkled up at her with a knowing smile. "Am I then to tackle Ajax again, my indomitable wife?"

She smiled unhesitatingly into his eyes, her heart pierced through by the tender fire that had ever shone in them for her. "When one is thrown, one must always climb back on. How many times have I heard you say that to the children? Ajax will be waiting when your arm is healed."

"Ajax will go to the auction block."

Emmaline's breath caught at that unexpected pronouncement. "But I thought—"

He touched an index finger lightly to her lips, stopping her flow of words. "Wiggens was right. The colt is a rogue. He might be broken, but he will never be won. Let someone else have the headache of a mount that can never be trusted. I value my neck too much."

"No more than do I," breathed Emmaline. Careful of his injured arm, she laid her cheek against his chest and stared into the candle flame. "Are you quite certain, William? I thought you placed great store in him."

She felt his hand moving over her hair in slow, even strokes, as if she were the one who needed comforting. "He has the look of a champion, but not the temperament. And he will pass his mean traits on to his offspring. The truth to tell, I shall not regret his loss. I have had my eye for some time on a foal sired by Lathrop's El Guererro." He paused, his hand going still. "Did you think, my dear, that I dared not walk away? I promise I shall not think less of myself for doing the sensible thing. I haven't the least wish to engage in a pointless demonstration of my manly prowess. It would prove nothing, save that I was mulishly stubborn and not a little dimwitted. And you know, my dear, I have always prided myself on being an eminently rational being.''

Emmaline's head came up, the anger bubbling up in her again. ''If that is the case, then why did you get on the beast at all? Wiggens warned you what he was. What in the world possessed you to suddenly abandon your eminent sense of rationale this morning?''

''I beg your pardon?'' Bancroft's eyebrows arched whimsically toward his hairline. ''What I did this morning was entirely rational. I had to make certain for myself what Ajax was. If I had not tried him just once, I should have gone the rest of my life wondering if I could have mastered the brute. As it is, I haven't the least doubt that he simply is not worth the bother, and I can now leave the entire matter behind me.''

''Perhaps *you* can,'' Emmaline protested, ''but what about our daughter? Or had you forgot she and I were to leave for Harrogate on Friday week?''

Bancroft winced. Egad, it *had* slipped his memory. So that was what had got his Emmaline in a dither. ''And no doubt you will still go, my dear,'' he answered bracingly. ''I assure you I am perfectly able to weather this little setback on my own. I should not dream of robbing you and Josephine of your holiday together.''

Instantly, the impatience went out of Emmaline. ''No, I know you would not,'' she said, cradling her palm against Bancroft's cheek. ''On the other hand, you know very well I cannot possibly leave you in the lurch. I should be in a pother the entire time, worrying how you went on. No, my going is out of the question. If only there were some way for Josephine to make the trip without me.''

''That seems easy enough, if you are resolved to keep me company. We shall simply find someone to serve as Josephine's companion. An older woman of gentility, of course, with a modicum of sense about her. We should not wish to saddle Josephine with a henwit or one of those gibble-gabblers who are more of a nuisance than a help. One possibly on a limited income who would welcome a little extra blunt coming in. I know it is rather short notice, but if we were to advertise . . ."

"On the contrary, Bancroft," exclaimed Emmaline, sitting up with a sudden gleam in her eye. "We do not have to advertise at all. We already have the perfect candidate. Oh, but you have come up with a brilliant solution to our problem. I can only wonder that I did not think of it myself."

"No doubt I am gratified that I could be of some help," offered Bancroft, clearly at a loss as to the reason for his wife's excitement. "Whom, precisely, did you have in mind?"

"My sister Regina, of course," exclaimed Emmaline. "Remember I told you she wrote to say Colonel Bickerstaff was kind enough to pension her off when the last of his five daughters no longer required a governess. It is a small stipend, but sufficient to her needs. I daresay if we sent for her immediately, she could be here before the end of the week."

"Yes, but Reggie—?" Bancroft ejaculated in stunned accents, only to immediately catch himself at his lady wife's suddenly sharpened glance. "You know I am as fond of your sister as you are, Emmaline, but you will admit Reggie was always a trifle out of the ordinary. And twenty years in the Orient with the Bickerstaffs has hardly served to blunt the sharp edges, now has it."

"Perhaps not," Emmaline replied, noticeably drawing up. "Still, Regina has helped to mold five girls into young ladies of refinement. You cannot think Colonel Bickerstaff would have kept her on all those years if she had not been perfectly unexceptional?"

"I should never dream of saying Reggie was exceptional,

only eccentric,'' Bancroft temporized, sensing how thin
was the ice on to which he had blundered. ''Are you certain
you wish to entrust our Josephine to a woman who believes
modern medicine is a grand hoax perpetuated by charla-
tans and quacksalvers for the sole purpose of lining their
purses? She fancies herself an orientalist, Emmaline. There
is no telling what she might dose Josephine with in the
event the child came down with something.''

''Rather say she is a naturalist, William,'' Emmaline
countered, ''who sees in nature the potential for healing.
It is true she has spent a great many years studying Oriental
thought and has come to believe in the efficacy of herbs
in treating illness. She also believes in moderation and
balance in diet in order to achieve and maintain one's
health. Is that really so outlandish or illogical?''

''No, only whimsical, my dear. It is highly doubtful that
eating will ever replace real medicine, after all. Or perhaps
one should say notional,'' he amended dryly, ''when one
takes into account that she has become a sun-worshiper.
I'm afraid that went out with the Zoroastrians.''

Emmaline awarded him a darkling look for that astute
observation. ''Really, Bancroft, I find your levity appalling
at times. Regina is a wholly sensible female. You may be
certain she would never do anything to harm Josephine.
And you cannot deny she would be the ideal companion
for one of Josephine's temperament. Besides being intellectual in her pursuits, she has always been of a cheerful
disposition. I daresay she is just what Josephine needs
right now.''

''Yes, well,'' commented Bancroft doubtfully, ''I suppose Josephine is old enough to come to her own conclu-
sions regarding her aunt's peculiarities. By all means, send
for Reggie. I daresay it is time at any rate we let go of the
leading strings.''

* * *

The decision having been made, Emmaline sent at once to her sister, Regina Moresby, who had retired to Oxford, to ask if she would be pleased to serve as Josephine's companion for a month's stay at Harrogate. The reply by return post assured Emmaline that Regina would not only be happy to oblige her sister in her request, but that she would undoubtedly arrive no later than Thursday next.

It was, consequently, with a feeling of unreality that nine days after her papa's untimely fall from a horse Josephine found herself ensconced in the old family coach and on her way to Harrogate in the company of her abigail, Annabel, and her aunt, who, in spite of her alleged eccentricities, promised fair to be a most congenial companion. She gave, in fact, every appearance of an unexceptional middle-aged woman of uncommonly good looks with fair hair, very like her sister Emmaline's, merry blue eyes behind rimless spectacles, and regular, well-molded features. Her disposition was cheerful without being garrulous, her manner open and friendly without being fawning or cloying. She had the gift of knowing when to engage in lively conversation and when to settle into a cozy silence.

Most gratifying of all to Josephine, however, her aunt Reggie, as she liked to be called, never once made allusion to the obvious—that her niece was rather too pale or too thin or altogether too delicate-seeming for a young woman of nineteen.

At first, buoyed by excitement and the eagerness to see everything, Josephine hardly noticed the passing miles in the ancient coach, which, in spite of its having been recently re-sprung and newly refurbished with red velvet padded squabs, demonstrated a distinct tendency to lurch and sway with a violence that Josephine soon came to feel was designed for the sole purpose of testing her will. It

was not many miles before she was made ruefully aware
of a persistent stab of pain in her side. By the time a halt
was made for a nuncheon of cold chicken, bread thickly
spread with butter and honey, and a tart cheese served
with apple slices, Josephine had become newly acquainted
with seemingly every muscle in her slender body.

Deprived of her appetite, she ate sparingly of the repast
and could only be grateful that her aunt appeared not to
notice. The last thing she wished was to be urged to eat
when she felt as if she had just escaped from a torture
rack.

She was mistaken, however, in thinking her aunt had
not taken notice of her lack of appetite. Regina Morseby,
after a lifetime of molding young girls into women ready
to take their allotted places in Society, was far too discerning not to have noted a great deal about her niece from
the moment of their first meeting the evening before.

Only an idiot or a blind man would fail to see the girl
was anything but robust. On the other hand, Josephine
was hardly a wilting hothouse flower. The girl had back-
bone and, in spite of her air of calm acceptance, a deal
of pride that chafed at being treated as a convalescent. It
had not taken Regina more than a few moments to surmise
that nothing was more certain to alienate the girl's
affections than to have her aunt attempt to mollycoddle
her. No, what the situation needed was tact.

After a single discerning glance at her niece's pinched
features, Regina busied herself replacing the leftovers of
their alfresco meal in the wicker basket.

"I had forgot how peaceful it is in the English countryside," she observed after a moment as she closed the lid
and leaned back to gaze around her at the sweeping dales,
shimmering purple and green in the sunlight. Smiling at
Josephine, she stood and dusted off her skirts. "I wonder,
would you happen to feel like stretching your legs a bit?

One should walk on a day like this. If nothing else, it should help to work out the kinks.''

Josephine, who had been contemplating with dread the time when they must return to the wretched coach, was not loath to reply in the positive. Stiffly, she climbed to her feet. "I believe I should like it above all things at the moment," she said with a rueful smile.

"Excellent," Aunt Regina applauded. "There is nothing like a daily constitutional to keep one's blood flowing." Hooking her arm in her niece's, the older woman started off at a leisurely pace. "India, for all its splendor, was never like this. There was always a certain feeling of uncertainty, a realization of how quickly one could succumb to any number of perils."

"What sort of perils, Aunt Reggie?" Josephine questioned, doing her best to ignore her numerous aches and pains as she kept pace with the older woman.

"Oh, any number of things—poisonous snakes, raiding bandits, cholera. I once witnessed a bearer being attacked by a tiger. It happened so suddenly that one moment Colonel Bickerstaff and I were discussing the probability of rain, and the next the poor man was gone—mauled to death in the most dreadful manner possible. Here, the very last thing one would feel moved to contemplate is an imminent and violent end."

"Yes, but then, there is always the waiting reality of that miserable coach," Josephine declared with a comical grimace. "I fear when, in my daydreams, I fancied myself junketing about the world, I failed to take into account the discomforts inherent in the actual traveling. What a miserable creature you must think me, but I must confess I feel as though I had been severely beaten."

"Nonsense. You are not used to traveling, that is all. You should try riding an elephant sometime. Many's the time that I have fallen into my cot after a day spent on one of those miserable creatures and felt like weeping from sheer exhaustion. Give it time, my dear. You might be surprised how resilient the human body can be.''

''Do you think so?'' queried Josephine a trifle wistfully. ''I am resolved that for once in my life I shall have what Francie calls 'a glorious grand adventure.' I know Harrogate must not seem like much to you after the East Indies, but for one who has never before been beyond the bounds of Greensward, it looms at the moment as marvelous as the Taj Mahal and nearly as inaccessible.''

''Inaccessible?'' Aunt Reggie gave vent to a chuckle, which was as infectious as it was melodious. ''You *are* feeling downpin, are you not. Come, where is your fighting spirit? You must learn to expand your horizons. Harrogate is only a skip and a jump from here. We shall arrive before nightfall, I promise you. Do you think you are ready now to brave that miserable excuse for a coach?''

''As a matter of fact, I am feeling somewhat better,'' confessed Josephine, surprised to discover the exercise had served to relieve her cramped limbs, not to mention the stitch in her side. ''You truly are a marvel, Aunt Reggie.''

''Gammon, my dearest Jo,'' scoffed her aunt, relieved to see a tinge of color had returned to the girl's cheeks. ''I have only lived a deal longer than you and learned a trick or two along the way.''

Indeed, Regina had experienced a great deal in her years junketing about with the colonel and his five daughters, enough to have felt certain doubts as to the advisability of a journey of even fifty miles or so for one of her niece's delicate appearance. Still, the child had seemed determined, and she had not wished to be the one to put a damper on things. Her misgivings had deepened as she watched Josephine's valiant efforts to maintain a cheerful front when, clearly, her meager inner resources were being taxed to the limit. The child was game as a pebble. If only her strength did not prove unequal to the task she had set herself!

Still, Regina was a firm believer not only in nature's ability to heal itself, but in the efficacy of balancing one's bodily needs with those of the spirit. If she had learned anything in the past few hours, it was that there was a hunger in Josephine to experience something more than the coddled existence she had known, and, by heavens, she should have the chance if Regina Morseby had anything to say to it! In the meantime, it would not hurt to give nature a little boost.

Once more in the coach, Josephine braced herself for the inevitable bone-jarring forward lurch of the coach, only to discover her aunt pressing a small vial in her palm.

"Here, my dear. A little something to help the miles pass," she was informed with a reassuring smile.

Josephine, who had had enough of medicines to form an intense dislike of all such liquid remedies, eyed the vial with obvious reluctance. "Really, Aunt Reggie, I should really rather not—"

"Nonsense," retorted the older woman in tones strongly reminiscent of Miss Gladdens, Josephine's former governess. "It is only one of my cordials. Pray drink it all down. I promise you will not regret it."

Josephine, scenting the aroma of chamomile mingled with peppermint and a hint of lemon, hesitated a moment longer, but at last, at her aunt's urging, she submitted to placing the vial to her lips and in a single swallow downed its entire contents.

"Good girl," Aunt Reggie applauded as she replaced the now empty vessel in a leather-covered box containing any number of vials, packets, and powders. "Now, that was not so bad, was it?"

Josephine, left with the rather pleasing aftertaste of peppermint, smiled and shook her head. It was on her tongue to ask her aunt what it was that she had just imbibed, but somehow she could not quite get the words out. Indeed, she had the curious sensation of being slowly enveloped by a marvelously soothing languor which rendered her strangely indifferent to the motion of the coach, the march of time, or anything else, for that matter, save for the wondrous sights and smells of the scenery passing outside her window. As the afternoon wore steadily away, she felt gloriously adrift in a marvelous dream in which grass had never looked greener or the sky more resplendently blue. At last, breathing in the sweet scent of wildflowers, she became entranced by the high, trilling note of a meadow-lark, so singularly lovely that she was quite sure she had never heard its like before.

Consequently, she never saw the curricle pulled by a pair of high-steppers sweep around a curve in the narrow road or realized with what consummate skill its driver caused his cattle to swerve out of the way to avoid an otherwise certain collision.

With a sense of unreality, she felt the unwieldy coach careen violently, heard the terrified scream of horses. Then she was flung bodily forward off the seat. She felt an agonizing blow to the head, which caused a myriad of lights to explode in her brain. And that was the last that she knew.

Chapter 2

Josephine frowned, made aware that things were not precisely what they should be. One did not normally awaken to the sensation, after all, of a persistent throbbing in one's skull, or, for that matter, to the harangue of voices nearby, one of them made shrill with excitement. Or was it hysteria, perhaps? she mused, feeling curiously detached from events going forth around her.

It came to her that she would be pleased if the din would stop. She had no wish to open her eyes. She had no wish to move or do anything that would disturb her. Not now, when she was preoccupied with trying to explain the far more intriguing question of why it was that she was being carried with the greatest of care in what gave every evidence of being a pair of exceedingly strong, masculine arms.

The gentleman—and, indeed, judging from the pleasing scents of clean linen, shaving soap, and the hint of tobacco that assailed her nostrils, she did not doubt that he *was* a gentleman—had a pleasingly firm chest, a steady heartbeat, and a firm, powerful stride that bespoke a man of resolve. A faint smile tugged at her lips as it came to her that, indeed, he had to be, for he gave every indication of one impervious to the scene fraught with shouting men, screaming horses, and at least one weeping female which was being enacted immediately behind him.

"God in heaven, she is dead!" wailed in doleful accents expressive of terrible doom. "Our poor wee lass what never harmed anyone. 'Tis the devil's work. And now he be taking her away."

"Nonsense. Pray get a hold on yourself. She is not dead, and this gentleman is not the devil. Lady Josephine struck her head in the carriage wreck. She will be all right, Annabel, I promise you. Indeed, I cannot believe she is greatly injured."

It was Aunt Reggie. As this last was uttered with considerably less assurance than that with which the rest had been delivered, Josephine felt compelled to give some sign that she was not in the least disposed to succumb to an untimely demise.

She opened her eyes and would have spoken out. She would have, that was, had she not found herself staring up at the most compellingly masculine countenance that she had ever before beheld.

Stern-lipped and forbiddingly harsh, it could not have been described as precisely handsome, at least not in the prevailing mode of Lord Byron. Neither was it precisely young. There were distinct lines etched at the corners of the eyes, and the thick, dark hair was touched with silver over the temples. The nose was forceful rather than aesthetic, the mouth rather too wide, the lips thinned at the moment to a stern, hard line. The eyebrows, set in a wide, intelligent brow, were thick and black and arrogantly masculine. Furthermore, she doubted not that the hard, lean jaw would be judged a deal too strong for purely fashionable tastes.

The eyes, however, could not be faulted, she decided. They were marvelous eyes, compellingly dark and at the moment exceedingly grim.

She thought him the most attractive male she had ever seen, and the most intriguing, she added to herself as she tried to assess the character of the man behind the rugged features.

His was obviously a forceful personality, strong-willed, arrogant, and probably overbearing. Still, the creases, one in either cheek, which, besides being decidedly sensual, lent a cynical cast to the features, might just as easily have owed their formation to a tendency to give way to laughter. The mouth bore strong evidence of a man capable of great passion, something which, she doubted not, he was at great pains to keep rigidly under control. In different circumstances, or perhaps at some earlier time in his life, might there not have been tenderness, too?

Who was he? she wondered, aware of a quickening of her pulse.

"Really, this is not necessary," she said at last, her voice colored with wry amusement. "I believe I am not greatly hurt. In fact, if you will kindly put me down, I daresay I could walk, sir."

The truth of that assertion was called immediately into question. He looked at her, a sudden piercing glance that had the peculiar effect of rendering her instantly light-headed.

"So, you are awake, are you? And with your wits about you, too, it would seem," commented the stranger, observing her far too closely for her own comfort.

"As you see, sir," Josephine responded with a hint of annoyance. She felt her cheeks color under his protracted stare. Unconsciously, her head came up, her eyes sparkling dangerously. "You undoubtedly mean to be kind, but I do wish you will put me down."

"Then I collect I was mistaken," replied the stranger with an abruptness that seemed characteristic of his harsh nature. "Obviously your wits are scrambled. From the look of the crease between your eyebrows, I should say you are clearly suffering a headache. Considering the size of the lump on your forehead, that is hardly remarkable. You are trembling. I daresay you are as weak as a kitten. Furthermore, Miss Powell, you know nothing about me. If you did, you would know that it is hardly kindness for which I am noted."

"No, I daresay it is rudeness," retorted Josephine, succumbing to a wholly uncharacteristic leap of temper at that bald assessment of her physical state, not to mention his self-avowed lack of a propensity for altruism. Instantly, she regretted her hasty tongue. He was, after all, playing the role, at least, of good Samaritan. "I beg your pardon. I should not have ripped up at you. Do you always have this effect on females you have never met before? Or is it only my misfortune to be the one you rub the wrong way?

In the norm, you would find me the most unruffled of creatures, I assure you, not to mention one who is at least moderately aware of the proprieties. I should feel better, sir, if I at least knew your name, especially as you already know mine."

She was rewarded for her efforts at conciliation with a sudden gleam of humor in his eyes and a cynical twist of his handsome lips. "I am Roth—Devon Roth. Or Raven-augh, if you prefer. And don't apologize, Lady Josephine. As it happens, I prefer dealing in plain pounds. In answer to your question, you will undoubtedly be interested to learn that I have been called far worse by any number of females, whether I have only just met them or not."

"A circumstance in which you obviously take great pride," observed Josephine, recalling from among her sister Florence's numerous anecdotes about the *ton* one concerning the Earl of Ravenaugh. A widower of several years standing, he had long been considered a Catch of the Marriage Mart. An unwitting grin tugged at the corners of her mouth. "Really, my lord, it is my considered opinion that you are a complete and utter hand."

"And you," he did not hesitate to inform her, "are a green girl hardly out of the schoolroom who should know better than to treat her elders to an impudent tongue."

That observation served to arouse the imp of perversity in her along with a gurgle of laughter. "I beg your pardon, but I have been out of the schoolroom for no little time now. I may look young, but I am all of nineteen. You, on the other hand, are hardly venerable. I daresay you are not as old as my father, who, after all, is only nine-and-forty."

"No, but I am old enough to *be* your father," he asserted, struck by the fact that, for a grown girl of nineteen, the impudent Miss Powell weighed hardly more than a child in his arms. But then, the aunt had said something about an illness, and she was on her way to Harrogate, presumably to take the waters. No doubt that accounted for the lack of meat on the girl's bones. It would account, too, for the arresting quality of Lady Josephine's singular appearance. Possessed of a delicate bone-structure and a pallor of complexion that served to enhance the deep blue-violet of eyes framed in luxurious dark eyelashes, the girl was not only strikingly, but ethereally, beautiful. Indeed, if anything, she gave the impression of one who was not firmly attached to this world.

She did, at least, he amended, until she gave rein to an obvious inclination for quick-witted verbal exchange, upon which her eyes took on a decided sparkle and her face a glow of animation that was wholly human and enchantingly feminine. Lady Josephine was possessed of a lively wit and a vitality of spirit that put to the shade many a female blest with a more robust constitution.

Still, he could not dismiss an uneasiness concerning her fragility of appearance. She had suffered a severe blow to the head in the carriage wreck, one which might have knocked the pins out from under a much stronger girl. In spite of her avowal that she was not greatly hurt, she was obviously shaken.

Hell and the devil confound it! he cursed, silently to himself. It seemed he found himself in a devil of a coil. Possessed of a strong constitution, he could not recall ever having been sick a day in his life. He could not begin to understand what it must be like for the young beauty in his arms. Still, it did not take a great deal of insight to see that pride alone would not permit a female of Lady Josephine's singular spirit to admit to any sort of weakness. In which case, he saw nothing for it, but to take matters into his own hands.

Clearly, even if her coach had not sustained a broken axle, she could not continue on to Harrogate in her present state. In addition to the fact that she looked worn to the nub, there was every possibility that she was concussed. At the very least she should be examined as soon as possible by a physician. Whether she could be made to see it or not, he was left with but a single viable solution.

His decision having been made, he did not hesitate to implement it.

Before Josephine could utter a protest, she found herself deposited gently but summarily on the seat of the earl's curricle. Only then was she given to see the sorry state of the venerable Powell coach, which, having come to rest with the right back wheel precariously off the road, leaned at a drunken angle, the rear axle snapped in two. She shuddered, realizing how close the coach had come to leaving the road altogether to hurtle willy-nilly down the hillside to the rushing bourne below.

Ever of a practical nature, she could hardly object when Ravenaugh turned to address Miss Morseby, who had only just succeeded in calming Josephine's overwrought abigail.

"I believe in the circumstances our wisest course is for me to take Lady Josephine to Ravenscliff, my home, which lies only a short distance from here. I regret, ma'am, that I have room only for two in the curricle. I shall, of course, send a conveyance to bring you and your servant to your niece as quickly as is possible."

Aunt Reggie's glance flew to Josephine, who assayed a reassuring smile. "It is very kind of you, my lord," the older woman said, obviously relieved at the sight of her niece, awake and with her wits about her, "and pray do not concern yourself. We shall be quite all right."

Reassured that the aunt had a sensible head on her shoulders, Ravenaugh turned and swiftly mounted to the seat beside Josephine. Pausing only long enough to cover the girl with a lap rug, he gathered up the whip and the reins.

"If you are ready, Lady Josephine?" he queried, glancing down into his passenger's composed countenance.

Josephine smiled back at him, a twinkle in the depths of her eyes at his solicitude. For a man who did not count kindness among his store of virtues, his lordship would seem to be uncommonly concerned for her welfare. But then, no doubt he felt a certain responsibility for having nearly run her coach off the road, she reflected, and did not believe for a moment that that was the sole reason for his generous treatment of her.

"I am quite ready, my lord," she said firmly, and, in spite of her aching body and throbbing head, meant every word of it. "I am, as a matter of fact, looking forward to the ride. In my entire nineteen years this is the first time I have ever been away from Greensward, and I intend to reap every enjoyment out of it."

Yes, and at no matter what the cost, surmised Ravenaugh with a wry quirk of the lips, as he observed the young beauty brace herself somewhat grimly for the forward lurch of the curricle.

Ravenaugh, however, was no mere whipster, and, perhaps fortunately, he had long since worked the edge off his spirited pair of high-steppers. The curricle eased smoothly forward and, gradually gathering speed, proceeded at a steady clip along the narrow, winding road.

Josephine, pleasantly surprised to discover the benefits of a well-sprung, modern carriage beneath her, soon found herself loosening her death grip on the side rail. She was moved, in fact, to release an audible sigh as she allowed her taut muscles to relax.

"Yes, that's more like," applauded Ravenaugh, turning into a well-maintained offshoot of the main road. "Better to allow yourself to give with the motion than to wear yourself out fighting it."

"No doubt you are in the right of it, my lord," replied Josephine in rueful accents. "But then, you have a marvelously well-sprung carriage. I daresay I should grow quite fond of travel in such comfortable circumstances."

"It would seem you do not entertain a similar fondness for the relic bearing your family arms," noted Ravenaugh with a suspicious twitch at the corners of his lips.

"I confess I should not be sorry to see it relegated to wherever one consigns conveyances designed for the express purpose of jarring one's teeth out," Josephine declared in no uncertain terms. "Papa would have replaced it years ago, but Mama has always held to the opinion that so long as a thing is not visibly succumbing to decrepitude, it would be shockingly wasteful to go to the expense of a new one. I daresay it is all due to her upbringing as a parson's daughter."

Ravenaugh, whose experience with the fairer sex had yet to include one who practiced frugality for frugality's sake or for any other sake, for that matter, glanced speculatively at Josephine. "You, however, do not share her point of view?" he asked.

"Not in the matter of the family coach," Josephine readily admitted. "I should replace it in a minute. On the other hand, *I* have not reared seven children. I daresay for the price of a new coach, Papa could have purchased Timothy or Thomas his colors, or Florence her coming-out gown, or Francie her beloved Jester. When one comes right down to it, it all depends on one's circumstances, does it not?"

"Oh, indubitably," Ravenaugh smoothly agreed. "And what has it purchased you, Lady Josephine?"

"A month at Harrogate, my lord," Josephine answered

without hesitation. "And I should not trade that for any number of new coaches."

A month at Harrogate, good God, thought Ravenaugh, who could little imagine a worse fate for a young girl than to be forced to spend so much as an entire day at the fashionable watering hole. Peopled with middle-aged matrons and aging aristocrats in search of a cure for a plethora of complaints, it would hardly offer much in the way of entertainment for a female of Lady Josephine's keen wit and intelligence.

"Pray don't look so horrified, my lord," Josephine said with a chuckle. "I am well aware that Harrogate would hardly be your cup of tea for a holiday. I daresay you would be bored to tears within minutes of being exposed to Lady Featherwait's liver complaints or Lord Galstone's gout. I, however, shall derive no little entertainment from merely observing how my fellowmen go on."

"You are even greener than I imagined," Ravenaugh returned, knowing full well when he was being baited, "if you expect me to swallow such a Banbury story."

"Am I?" Josephine laughed, thinking how little his lordship truly comprehended her situation. "Then perhaps you are right. On the other hand, I have no intention of spending my entire time away from home indulging myself with Lord Galstone. There is a deal to offer in the way of interest within easy reach of Harrogate. I intend to see and experience as much as I can while I am here. I have already come to within a hairs-breadth of losing my life in a carriage accident, after all, and find myself now with a gentleman whom I have never seen before and who has kindly insisted on transporting me to his home. That is already far more than I had hoped for—far more than I have experienced in my whole life. Surely one could not ask for a better beginning to one's holiday, even if it is to be spent at a watering spa?"

Ravenaugh, who could think of few things less enjoyable than rounding a bend to find oneself on the point of colliding with a cumbersome coach, only moments later to extract from the wreckage the seemingly lifeless form of a slender girl, could only marvel at Miss Powell's singular manner of viewing events. No doubt her unique interpretation could be attributed to extreme youth. Certainly no one else in his right mind would treasure a brush with death as a bright beginning to bigger and better things yet to come.

The road, which had been steadily climbing, allowed an unobstructed view of a sweeping panorama of the Yorkshire dales intersected with serpentine stone hedges. In the distance a craggy ridge basked in the late afternoon sunshine, a beech wood nestled at its feet, while the downs unfurled in neat fields dotted with haystacks and grazing black-faced sheep. It was a portrait of tranquillity rendered in green and gold, thought Josephine, and yearned for the blue haze of far away peaks obscured in mist.

Moments later the scene was lost, the road swallowed up in a pine wood. Somewhere in the distance, the rush of water filled the silence. Josephine breathed in a long breath scented with pine needles and damp earth and let it out again in a gusty sigh.

"Rest assured. We are almost there."

Ravenaugh's deep voice jarred her to an awareness that, lost in contemplation of the countryside, she had all but forgotten his presence.

"I beg your pardon," she blurted, color flooding her pale cheeks. "I have not been very good company, have I?"

Ravenaugh smiled in wry amusement. It was not often that he found himself in the position of being ignored by a beautiful young woman. On the other hand, it was not often that he encountered a female who had a gift for companionable silence. He found the novelty of the experience refreshing somehow.

"You should have learned by now that a beautiful woman need never apologize," he ventured, thinking, no doubt, to relieve her of any embarrassment. Miss Powell, however, soon proved cast of a different mold from other young beauties he had known.

"If that is the case, then beautiful women must tend to be exceedingly spoiled," Josephine observed in a practical vein. "It is gracious of you, however, to include me in that exalted category."

"Baggage," remarked Ravenaugh, noting the impish gleam in her remarkable eyes. "You know as well as I that you are a diamond of the first water."

"Do I?" Josephine's answering smile was whimsical. "You will no doubt pardon me if I confess to never having thought of myself in that way. It has always been my belief that gentlemen prefer pleasingly plump beauties, who fairly exude an air of vulnerability."

"And that, of course, does not include you," Ravenaugh countered dryly.

"Hardly, my lord. I am, after all, much too thin, and, though I may give the impression of vulnerability, I soon ruin everything by unloosing my unruly tongue on anyone unfortunate enough to try and treat me with pity. I simply cannot help myself. I fear I suffer from an unwieldy pride, which is ever my undoing."

He laughed at that, a rich, full-bodied chuckle, which had the effect of sending a ripple of pleasure coursing through Josephine. "But then, 'How much better it is to be envied than pitied,' " he quoted. "I daresay you cannot be blamed for your pride."

"Perhaps," Josephine reflected, pleased to recognize the words of Herodotus. "On the other hand, Montaigne advises that 'One may be humble out of pride.' If so, I have failed abominably to master the concept. I am, at any rate, a poor actor at best."

"No, you are far too honest for that," he concurred bluntly. "If I were you, I should change nothing. Humility as a virtue has been vastly overrated. I myself find it a dead bore. And you, my dear, are anything but boring."

"You say that to be kind, my lord," Josephine demurred, pleased nonetheless. "I am, in the norm, considered a dull creature. Never having experienced anything outside the province of books, I have little to offer in the way of scintillating conversation. I have no acquaintanceship outside of my family and a few family friends. Consequently, my store of amusing *on dits* is severely lacking. In short, while I may be able to quote Herodotus and Pindar, I haven't the foggiest notion what Sally Jersey said to Lady Fitzhugh only last week over tea."

"Very likely it was 'Two lumps of sugar, and cream,' " submitted Ravenaugh, straight-faced. "Certainly, it could not have been more momentous than 'The word outlives the deed.' "

"You are determined to be difficult, are you not?" Josephine said, giving way to a burble of laughter at his flight of fancy. The quotation, of course, was Pindar's. "You know precisely what I am getting at. Only blue-stockings and gentlemen scholars stand around discussing literature. Everyone else is interested in a neat turn of phrase and the events going forth in the immediate world around them."

"Not everyone, Lady Josephine," Ravenaugh said. "I daresay you might find not a few who appreciate intelligence and originality of thought." Coming to the edge of the trees, the earl pulled up, presumably to breathe the horses. "Nor does every moment cry out for scintillating conversation." Unaccountably, Josephine's heart began to pound as he looked her straight in the eyes. "As it happens, I have enjoyed your company very much."

"You cannot know how relieved I am to hear it," replied Josephine, feeling curiously as if she had known Ravenaugh all her life, or in some previous existence, perhaps, in which they had been very dear friends. "As for me, I believe I should never have found the notion of ending up in a carriage wreck quite so agreeable had it not led to my making your acquaintance. This has undoubtedly been the most singular day of my life, and for that, and so much more, I thank you."

"Pray think nothing of it," Ravenaugh returned, as though he were perfectly accustomed to running into the coaches of any number of young women purely for their entertainment, a conceit which did not in the least fool Josephine.

She smiled at him in perfect understanding.

"Quite so, my dear," murmured Ravenaugh, and, lifting the reins, sent the curricle forward out of the wood.

The scene that leaped into view took Josephine's breath away. She was made dizzy by the sight of grey stone cliffs plunging sheer into the depths of a gorge at the bottom of which a rushing stream, white-feathered with rapids, leaped over and around moss-covered boulders. A waterfall, trailing clouds of steam, hurtled over the cliffs into a boulder-strewn pool fully seventy feet below. Spanning the chasm was a stonework bridge, which evoked visions of plumed knights riding forth to do battle. Her breath caught at sight of the great turreted manor set on craggy stone cliffs on the far side of the gorge. Its grey stone walls seemed forged from the cliffs themselves, a living extension of the wild environs of Ravenscliff.

And, indeed, it was a wild, secluded place, unlike anything Josephine had ever known before. She felt a sudden stirring, an awakening of something that had long lain dormant in her—a yearning to feel wonderfully and terribly alive.

"Oh, but it is magnificent!" she breathed, her eyes shining with rapture. "A castle out of a storybook."

"It is cold in the winter, and draughty, no matter what the season," answered Ravenaugh, observing her reaction to the scene with the faintest of smiles. "And it is hardly a castle."

"No, it is a stately manor, a dream palace." She laughed. "How far away the world must seem to you when you are seated before the fire, the door shut against the night and a pair of hounds at your feet. I believe I should never feel lonely here, not with the roar of the falls to bear me company."

Ravenaugh's eyebrows shot together over the bridge of his nose. Her words evoked memories of another time, when he had known just such domestic comforts as she had described, even to the two hounds stretched out before the hearth, absorbing the heat of the fire. The memory was not a kind one. "I fear not everyone would share your sentiments," he said abruptly, his voice perhaps harsher than he had intended. "My daughter Clarissa, for example, is fond of referring to Ravenscliff as a 'Fortress of Melancholy,' a prison in which her spirit is doomed to languish eternally. It is, of course, something of an exaggeration," he added dryly, sending the horses pounding over the bridge. "She will have her come-out in London next spring."

Struck by his sudden change in mood, Josephine favored Ravenaugh with a penetrating glance. "She sounds a girl of keen sensibilities with a vivid appreciation for the dramatic, rather like my sister Florence. I shouldn't worry, my lord. It is not unusual for a girl of her age to experience a certain disaffection for the things of childhood. It is the time when children are most driven to test the patience of their parents. Having observed the phenomenon in each of my elder siblings in succession, however, I daresay she will in time outgrow it."

If she had meant to banish the grimness from Ravenaugh's countenance, she succeeded admirably. A gleam of startled humor leaped in the look he bent upon her.

"You sound as if you speak from a world of experience, Lady Josephine," he said with only the barest hint of irony. "Dare I remind you that you are nearly of an age with my daughter?"

"Strange," Josephine replied somewhat whimsically, "but I feel a deal older. Or perhaps it is not so strange at all when one takes into account the fact that all my life I have had to live vicariously through others. I have felt at times that I am rather like a household pet, greatly coddled and held in no little affection, but seldom noticed or taken seriously. It has given me the opportunity to observe a great deal others take for granted simply because they are too busy experiencing life to make note of it."

It had, in fact, given her the air of one who had been robbed of her childhood, reflected Ravenaugh, suffering an unwonted stab of sympathy for the girl, which made him distinctly uncomfortable.

Careful, he cynically chided himself, as he pulled the horses to a halt in the cobblestone drive before the manor. In spite of her air of maturity, Lady Josephine was little more than a child. And he was far beyond the age of falling victim either to a pretty face or the wiles of an innocent. There were few surer ways to end up in Parson's Mousetrap, and he, he reminded himself, was old enough to be her father.

Damn the chit! he thought, inexplicably nettled at the fact that he had found himself even following such a line of reasoning. He had not asked to have the girl dropped into his lap. Some vagary of fate had brought them unavoidably together, but that was all there was to it. He would put his troublesome charge up for the night, and on the morrow he would send her on her way. And that would bloody well be the end of it, he told himself as, stepping lightly down from the curricle, he turned back to meet the spell-binding, blue-violet gaze of the unasked-for complication in his life.

"I am afraid my aunt and I have been a deal of trouble for you," she had the gall to say to him with a directness that was as guileless as it was disarming. "Indeed, I daresay you may be wishing us at Jericho. And now we must impose on your kindness even further. I should be ever so grateful if you will send at once, my lord, to summon a post chaise from Harrogate. My aunt and I should be on our way as soon as possible if we are to have any hope of reaching our destination before nightfall."

Even as it occurred to him to wonder if Lady Josephine possessed the gift of reading his mind, Ravenaugh sustained a decided twinge of conscience for his earlier, unkind thoughts, a circumstance which did little to improve his temper.

"Pray don't be absurd," he answered with brutal honesty. "You do not pose an imposition. Nor is there the remotest possibility that you will reach Harrogate today. Even if a post chaise could be brought here before nightfall, which is highly unlikely, you are hardly in any state to continue your journey at the present time. You require at the very least a good night's rest and a physician to make sure you have sustained nothing worse than a sizeable goose egg."

"I see," murmured Josephine, struck not by the content of his words, which on the surface, at least, were solicitous, but in the manner of their delivery, which seemed meant to cut her to the quick. Why? she wondered. What had there been in her innocuous observations to bring a bleak, hard cast to his face? "Nevertheless, I am afraid I must insist, my lord," she added with a firmness borne of the conviction that he found her presence at Ravenscliff infelicitous somehow. "My aunt and I are most anxious to reach Harrogate as soon as possible, and you have already been more than kind."

Had Ravenaugh meant to quash any false perceptions the girl might have entertained about him, he saw at once that he had failed abominably. Far from inciting her loathing, he found himself being treated to a gently probing look, which, besides unsettling his equilibrium, had an immediate chastening effect on his mood.

"The devil I have," he said, relenting with a wry twist of his lips. "You are as aware as I that I was being nothing of the sort just now. Come inside, Lady Josephine. Far from wishing you and your aunt at Jericho, Clarissa and I should be pleased if you would stay the night with us. We do not often have the pleasure of feminine company."

He was rewarded for his efforts with a grave smile, which did little to alleviate the discomfiting conviction that this intriguing child had behaved in a far more mature manner than had he. "In that case, my lord, my aunt and I should be pleased to accept your generous hospitality. With the exception, that is, of a physician's visit. There is nothing wrong with me that cannot be fixed with willow bark tea and a cold compress of comfrey leaves, both of which I am reasonably certain Aunt Reggie can provide. Promise me, Ravenaugh," she added, when she saw he meant to offer an objection. "No doctor. I have been poked, prodded, examined, and dosed by doctors all my life. I do not wish to begin my holiday away from home by having another inflicted on me."

No, naturally she would not, reflected Ravenaugh. No doubt she had borne with the cursed leeches and cups and prescribed medicines of physicians with a fortitude of which few others could boast. He had done enough to put a blight on her spirits. He would not add to it by going against her wishes. "I promise, Lady Josephine," Ravenaugh acquiesced, albeit with reservations. "So long as you remain in reasonable health, I shall not try to force a physician on you. And you, in return, will allow me to carry you inside, where you will immediately lie down and rest."

Josephine, who was feeling a deal wearier than she wished to let on, was not loath to comply with his demands. She was even willing to suffer the ignominy of being carried like a child rather than risk utterly disgracing herself by having her traitorous limbs give way beneath her. Besides, she had the sneaking suspicion that she rather liked the novelty of being cradled in the strong, gentle embrace of a man who had the distinction of not being even remotely related to her. Certainly, the uniqueness of her position evoked a whole array of intriguing emotions, not the least of which was a strange feeling of rightness, as if she belonged precisely where she was, never mind that the gentleman in question was for all practical purposes a complete stranger to her.

And why should she not derive some little enjoyment from her unlooked for adventure? She was ruefully aware that this was probably the only opportunity she would ever have to experience at least the similitude of being cherished by a strong, virile man, especially one for whom she had felt an almost instinctive liking from the moment she had opened her eyes to his harsh, manly countenance. She resolutely ignored the small persistent voice of conscience, which chided her for her shocking lack of morals, even as she resisted the almost overpowering urge to allow her head to rest against his broad shoulder, seemingly so conveniently placed for that very purpose.

Clearly there were facets to her character that she had

never before suspected she had, and instead of being embarrassed by them or ashamed, she found the discovery wholly fascinating. A pity she would not have the chance to explore them further, she thought, as the door was opened to them by one of those august breeds of superior servants, an English butler.

"I'm afraid there has been an accident, Phelps," Ravenaugh announced, striding past the astonished servant. "While we were fortunate Lady Josephine's coach suffered the only serious injury, the lady herself was a trifle shaken up. You will summon Mrs. Carstairs to see to her needs. I shall send Ridings to fetch her companion and servant to her."

"At once, m'lord. And might I suggest the Floral Suite? Besides boasting a cheerful decor, it has the added benefit of an adjoining room for her ladyship's companion."

"Thank you, Phelps," murmured Josephine, smiling, "for your thoughtfulness. The Floral Suite sounds perfectly delightful."

"You will, I trust, be comfortable, my lady." Phelps bent his starched form in a bow and retreated to fetch Mrs. Carstairs.

"Oh, but this is lovely," Josephine breathed, a trifle awed by the great parquetry-tiled hall, rising to a domed ceiling graced by a magnificent crystal chandelier. Embraced on either side by twin staircases, gracefully curved to meet in an open gallery at the back, and adorned with objets d'art arranged with tasteful elegance, the muraled hall somewhat reminded Josephine of the parlor in the rectory, which, preserved in stately perfection in the unlikely event that her grandfather's patroness Lady Fontesquieu might call without warning, had been forbidden to the host of boisterous Powell hopefuls. And, indeed, she could not imagine a place less suited to the ringing laughter and unbridled vitality of children than the cold grandeur of Ravenscliff.

Or perhaps that was precisely what was needed here, she mused, listening to the hollow echoes of Ravenaugh's bootsoles reverberate through the pristine silence—a whole host of noisy, rambunctious children.

Chapter 3

It was amazing what a cup of willow bark tea in conjunction with a three-hour nap could accomplish, reflected Josephine, as Annabel applied the finishing touches to her mistress's toilette. Aside from a small, persistent headache and a few bumps and bruises, Josephine felt wondrously refreshed. She was pleasantly surprised, in fact, to discover she was looking forward to the evening meal with an unusually keen appetite.

That she was also aware of a flutter of excitement at the prospect of dining with the earl and his daughter, she refused to analyze too closely for fear that she might spoil it. The mere feeling, coursing, light and a little intoxicating, through her veins, was as novel to her as was the subtle tinge of color that it lent to her cheeks.

"There you be, m'lady," said Annabel, stepping back to view the results of her handiwork with no little satisfaction. "It's all hid away, neat, beneath your curls. Not a soul would ever guess you'd taken a bump to the head the way you did."

"Annabel, you have outdone yourself!" Josephine stared, pleased with the soft profusion of ringlets allowed to spill in fashionable disarray over her forehead. The result was surprisingly becoming. Not only did it serve to conceal the glaring reminder of her earlier mishap, but it lent her an unwontedly gay, frivolous look that was wholly unlike her normally serene and rather otherworldly appearance. If only her eyes did not spoil the effect, she thought with a small moue of disgust. They stared back at her, great, luminous pools, seemingly too large for her face. Still, she could not deny that she had seldom looked better. The knowledge a certain gimlet-eyed nobleman would see her thus unwittingly sent a soft thrill of excitement careening about in the pit of her stomach.

Faith, what was this? she chided herself sternly. The earl was a virtual stranger to her. Nor was she likely ever to see him again after she left Ravenscliff. It was patently ridiculous to allow herself to imagine there was anything out of the ordinary in sitting down to dinner with the gentleman. The silent remonstrance, however, changed nothing, save, perhaps, to cause her lovely orbs to sparkle with an added sense of anticipation.

"Indeed, Annabel," she announced, secretly amused at herself, "I believe I like my hair even better this way."

Josephine stood and shook out her skirts before the oval looking glass. The Persian silk of her evening dress, flowing from an Empire waist to a short train at the back, shimmered, blue-violet, in the candlelight as she moved. It was an exquisite creation, one her mama had insisted she have in spite of Josephine's protestations that she would hardly require anything so fine at Harrogate. "One never knows," Emmaline had said with one of her cryptic smiles, which Lucy had more than once likened to the all-knowing grin of the Sphinx. "It never hurts to be prepared."

That Emmaline had also instructed Annabel to pack the ball gown that had been intended for Josephine's coming out ball, not to mention the wardrobe of dresses, pelisses, two riding habits, and all the accoutrements that had been purchased for her missed Season in London, had caused Josephine to secretly question her mama's rationality. Harrogate was hardly London, after all. While it was not beyond the bounds of reason to suppose there might be the usual assembly rooms for dances, it was highly unlikely they would require anything so formal as a ball gown. As to the rest, she supposed she might as well put on an elegant front, since her mama had gone to the expense of a wardrobe for London. It would, after all, be a shame to waste it.

Regina, entering the room, halted at sight of the lovely vision in blue-violet. "Josephine, my dear," she exclaimed softly, "you take my breath away. You remind me of your mama, the night she announced her engagement to Bancroft."

"Do I?" Josephine turned to smile at the older woman. "Are you sure it is not too much for the occasion?"

"On the contrary," said Regina, calling to mind the Earl of Ravenaugh's hard countenance. In spite of his lordship's kindness to them both, the man had reacted to her niece as if he had not seen her at all. It occurred to her that their host was a singularly lonely man, who could stand to have the wind knocked from his sails, and, if Josephine's appearance tonight failed of that purpose, then, clearly, Ravenaugh must have ice-water in his veins. "I think it is precisely what the occasion demands."

The dinner bell had only just sounded, when an under-footman in black and silver livery arrived to conduct Josephine and Regina along echoing corridors lined with closed doors interspersed with staring portraits. Josephine shivered, touched by the chill fingers of a draught. Despite the lighted wall lamps, the halls seemed uncommonly riven with shadows.

She was absurdly relieved when at last they came to gold embossed doors, which opened to reveal a large, well-appointed withdrawing room, softened and made rather more cheerful by candlelight and the companionable leap of a fire in a white marble fireplace. Ravenaugh, quietly elegant in black evening dress, stood with his arm propped casually along the top of the mantelpiece, a glass of red wine in his hand, as he contemplated a young beauty in pale pink pacing fitfully before him.

"But if she was ill," commented the young lady, with a doubtful shake of her raven curls, "perhaps she will not feel strong enough to come down, and I did so wish to make her acquaintance." She lifted speculative brown eyes to Ravenaugh's face. "You did say she was young, did you not, my lord? Nearly my own age. Is she of a friendly disposition? You did say you did not think her high in the instep."

At Josephine's entrance, Ravenaugh's gaze lifted and held.

Unaccountably, Josephine felt a warm rush of blood to her cheeks.

"I believe," Ravenaugh remarked slowly, "you will find she is everything that is charming." Deliberately, he straightened. "Lady Josephine Powell, Miss Regina Moresby, I should like to present my daughter, Clarissa Roth, who is *most* eager to make your acquaintance."

"Oh, really, Father," exclaimed the girl, dropping a curtsey. "Still, he is right, you know," she added, rising to meet Josephine's eyes with unabashed curiosity. "I have been on pins and needles, hoping you would come down. Miss Morseby, I am most happy to meet you. I do hope you are feeling better after your rest, Lady Josephine."

Josephine warmed immediately to the girl's frank and lively manner. She was a slender girl, somewhat above average height and possessed of a creamy complexion and finely molded, delicate features. There was the distinct promise of a passionate nature about the wide, sensitive mouth so like her father's, and the golden brown eyes sparkled with an inner vitality that would surely devastate more than one masculine heart. "I am feeling much better, thank you, and I am very pleased to make your acquaintance. Please call me Jo. It is what I have been used all my life to hearing my brothers and sisters call me, and I find, now that they are all grown up and gone, that I miss it exceedingly."

"How many brothers and sisters have you?" queried Lady Clarissa, drawing Josephine to a settee near the fireplace.

"I am the youngest of seven—three boys and four girls. Although sometimes it seemed as if there were twice that many of us. I'm afraid we were a rather boisterous lot, growing up."

"But how simply splendid," breathed Lady Clarissa, her lovely face expressive of envy. "I have always wished for brothers and sisters. Or at least a handful of cousins. You cannot imagine how dreadfully boring it is being an only child, especially in the 'Fortress of Melancholy.' I never see anyone my own age."

Josephine was moved to laughter at the girl's dour grimace. "I was fourteen when my sister Francie married and left Greensward. I have been for all practical purposes an only child for the past five years. It can be exceedingly lonely at times. His lordship, however, has informed me that you are soon to have your come-out in London. Surely that is something for which to look forward."

"It is ten months away," complained Clarissa with a long sigh. "Almost a lifetime. Sometimes I think I shall never be allowed out of the schoolroom, let alone presented at my first ball."

"Having postponed my curtsey in polite society for the

second Season in a row, I do sympathize,'' Josephine smil-
ingly assured the girl. "I shall be at Harrogate for a month,
however, if you would like to come and see me sometimes.
We should be happy to have the company, should we not,
Aunt Reggie?''

"I daresay there will be more than enough room in the
cottage for a guest or two," declared Regina, who could
not but think such an arrangement would profit both girls.

"Well, then," Josephine said. "It is settled—if, that is,
you have no objection, my lord," she added, glancing
quizzically up at Ravenaugh, who had been noticeably
silent during this exchange.

"Oh, please, say I may," Clarissa interjected, turning a
luminous gaze on her father's impassive countenance.

The devil, thought Ravenaugh, who had every objection
to imposing on Lady Josephine's good nature. She did not
know his daughter and consequently had not the smallest
notion what she was inviting. The long succession of governesses who had been variously employed over the years
might have enlightened her, he reflected humorlessly. On
the other hand, Miss Moresby, he suspected, was a cut
above the best of those poor, unsuspecting females who
had taken on the task of governing his daughter. She had
not the look of a woman who would be easily taken in by
an overimaginative girl who had a gift for pulling the wool
over the eyes of anyone who came in her sphere of influence.

More pertinent, however, than any imposition on his
two guests, he had not lived to be eight-and-thirty without
having gained a deal of worldly experience. Having spent
an hour in the wholly captivating Lady Josephine's company, he envisioned in any sort of intimacy between the
young beauty and his daughter any number of complica-
tions, none of which could possibly benefit either Josephine or himself, let alone Clarissa. There would be talk,

the whole miserable thing dredged up again, the rumors and innuendoes. His daughter should be spared that much at least.

"But I do object. It is, in fact, out of the question," he stated baldly. "Lady Josephine is far too young to wish to play nursemaid to a schoolgirl. You did say this was your first holiday away from home. I suggest, Lady Josephine, rather than saddle yourself with an obvious impediment, you enjoy yourself."

He saw his blunt speech had the effect of bringing a flush to Lady Josephine's cheeks, and, though she was quick to hide it, he could not mistake a glimmer of hurt in her eyes. The devil, he thought.

"That's not fair," declared Clarissa, her face clouding over. "I should not be an impediment. Should I, Jo?"

Josephine, startled and not a little puzzled by the earl's harsh reaction, leaned quickly forward to pat the girl's hand. "No, of course you would not."

"Miss Powell is being kind, my dear," Ravenaugh observed, his face an impenetrable mask of ennui. "She is, after all, a lady in the truest sense of the word. I suggest you emulate her example and allow that, until you have made your curtsey in polite society, you would prove at the very least an inconvenience to her."

"Oh, but you would like that very well, would you not?" retorted Clarissa resentfully. "You are determined, as always, to be disagreeable. It is quite useless, Jo. Ravenaugh never changes his mind once it is made up. I daresay he enjoys seeing me unhappy, since he will never let me do the least little thing. And I—I dislike him prodigiously."

"Hush," said Josephine, appalled at the furor her innocent invitation had aroused. "You do not mean that. If it is your custom to behave toward your father in so uncivil a fashion, I daresay he can hardly be blamed if he is prone to be stern with you."

She was gratified to see Lady Clarissa flush and duck her head. At least the girl was not entirely lost to all sense of the behavior proper to a young lady of refinement. Nor would Josephine attribute the child's outburst to a spoiled or unruly nature. There was something else beneath the surface that she did not understand, something she had felt from the moment she crossed the threshold into Ravenscliff, indeed, something she had glimpsed upon occasion in Ravenaugh's eyes—a shadow, she thought, lifting her gaze to Ravenaugh's.

His harsh features wore a distinctly cynical expression. Instantly, her heart went out to him. Clearly, he was not impervious to his daughter's avowal of disaffection.

"On the other hand, I daresay your father has over-looked the obvious," she gently pointed out. "I am, after all, wholly unacquainted with anyone at Harrogate and consequently should be glad to have a friend to visit me. I assure you, my lord, you would be doing me a favor by letting Lady Clarissa come to me."

Ravenaugh, transfixed by eyes which he had already discovered had the discomfiting effect of rendering him peculiarly prone to examine his own conscience, smiled mirthlessly. "I daresay you will have any number of friends, Lady Josephine," he countered dryly, "the instant you make your appearance at the Royal Pump Room. It could hardly be otherwise." He watched, fascinated, her eyes, glimmer and darken with mingling pleasure and protest. The ridiculous child had not an inkling of how lovely she was, he thought. "However," he next heard himself with a vague sense of incredulity saying, "when you and your aunt have settled in, if you still wish Clarissa to come to you, then naturally I shall reconsider my objection."

He was rewarded for his unprecedented change of heart with a squeal of delight from his daughter and a look from Lady Josephine that left him with the peculiar impression she saw through his habitually satyric front to something no one else had been given to see in a very long time. The thought brought a cynical twist to his lips. But then, Lady Josephine would seem to be a singular female, quite unlike any other he had ever encountered. He could almost envy the man who would one day win her heart.

Immediately he chided himself for a bloody fool. Even if she were not too young for him, he had had enough of marital bliss to last him a lifetime, he reminded himself. Downing his wine in a single swallow, he set the glass aside.

"Dinner, I believe, is served," he announced abruptly and offered his arm to Miss Morseby. That worthy awarded him a sapient look over the tops of her spectacles. "Quite so, Miss Morseby," he commented dryly, and conducted the ladies into the dining room.

Dinner proved, in spite of its somewhat uncertain beginnings, to be a festive affair. This was due only in part to Lady Clarissa's ebullience of spirits. Ravenaugh, Josephine quickly discovered, was capable of immense charm, when he chose to display it. That he did so this evening, she suspected, was as much for his daughter's benefit as for hers or Regina's. Certainly, it seemed that this was a facet of his character that Clarissa had not seen before. Wary at first, the child came at last to blossom under the influence of her father's light teasing and disarming ease of manner. He had traveled a great deal the past several years on what Josephine soon came to suspect were undertakings that had had more than a little to do with the war. It was not his anecdotes which led her to believe his travels were attended with peril, however. They were light and meant to be entertaining. It was rather something she sensed behind the charming descriptions of scenes and people—

a feeling that he was leaving out far more than he was telling.

Whatever the case, Josephine found she was enjoying herself immensely. She had never been given to shyness and was possessed of a keen and lively wit. When drawn out, she was not averse to relating any number of amusing tales of Greensward and the Powell progeny who had grown up there. She could not know that, when she talked about her siblings and their numerous misadventures, her eyes tended to sparkle with humor or that her face lit up with animation.

Ravenaugh, however, was acutely aware of it, and of the lovely picture of unaffected innocence she presented. Still, it was hardly a childish innocence, he reflected, struck by the contrast between Lady Josephine's laughing composure and his daughter's gurgling bursts of exuberance. She might be young, but she was a woman, beautiful, charming, and infinitely desirable. What was more, she had an engaging manner and an informed intellect, which did not bore him. He found himself thinking that she deserved better than anything Harrogate had to offer. She was meant to reign in London. Indeed, he thought, watching her charm his daughter, Lady Josephine at Harrogate was equivalent to an exquisite diamond relegated to a brass setting.

When the sweetmeats and jellies had gone the rounds, Ravenaugh surprised them all by foregoing a gentleman's prerogative of indulging in brandy and cigars in masculine solitude.

"After our congenial meal, I find little to recommend in being left to enjoy my own company." Ravenaugh's unfathomable gaze rested on Clarissa's rapt young face. "Besides, I have it from a reliable source that my daughter has acquired a certain proficiency at the pianoforte. Perhaps if no one is ready for bed, a small impromptu musicale would be agreeable with everyone. As it happens, I had the foresight to order a fire laid in the Music Room.''

"I, for one, should love to hear Clarissa play,'' Josephine was quick to exclaim. "And I am not in the least ready for bed.''

Regina professed that she liked nothing better than to listen to music before a repose. "It is, after all, soothing to body and soul,'' she declared.

Clarissa, alone, seemed less than pleased at the proposed entertainment. "But the Music Room?'' she blurted in an odd voice. "Must it be there, my lord?''

"It would seem the most appropriate setting,'' observed Ravenaugh with quizzically arched eyebrows. "The school-room, after all, would offer rather cramped quarters for our guests, don't you think?'' The look that passed between father and daughter was almost palpable with the clash of wills behind it.

"Yes, I suppose it would,'' Clarissa murmured at last, dropping her eyes from his.

"Well, then.'' Smoothly rising from his chair, Ravenaugh addressed Lady Josephine and Miss Morseby. "Ladies? If you are ready?''

Ravenaugh led the way out of the dining room and along the corridor. Josephine, more than a little puzzled at the undercurrent of emotion she had sensed between father and daughter, fell into step beside the girl.

"If you have no wish to play, I daresay we should all understand,'' she said quietly, as she slipped her arm through Clarissa's.

Clarissa, startled, glanced up, then quickly away. "No, it isn't that. I should be happy to play for you and Miss Morseby. It is only that—''

"Yes?'' Josephine gently prodded, when it seemed the girl would not go on. "It is only what?''

Clarissa appeared prey to a brief inner struggle with

herself. At last drawing a breath, she blurted in a low whisper, "It is Ravenagh. I have never seen him like this. If I did not know better, I should say he was bewitched. He is, at the very least, in a fey mood." Her eyes lifted to Josephine's. "He has not set foot in the Music Room since Mama—"

The girl's voice faltered and broke off. Instinctively, Josephine caught the child's hand and squeezed it. Faith, what was this? Clarissa's hand trembled in hers. Nor could Josephine be mistaken in thinking she had glimpsed a glimmer of something very nearly resembling panic in the girl's eyes. Then Clarissa had turned her head away and withdrawn her cold hand from Josephine's. The moment gone, Josephine was no longer certain what she had seen.

She knew, however, what she had sensed, and it was far more than a young girl's nervousness at displaying her musical accomplishments before guests, not to mention her aristocratic father. Clarissa entertained a dread of the Music Room. Josephine was quite certain of it.

No doubt it was merely an overexaggerated sense of anticipation that caused a shiver to course down Josephine's spine at her first glimpse of the Music Room. It was, after all, a splendid example of its kind, with a high, vaulted ceiling, painted in murals, and a comfortable array of settees and chairs arranged for comfort. A standing harp and a concert grand by Broadwood occupied places of honor at the front of the room, while a magnificent harpsichord with double keyboards and an elaborately carved case stood in solitary splendor to one side.

It was not the musical instruments, splendid as they were, however, that captured and held Josephine in rapt fascination, but a portrait, marvelously rendered, of a young beauty playing the harp. And how not, Josephine thought, feeling herself drawn into the huge, haunted eyes. The portrait, hanging in state over the Adams fireplace, dominated the room. The artist had captured his subject, lost in the melody. Garbed in a white Grecian gown, her raven curls graced with a garland of lavender flowers, she was hauntingly lovely, and not a little tormented, mused Josephine, hardly wondering at Ravenaugh's reluctance to visit the room.

"She was my mother," said Clarissa, coming up beside Josephine, who had halted just inside the doorway. "Her name was Eugenia. Father had the painting commissioned just weeks before she died. She loved music. This was her favorite room."

"She is beautiful," Josephine answered, slipping her arm about the girl's waist. "You are very like her."

"Everyone says so. Sometimes I think that is why Papa—" She stopped.

"Why he has been gone so often?" Josephine gently queried. Then, when the girl did not answer, "He must have loved her very much, Clarissa. It is obvious he cares a great deal about you."

"Does he?" Clarissa shrugged. "He has a curious way of showing it. He is never here, and he never talks about her. They were childhood sweethearts, so I daresay he must have cared once. Still," she pulled away, her expression suddenly closed, "it was all a very long time ago. I hardly remember her anymore."

With a feeling that there was a great deal that was troubling at Ravenscliff, Josephine watched Clarissa cross the room to the pianoforte before she herself took a seat in an arm chair. Indeed, she could not but see a striking similarity between mother and daughter as Clarissa began to play. But then, it soon occurred to her that it was hardly by chance that the little minx had chosen a ponderously solemn piece, a dirge, in fact, designed to depress the senses.

Had Clarissa meant to deliberately put a pall on the evening, not to mention her father's mood, she was succeeding admirably. Not only was the girl a great deal more than merely competent at the pianoforte, but she was obviously a consummate actress as well, Josephine decided, observing the soulful nuance of facial expressions that accompanied the mournful musical rendition.

A single glance at the grim leap of muscle along Ravenaugh's lean jaw was proof of the pudding. The entire performance was meant for his benefit, but why? wondered Josephine, exchanging a sapient look with Aunt Reggie. It would seem a poor payment for Ravenaugh's earlier concession in the matter of his daughter's proposed visit to Harrogate. Whatever her motives, however, it would never do to allow the child the satisfaction of seeing she had succeeded in her intent, thought Josephine, who was exceedingly knowledgeable in the art of practical jokes. It would only encourage the little baggage to more and ever greater efforts at manipulation.

Josephine, who had long ago learned the best way to turn a practical joke back on one of her siblings was to refuse to take the bait, was prepared when Clarissa came at last to a particularly long and affected ending.

"That was lovely, Clarissa," she applauded, rising from her chair, when the final, languishing note had died away. "I daresay my sister Florence could not have given a more moving performance, and she was always noted for her flair for the dramatic. Her tastes, of course, have changed a great deal since she has become one of London's leading hostesses. I'm afraid she has not indulged herself in anything quite so daringly sentimental since William's tutor announced he was engaged to Miss Alice Fogarty and would be leaving at the end of his term. Florence, as I recall, was thirteen at the time.'' She had the satisfaction of seeing Clarissa's studied expression of a soul in torment alter to the chagrin of a seventeen-year-old caught in a childish prank. ''As for myself,'' she added, seating herself on the bench beside Clarissa and lightly running her fingers over the keys, ''I fear I am hopelessly given to a preference for 'Jest, and youthful Jollity.' '' Her laughing eyes met Ravenaugh's across the pianoforte.

She was rewarded with an appreciative leap of sardonic humor in their depths. '' 'Quips and Cranks and wanton Wiles, Nods and Becks and wreathed Smiles'?'' he murmured quizzically.

''Exactly so, my lord.'' Naturally, he was familiar with Milton. She had known he would be.

Josephine laughed and launched into a gay piece. And when she took up the lyrics in her rich contralto, Aunt Reggie added her lilting soprano. Josephine flashed a smile at her aunt. Her fingers nearly faltered, however, when a deep baritone, too, sounded at her shoulder and she realized Ravenaugh had come to stand behind her. She suffered a soft thrill of gladness mingled with other less easily explained emotions due solely, she did not doubt, to Ravenaugh's proximity. If only Clarissa would cease to pout, Josephine was moved to reflect. Nudging an elbow lightly into the girl's side, Josephine winked. Clarissa gave a dour grimace, then, giving in with a final show of reluctance, grinned wryly and at last joined in the singing.

It seemed, then, that the spell that had hung over the Music Room, if indeed there had truly been one, was banished before the lively sounds of song and merriment.

Down the hall in the dining room, Phelps paused in his evening task of polishing the silver just as Mrs. Carstairs emerged suddenly from the kitchens to stand, drying her hands in her apron skirt.

"What is it, Mr. Phelps?" she queried. "It sounds like music."

"Aye," said Phelps.

"And laughter," added Mrs. Carstairs.

"Aye," agreed the butler, turning back to his polishing.

"Well, I never," declared Mrs. Carstairs, smiling and shaking her head. "Belike it's the young lady. She has a merry way about her in spite of her looking so frail and all." Still smiling in wonder, the housekeeper retreated belowstairs, while behind her Phelps paused once more in his polishing.

"Aye, belike," he murmured, the seamed countenance expressive of a strange satisfaction. Then humming quietly, he applied his cloth to the silverware.

"Naturally, I am sorry that your coach was wrecked," declared Clarissa a great deal later, as she paused in the doorway to the Music Room. "Nevertheless, I cannot but be glad, too, Jo, because it brought you and Miss Morseby to Ravenscliff."

"I daresay we are just as glad to be here," Josephine replied. "Certainly, I have seldom had a more enjoyable evening. For which I must thank you and your father."

"You could not have enjoyed it half as much as I did," Clarissa averred, flashing a sidelong glance at the earl. "I wish it had not to end quite so soon?"

Upon which Ravenaugh pointedly interjected, "Good-night, *enfant*. It is long past your bedtime."

"Pooh," Clarissa retorted with a comical grimace. "I am almost of the age to stay out all night, dancing. Still, I shan't be greedy just this once. I have had too splendid a time to spoil it. Goodnight, everyone." Once more, before stepping through the doorway, she paused to smile happily over her shoulder at Josephine. "I can hardly wait until tomorrow, Jo. There is so much that I wish to show you. Pray sleep well."

Then turning before Josephine could reply, Clarissa fled.

"I'm afraid it is past my bedtime, too," declared Aunt Regina, who could hardly fail to note the look in Ravenaugh's eyes as they came to rest on Josephine. "I must thank you, my lord, for a most pleasant evening."

Ravenaugh inclined his head. "The pleasure, I assure you, Miss Morseby, was all mine."

"Can you find your way, Aunt Reggie?" queried Josephine. "I discover, after all the excitement, I am not in the least inclined for sleep. If his lordship has no objection, I believe I should like to borrow a book to read in bed."

"I found my way across the Punjab once," Regina submitted dryly. "I daresay I can find my way to my room. Goodnight, dear."

"Goodnight, Aunt," Josephine called after Regina's retreating figure. "I shall be up directly."

Alone with Ravenaugh, Josephine became aware of the empty chill of the Music Room at her back. Inexplicably, she shivered.

"You should be in your bed," Ravenaugh observed roughly. "You are cold. And you are probably feeling the effects of the accident."

Josephine smiled at his abruptness. "I am fine, my lord. Really. And, after all, you did warn me." A single arrogant eyebrow shot quizzically toward Ravenaugh's hairline. "You said Ravenscliff was cold and draughty no matter what the season. I should have dressed more appropriately. I fear, however, that I am far too vain to have wished to appear at dinner in an unbecoming, if wholly practical, gown of grey woolen."

Ravenaugh's hard eyes glittered in the candlelight. "Then, my child, you are guilty of the height of folly. On you, the grey woolen would have made little difference. I daresay you would look fetching in sackcloth and ashes."

"No, how can you say so?" Josephine laughed, not in the least intimidated by his harshness. "Sackcloth and ashes? You defeat the whole purpose of a woman's toilette, my lord. And I was so sure you would like me in this gown. It is quite the finest I have ever worn."

"Little devil," growled Ravenaugh feelingly. "You are perfectly aware that I like you very well in that gown. On you, it is stunning."

"And I like you, too," Josephine shot instantly back at him, "no matter what you might happen to be wearing. Do you find that surprising, my lord? I confess that I do, a little. You have, after all, done your best to convince me that I should do nothing of the kind. I warn you, however, that circumstances have made me a student of human behavior. I have been accused more than once of possessing a keen insight into people."

"Kind of you to warn me," Ravenaugh drawled acerbically. Taking Josephine's arm, he led her out of the Music Room and along the hall to the stairs. "On the other hand, it comes a trifle late. I believe those intriguing aspects of your character were amply demonstrated this evening— with Clarissa. Are you certain you are the youngest of the Powell progeny? You handled my daughter with the consummate skill of a veteran. I have seen case-hardened governesses fail, where you succeeded in disarming her with apparent ease."

"Dear me, was it so bad as that?" Josephine exclaimed, wrinkling her nose in consternation. "You make me sound the veriest managing female, and I detest people who are always meddling in affairs that do not in the least concern them."

"Then you may rest easy," Ravenaugh did not hesitate to inform her. "You are neither meddling nor managing. On the contrary. It is obvious you are guilty of nothing worse than being prey to a generous nature and an all-too-discerning heart."

Halting at the top of the stairs, he turned her to face him. Josephine's heart seemed to skip a beat as she looked up into the earl's dark, compelling gaze. "It was worth a great deal to me to see Clarissa laugh in my presence," he said quietly. "I believe you are good for her."

Josephine searched his eyes. "But you would rather she did not come to me at Harrogate," she answered. "Why?"

"I told you why."

"Because I am too young."

"Because you are *young* and should be concerned only with enjoying your holiday." With a hint of impatience, he turned away down the corridor. "Clarissa would be an unnecessary complication, not to mention a drain on your energies."

"I see, so it is my health that concerns you," Josephine replied, hurrying to keep up with him. "But I assure you I do not intend to make Clarissa a permanent houseguest. I haven't the least desire to have her under my charge. It would, after all, be highly improper. A day or two at a time, or perhaps an afternoon now and again, was all I had in mind. I daresay, with Aunt Reggie to help, I am up to that much at least. But then," she added as Ravenaugh came to a halt before a heavy oak door, "that is not the real reason you are against the idea."

Ravenaugh's hand froze on the doorhandle for the barest instant. Then giving it a quick downward jerk, he pushed the door open.

"Is it not?" he said, stepping aside to allow Josephine to go in before him. "You would seem to know a deal more about my motives than I, my lady."

"I told you," Josephine smiled. "I am possessed of a keen insight. Besides, it is the only logical explanation." She turned from gazing about her at the walls lined with ceiling-high bookcases replete with an imposing collection of leather-bound volumes. "You know perfectly well Clarissa would be on her best behavior with Aunt Reggie and me, and Harrogate is hardly Bath or London. You cannot possibly think it would be improper for Clarissa to accompany us to whatever social engagements there are to offer. You know as well as I, in fact, that she would benefit from gaining a little experience before her actual come-out. Therefore, I can only assume that, either you are being merely arbitrary, which would seem to me highly inconsistent with what I have seen thus far of your character, or you entertain some other reason, known only to yourself, for viewing my invitation with disfavor. I daresay it has something to do with me." Taking a book from a shelf, she briefly leafed through it, then put it back in order to reach for another. "It cannot be, surely, that you disapprove of me as a companion for your daughter."

"I do disapprove. Strongly," Ravenaugh stated baldly. Crossing to a sideboard, he poured a brandy from a decanter. "After this evening, I am, in fact, convinced that you are wholly unfit to have Clarissa foisted on you."

Had he meant to put her off her balance, he was soon to discover he had failed abominably.

"Are you?" Lady Josephine had the gall to answer him, her lovely face lighting with interest. "But how delightful. You cannot know what a dead bore it is to be the wholly unexceptional Lady Josephine, who not only has never done anything the least objectionable in her life, but, indeed, has never done anything to incite the smallest interest. It has always been rather lowering to realize that I have never been the object of even the most innocuous gossip, never mind a truly scandalous offering. What, exactly, my lord, have I done to impress you with my unsuitability?"

"Impudent baggage," growled Ravenaugh with obvious feeling. "You know I was not referring to your character, which, besides being hopelessly obdurate and not a little given to a reprehensible delight in twisting to suit your meanings that should otherwise be simple and straightforward, is wholly lacking in a proper understanding of what is due your elders."

"An excellent beginning, my lord," applauded Josephine, her eyes alight with twin imps of laughter. "You must not be afraid to open the budget, you know. Did you by any chance fail to mention my unruly tongue?"

"That, too," agreed Ravenaugh with no little satisfaction. "While you may have a great deal to offer my daughter, it would hardly be a reciprocally beneficial arrangement. Whether you will admit it or not, Miss Powell, you would soon find putting up with Clarissa and the sort of companions suitable for a girl of her age not only unutterably insipid, but, frankly, a dead bore."

"Dear, I wish you will make up your mind," Josephine rejoined with a soulful air. "A moment ago I was too young to have Clarissa with me. Now it seems I am too old for your daughter. Surely you cannot intend to have it both ways, my lord."

Ravenaugh awarded her a darkling glance. "Do not talk flummery to me, my girl," he warned with grim humor. "You know as well as I actual age has little to do with it. It is a matter of compatible levels of maturity."

Ravenaugh was given the immediate impression that he had been masterfully maneuvered into a trap of his own making, a realization which would seem immediately to be confirmed by Lady Josephine's suspiciously demure aspect.

"Quite so, my lord," she said, firmly closing the book

she had been holding. "Indeed, I could not agree with you more. Age differences between two people are clearly of no significance when there exists a compatibility of thought and temperament, not to mention a strong inclination to friendship." Replacing the book on its shelf, she lifted guileless blue-violet eyes to his. "I daresay between two kindred souls, age would be of the smallest consideration."

Ravenaugh stared at her. Clearly it was not Clarissa about whom she was talking.

"Not always, I'm afraid, Lady Josephine," he said quietly after a moment, never taking his eyes off hers. "Sometimes there are other considerations, which make the years an insurmountable barrier."

Josephine held his eyes a moment longer, as though weighing his conclusion carefully. Then, with an unwitting pang of something very nearly resembling regret, the earl saw her accept it.

"I see," she said, and, taking in a deep breath, withdrew her gaze from his. "Well." Unnecessarily smoothing the front of her gown, she glanced around her. "I believe I shall not need a book after all. Indeed, I am convinced it must be growing unconscionably late." She looked at Ravenaugh, her smile not quite reaching her eyes. "I suppose I should be saying goodnight, my lord. And, thank you for a lovely evening." She held out her hand to him. "I shall not forget it, or your kindness to two strangers, for a very long time to come." This time a gleam of humor did reach her eyes. "It is, after all, very likely the only adventure I shall have to tell about when I reach home."

"Not at all, Lady Josephine." Absurdly, Josephine felt a small quiver in the pit of her stomach as Ravenaugh's strong fingers closed over hers. "You have a whole lifetime of adventures awaiting you."

"Yes, of course." As the earl released her hand, it came

to her, however, that none of them would equal what might have occurred had Ravenaugh not just closed the door to what had seemed destined to be a burgeoning friendship. "Well," she said again, and turned to take her leave. "No. No need to see me to my room. Pray finish your brandy, my lord. Goodnight."

"Goodnight, Lady Josephine."

Ravenaugh watched her as she let herself out the door. For a moment he stood, lost in apparent contemplation. Then, seeming to shake himself, he reached at last for his brandy.

"Hell and the devil confound it!" he uttered savagely and, tossing back his head, emptied the glass all in a single swallow.

Chapter 4

"I am feeling fine, Aunt Reggie, I promise. Whatever you gave me last night to make me sleep worked wonders," declared Josephine, equally gratified that the cold compress of comfrey leaves had served to reduce the bump on her forehead overnight. It was hardly noticeable in the morning light, even without the concealing curls.

"Of course you are, my dear," Regina readily agreed. "Still, Ravenscliff is a pleasant enough place, and his lordship and Lady Clarissa seemed not displeased with our company last night. I should have thought another day here, merely as a precautionary measure, would not be distasteful to you."

"No, not distasteful," Josephine agreed with an oddly twisted smile. "Hardly that. But exceedingly unwise, I'm afraid." Giving her curls a final pat, Josephine set the handmirror down on the dressing table and turned to face her aunt. "I believe that we have imposed on Ravenaugh's hospitality quite enough," she stated flatly, before Regina could give voice to the question writ plain on her face. "What *did* you give me, by the way—last night and yesterday in the travelling coach?" she inquired, in the hopes of turning the subject. Aunt Reggie, she had begun to suspect, was possessed of a formidable perspicacity, which might lead her to come a deal closer to the truth of Josephine's motives in wishing to leave than Josephine would wish her to do. "I had the most peculiar sensation that every muscle in my body had suddenly turned to soft wax."

"Only an herbal potion I picked up in the Orient," Regina answered evasively. "Peppermint, chamomile, a dash of hops and lemon balm, a measure of passionflower and a few drops of valerian, among other things. It is all perfectly harmless given in small doses, I assure you. On the other hand, it might give you a false sense of well-being. I should not wish you to overdo, Josephine, out of a mistaken notion that you are more recovered than you actually are. I should naturally blame myself if you suffered a relapse on account of something I had done. Which is why I urge you to reconsider leaving so soon."

"Now you are being absurd," exclaimed Josephine, who could not but speculate if her aunt might have some other reason for wishing to remain at Ravenscliff. At forty, after all, Regina was closer in age to the lord of the manor than Josephine herself. It was not inconceivable that her aunt might feel an attraction for the compelling Earl of Ravenaugh. Unaccountably, she suffered a peculiar stab in the vicinity of her breastbone at the thought. Still, she dared not stay another night under the earl's roof, not even for Aunt Reggie, she told herself. "I am perfectly ready to continue to Harrogate as soon as our means of transport can be arranged. I daresay his lordship would not be averse to lending us the use of his coach for that purpose. Wiggens can return it later in exchange for our own."

"Yes, I'm sure he can," Regina said, wondering what bee had gotten under her niece's bonnet. Last night, she had not seemed in such a hurry to quit the earl's company. If anything, they had given every impression of two people who enjoyed a remarkable compatibility, which was demonstrated in a lively exchange of ideas, a sharing of laughter, and a mutual enjoyment of a wide range of interests. Had she been in the match-making line, she might even have been congratulating herself on what gave every appearance of becoming *un fait accompli*. She might have, that was, until Josephine informed her in no uncertain terms that they would be leaving as soon as possible, that very morning if circumstances permitted.

"Very well, if you insist on going," Aunt Reggie said, quelling the urge to shake her head in perplexity, "I shall pack right after breakfast."

"Oh, but you *cannot!*" declared a feminine voice from behind the two women. "Not yet. I was counting on you to stay at least another day or two."

Startled, Josephine turned. "Clarissa, for heaven's sake," she exclaimed, holding her hands out to the girl, standing just inside the doorway. "I did not hear you come in."

"I beg your pardon. I should have knocked. Indeed, I was on the point of announcing my presence, when I heard you say you were leaving. Please say you won't, Jo," Clarissa pleaded, crossing to the older girl. "I have been waiting for you to wake up to show you my horses, and the deer park above the falls, and Miss Priss's kittens in the hayloft over the stables, and my diary. You promised we should be friends, Jo. You know you did."

"And so we are. I daresay we are destined to be bosom friends since you are very nearly my only friend," Josephine laughingly assured the girl. Strange, she thought, a little startled at the child's insistence. How quickly Clarissa would seem to have formed an attachment for her unexpected guest! But then, she could not but admit the entire company, including Aunt Reggie, had made a merry gathering. That was, after all, one of the reasons she had awakened determined to leave Ravenscliff, Josephine firmly reminded herself. "And, after all," she added brightly, "your father has promised you might come to see me at Harrogate. Aunt Reggie and I have a cottage all to ourselves. Should you come for a visit, we can talk to our heart's content."

Briefly, Clarissa's glance fell before Josephine's. "Naturally, I shall like that above all things," she said, then lifted her gaze once again. "Still, I wish you would not go today. There is so much that I should like you to see."

"I daresay there will be time to see a few things," Josephine smiled. "I haven't left yet, after all. We have still to discover if his lordship can oblige us with a conveyance of some sort."

"He will, you may be certain of it. But then, he has already gone this morning to see to the repair of your coach." Clarissa glanced hopefully at Josephine. "I doubt he will be back before tea."

"Well, then," Josephine replied, rising with alacrity from the dressing table. "I suggest we had better hurry down to breakfast if we are to visit the stables and the deer park before his lordship's return. As for your diary, you can bring that with you when you come to visit," she added, suffering a small twinge of conscience.

Josephine deemed it exceedingly unlikely in the wake

of her discussion with the earl that any such visit would ever transpire. If nothing else, Ravenaugh had made it clear he had little wish to further an acquaintanceship, which might easily have blossomed into something rather more intimate. Why? she wondered, only half-listening to Clarissa's chatter as they descended to the breakfast room.

He had liked her, just as she had immediately liked him. She could not be mistaken in that. If anything, their first meeting and her subsequent exposure to his compelling presence had had all the elements of what her sister Lucy had been wont to describe in her novels as a "sublime illumination," a moment of discovery in which two people of kindred souls meet and are awakened to a sympathetic awareness of one another. Not that she would have subscribed to the notion of any romantic involvement, she told herself firmly. She was not so green as to expect a man of Ravenaugh's obvious experience to fall head over ears in love with a provincial, not all in a single moment or even in a hundred years. Nor did she entertain the belief that she had lost her heart to a man she had only just met. She had, however, allowed herself to think that she might have found *someone* with whom she could at last share, not only her love of knowledge and books, but her keen sense of the absurd. She and Ravenaugh were in so many ways in perfect accord with one another. She did not doubt that, had circumstances been different, he might in time have been her very dear friend.

Little wonder, then, that she had found herself perplexed by the dawning suspicion that the real reason Ravenaugh did not favor Clarissa's coming to Harrogate was *because* he felt himself drawn to Josephine. Having been well-versed from an early age in logic, Josephine was not long in deducing that he considered himself too old to pursue a friendship with a female of nearly the same age as his daughter. It was, of course, all patently absurd, as she had not hesitated to demonstrate to him—to little effect, as it turned out, since he had remained stubbornly determined that nothing more should come of their chance meeting.

And that was that, she told herself, just as she had done in the middle of the night after examining the situation from every possible angle and before Aunt Reggie, coming in to check on her charge and, finding her still awake, had given her an herbal potion to help her sleep. There simply was nothing more to be done, and, rather than make a worse fool of herself than she had already done, she had seen nothing for it, but to remove herself from Ravenscliff as soon as was possible.

It really was too bad, she thought, as she sat down to a breakfast of tea and toast, for which she had not the least appetite. She would have liked the chance to at least *try* and chase the shadows from Ravenaugh's eyes.

"It is only a little farther," Clarissa called over her shoulder to Josephine no little time later, as she clambered ahead of the older girl along a narrow path hedged by craggy pines and boulders. "It was used to be my favorite place. Mama used to bring me, a long time ago. Then Papa, for no reason at all, said I was not to go anymore, unless he went with me."

"Then perhaps we should have waited, Clarissa. Indeed, you should have told me." Josephine, panting a little from her recent exertions, came up beside Clarissa, who had stopped and, standing curiously still, was staring ahead at a barren outcropping of rock some distance away. "I should not like to go against his wishes."

"Pooh! What do I care for his wishes? He cares nothing for mine. Besides," Clarissa added, glancing at Josephine and then away again. "After last night, I had to come."

Lifting her skirts, Clarissa darted off again. "Come, Jo. You cannot see anything from here. The falls are just ahead."

"Clarissa—*wait.*"

The roar of the falls was much louder here, and plumes of mist could be seen where the bourne plummeted over the cliff. Clarissa, hastening toward the outcrop, either did not hear or chose not to heed Josephine's call. In an instant she had vanished into a thick copse of trees and brush.

"Now what in heaven's name," muttered Josephine, mystified at Clarissa's odd behavior, not to mention her rather cryptic utterances. Then mindful of being left behind, she started after the girl.

Moments later, Josephine, picking her way over slippery boulders, was heartily wishing her young companion, if not precisely to the devil, then most certainly to a lengthy solitary confinement on bread and water. Had she known she would be required to go on a walking expedition, she might have eschewed her blue velvet half-boots for her rather disreputable, but otherwise far more practical, brown leather walking boots, she reflected. Wryly she noted the scuff marks on the toes of her fashionably shod feet, as she stepped at last out on to the ledge overlooking the chasm.

She was brushing ineffectually at her soiled skirts, when, straightening, she froze, a wave of fear washing over her at the sight of Clarissa.

The girl stood, poised at the stony lip of the precipice, her face wearing an expression of total absorption and her gaze fixed in seeming fascination on the falls, hurtling away at her feet. Good God, thought Josephine, who, though she might take being involved in a carriage wreck all in stride, especially while under the influence of one of Aunt Reggie's euphoria-inducing herbal concoctions, had never entertained an ambition for performing balancing feats at dizzying heights, let alone a fondness for flirting with almost certain death. No doubt this was what came of wishing for a little adventure in one's life, she reflected with sardonic appreciation of the dilemma in which she now found herself.

Ever of a practical nature, it could not but occur to her that the smallest distraction might very well be sufficient to set the child off her balance, with disastrous results. She quelled a queasy sensation at the inevitable image of Clarissa, plummeting over the edge to the rocks below. Nor could Josephine dismiss the distinct possibility that any attempt to forcibly draw the girl away from the edge of the cliff might very well result in Clarissa's taking her would-be rescuer with her.

The devil, she thought. Ill-equipped as she was for heroic gestures, she could hardly stand by and do nothing. Plainly what was called for was clear thinking and a calm approach.

It could not but occur to Josephine, as she steeled herself to take the first step, that whatever pleasure there was to be had in adventures of a hair-raising nature must occur only afterward—in the telling. Certainly, she found little to relish in her present circumstances, unless one were to count a highly elevated heart-rate and a clamp, like a vise, on her vitals. Drawing a deep breath, she strode resolutely out to the edge of the cliff beside Clarissa.

She could not but notice the girl gave every manifestation of one wholly oblivious to the addition of another person, teetering precariously, on the cliff beside her. "It's magnificent, isn't it," Josephine ventured at last, forced to shout above the din of the falls. With great care, she avoided looking down. Then, when it seemed no response was to be forthcoming, she felt her much vaunted patience stretched to the limit. "Clarissa!"

Clarissa blinked and lifted startled eyes to Josephine. "Jo?" she exclaimed. "You did come, after all."

"As you see," Josephine observed with more than a hint of irony. "Which is more than you deserve. I shall thank you not to run off like that again. You may be able to cavort over rock cliffs like a mountain goat, but I, I fear, cannot."

The effect of this telling speech was like a dash of cold water in Clarissa's face, which was just what Josephine had intended. It was one thing to abandon one's guests to the wilds, but quite another to lead them on to perilous grounds. Josephine was not amused. She was, however, intrigued in spite of herself. *Something* had provoked Clarissa's exceedingly odd behavior. Indeed, Josephine could not imagine that she herself would be standing at the edge of a seventy-foot precipice if there were not some very good reason for it.

"You are right, of course," Clarissa had the grace to answer, albeit a trifle grudgingly. "It was wrong of me. I'm afraid I can offer no excuse for my behavior."

"No, I daresay you cannot. Perhaps you *can* tell me, however, what, precisely, we are doing here."

"But I should think it would be obvious." Clarissa embraced the falls and the spectacular drop with a sweeping, and, to Josephine's way of thinking, exceedingly reckless, gesture of an arm. "The view, of course."

"I've said it is magnificent," observed Josephine, who had really preferred not to be reminded of the breathtaking aspects of her vantage point. Drawing a deep breath, she willed the butterflies in her stomach to cease their fluttering. "Must we stand so close to the edge? It tends to make one a trifle dizzy, does it not?"

"Dizzy?" Clarissa laughed and, flinging out her arms, pirouetted with heedless abandon at the edge of the projecting bulge of rock. "It's like standing at the top of the world. Mama said it was the one place where her spirit could be free. Here, nothing could ever touch her. Funny, isn't it," she added with a strange hint of bitterness.

"Funny? I see nothing funny in it," Josephine declared in no uncertain terms. "If you are trying to frighten me, you are doing an excellent job of it. I daresay your spirit will indeed be free—irrevocably so—if you continue in that manner."

To Josephine's dismay, the child's face went deathly pale at that observation. "Clarissa—dear," she exclaimed, reaching a hand out to the girl in alarm. "What is it? You look ill. Pray come away from there."

Abruptly, Clarissa yanked her arm from beneath Josephine's touch. "I am not in the least ill. And nothing is the matter." Hastily, she turned away. Not, however, before Josephine was given to glimpse the glimmer of tears in the other girl's eyes.

Josephine caught her bottom lip between her teeth. Faith, she thought, what was this? The girl was as changeable as quicksilver. "Clarissa, I can see that something is wrong. Please tell me what it is. How can I help you if you will not talk to me?"

"Help me?" Clarissa came sharply around, bridling with defiance. Josephine felt her heart sink. "What makes you think I need your help?" said Clarissa with a haughtiness that would have done Josephine's sister, Florence, credit. "I am not a child, Jo. Pray stop treating me like one. You, after all, are not so very much older than I."

"No," agreed Josephine, who not only thought of herself as eons older than the Earl of Ravenaugh's only offspring, but felt herself rapidly aging with every moment spent in her company. Josephine had not grown up in a family of seven children, nevertheless, without learning to recognize when she was being manipulated. "I am old enough, however, to realize the edge of a cliff is hardly the place to behave like a perfect gaby. I am truly sorry if I have in some way hurt you, Clarissa. But whatever I have said or done to elicit such a response, things have gone far enough. I am going back to the manor now, and I should hope you will go with me."

"Then go. I am sure I do not care what you do." Holding her arms out at her sides, the young miscreant began to give a superb imitation of an acrobat performing a balancing act.

"Gammon," pronounced Josephine, schooling her features to betray nothing of the terror she felt, watching Clarissa deliberately court disaster. "I know that you do care. But it changes nothing. I will not stay and play the dupe. Goodbye, Clarissa. I shall always be sorry we could not be friends."

Backing firmly away from the gorge to safety, Josephine turned—and beheld in the distance the powerful figure of the earl making his way toward the outcrop with what gave every manifestation of strong purpose.

"No, wait, Jo," Clarissa called from behind her. "Please don't go."

Josephine could not but think it was a trifle unfortuitous of Ravenaugh to appear just when she was on the point of luring his daughter away from the one spot he had forbidden her to be. It had become increasingly obvious to her in the past twenty-four hours that there was already a deal of hurt and misunderstanding between father and daughter. She could not imagine that any good could come from a confrontation between the two at such a time and in such a place. Very likely it would lead to dire repercussions.

Or perhaps it had nothing at all to do with chance, she thought suddenly, fortuitous or otherwise.

A glint in her eye, she turned back to Clarissa.

"Very well, Clarissa, I shall stay," she said in measured tones, "but only if you come away from there at once."

"Why? I am perfectly safe where I am," declared Clarissa, showing no immediate inclination to leave her lofty perch. "I was used to come here as a child without anyone the wiser. Strange. I thought, you, of all people, would understand, Jo. It is why I wanted most especially to bring you here."

"But I do understand—more than you know," Josephine answered, her heart leaping to her throat as Clarissa, her skirts billowing in a gust of wind, swayed perilously close to the edge. "It is, at least in part, because of your mama."

Clarissa's head came up, her aspect challenging. "I haven't the least idea what you are talking about. I cannot think what my mother could possibly have to do with anything."

"Pray save your breath, Clarissa. Missish airs are quite wasted on me. Of course it is your mama. You all but told me. She used to bring you here, you said. It was her special place. Last night brought the memories back, and you began to miss her all over again, did you not? But that is only part of the reason you lured me here today. What you really intended was to annoy your father. And that, I find particularly inexcusable. I dislike being used, Clarissa. Especially in a childish ploy to gain your father's attention. And pray do not deny it. He is on his way here at this very moment, just as you intended he should."

"So, what if he is," retorted the girl, perhaps not nearly so confident as she would like to appear. Her eyes darted beyond Josephine to the curve in the path where she had earlier pointed out the jut of cliff to her guest.

"I daresay you cannot see him now," Josephine said. "He will be out of sight, where the path winds among the trees. But he is there. I saw him coming. Before he arrives, you might at least tell me why you have gone to all this trouble to discredit me, not to mention yourself, in his eyes. I think you owe me that much.''

A shadow of uncertainty flickered in Clarissa's eyes. ''I don't know why. I never know why,'' she said strangely. ''Perhaps it is because he called you a lady. He wanted me to follow your example, someone with whom he was hardly acquainted. Have you any notion how that made me feel?''

''I should think it must have hurt your feelings,'' Josephine ventured. ''I daresay it might even have made you wish to show him how far removed from a lady you could be, if you wanted to. I have noted that very often we are moved to live up to what we believe others think of us.''

Clarissa, Josephine wryly noted, appeared not to have even heard her. ''I'm sure that must be it,'' she said, her gaze oddly vague. ''I *could* not bear it that he liked you better than me, especially when he has never made the smallest effort to come to know me. Perhaps just once I thought to make him actually see me. Perhaps I thought that here—'' Josephine held her breath, as Clarissa, in her distraction, stepped toward her, away from the precipice. ''But, no. It was a stupid idea.'' Clarissa stopped and turned to stare at the falls again. ''I see that now. The truth is, I am just what he thinks I am. Unruly and hopelessly headstrong. I daresay it is little wonder that he cannot bear to be near me.''

''Now you are being absurd,'' said Josephine, who could not but wish Clarissa had chosen a more felicitous setting in which to do her soul-searching. ''You needn't feel that I am trying to displace you in your father's affections. No one could ever do that. You are his daughter. I am nothing more to him than a chance acquaintance, surely you must see that.'' Josephine held out her hand to the girl. ''But I should like to be your friend, if you still want me to. I haven't so many friends in the world that I should like to lose even one.''

Clarissa's head came around. "Do you mean that? Do you?"

"But of course I do, Clarissa." It was on Josephine's lips to add that she was perfectly willing to forget the morning's events had ever happened, when, from out of nowhere, disaster struck.

Josephine could never recall precisely what happened next. One moment, Clarissa had turned and was reaching for Josephine's hand, and the next, to her horror, the girl's feet appeared simply to slide out from under. All in an instant, Clarissa was sprawled face-down at the very edge of the cliff, the gorge falling away before her eyes.

"Clarissa!" shouted Josephine, paralyzed with horror. "Clarissa, don't look down! Look at *me!*" The girl remained frozen, her eyes fixed in horrified fascination on the sheer drop before her. "Clarissa, push yourself away from the edge. Crawl, if you must, but come here to me at once!"

"I can't!" Closing her eyes, Clarissa clung to the rock. "Faith, what a mull I have made of things. It is just as Mama said it would be. Girls who tell lies and misbehave come to a bad end. It was the last thing she ever said to me. Why did I not listen!"

Josephine, considerably enlightened, took a step toward Clarissa. "Clarissa, it is not your fault she is gone. You were only a child, caught in some childish indiscretion. Your mama loved you. She would never have wished you to blame yourself."

At that, Clarissa did look around, her eyes filling with tears.

"It isn't fair, Jo. I never even got to say goodbye."

"No doubt I am very sorry for you," said Josephine, driven at last to desperate measures. "On the other hand, it is not fair either that you dragged me out here. If you must know, you have given me a splitting headache.

Indeed," she added, artfully lifting the back of her hand to her forehead, "I am very much afraid that I am about to be exceedingly unwell."

Closing her eyes, Josephine exhaled a long sigh and, without further preamble, crumpled to the ground.

She was to have the immediate gratification of hearing Clarissa shout her name in alarm and scramble instantly to her aid—as Josephine had been certain she would, indeed, had been counting on—and the less satisfying, and far more mortifying, sensation of having Ravenaugh arrive scant moments later.

It was all Josephine could do not to betray herself as she felt the earl drop to his knee by her side, then, firmly lifting her in his arms, carry her away from the scene of near disaster.

"It is all my fault," Clarissa sobbed, plucking ineffectually at one of Josephine's limply hanging hands. "Please say she is all right. You must believe I never meant for this to happen. I never thought—"

"No, I daresay you did not. But you must think now," rumbled Ravenaugh's voice over Josephine, as she felt herself lowered to a grassy mound, her back propped against the trunk of a tree. Strong, but gentle fingers felt for a pulse at her wrist. "You are no help to her in your present state. If you wish to be of use, I suggest you cease at once to be a watering pot."

"But, Papa—"

"At *once*, Clarissa," he said. Then, in a voice that, while firm, was a deal gentler than the one he had used before, "Lady Josephine has merely fainted. No doubt the climb was too much for her. Still, we must get her away from here. Are you listening, Clarissa?"

"Y-yes, Father," Clarissa answered with a watery hiccough. "I am better now, I promise."

"Good. I require you to run ahead and inform Miss

Morseby what has happened. Tell her not to be alarmed, that I am bringing her niece home to her. We shall discuss your behavior—later, when I have seen to Lady Josephine. And, Clarissa—''

''Yes, Father?''

''Take your time going. It will serve no one, least of all Lady Josephine, if you fall and hurt yourself.''

Josephine, tingling with the awareness of Ravenaugh's nearness, not to mention the masterful way in which he had calmed his daughter's hysteria, heard the scuffle of Clarissa's retreat. Only then, with the realization that she was alone with him, did it occur to her that it was time she was coming out of her swoon.

It was, consequently, with no little surprise and a deal of mortification that she heard the maddening earl announce in exceedingly dry tones, ''Clarissa is gone, my dear. You may open your eyes now.''

''Wretch,'' pronounced Josephine in rueful accents. Opening her eyes, she sat up. ''How did you guess I was shamming it?''

A single arrogant eyebrow arched toward Ravenaugh's hairline. ''How not? We did agree, after all, that you are a poor actress, did we not? You are clearly, however, a resourceful female. As it happens, I arrived in time to witness the finale to your dramatic performance and surmised its purpose almost at once. I believe I owe you my daughter's life. Having said that, I do not hesitate to inform you that, were *you* my daughter, I should gladly put you over my knee for pulling such a stunt. What the *devil* do you think you were doing, Miss Powell? I might have expected this of Clarissa, but hardly of you. Any fool could see at once that the falls are hardly a felicitous spot for sight-seeing.''

If he had thought by that to impress her with the enormity of her transgression, he was to be distinctly disappointed.

"Dear, you *are* in a rare taking, are you not?" queried Josephine, apparently without the slightest chink in her composure. Climbing stiffly to her feet with Ravenaugh's help, she proceeded to his silent amazement to calmly dust herself off. "I suppose I can only be grateful that you are not my father. Had he been here, he would undoubtedly have confined me for an entire year to chess lessons for my misjudgment in this matter." Straightening, she gazed soberly into Ravenaugh's eyes. "You have every right to be angry, my lord. It was remarkably ill-considered of me to ask Clarissa to show me the falls. I can only hope you will accept my sincerest apology for all the trouble I have caused."

Ravenaugh's gaze narrowed sharply on Josephine's lovely countenance. Hell and the devil confound it. The redoubtable Lady Josephine had no right to appear as if she were perfectly used to dealing with any number of crises involving adolescent girls with an excess of sensibilities and a flair for the dramatic. He wished never again to experience the dreadful moment, when, upon arriving home, he was handed Clarissa's note pointedly informing him she had acquiesced to take Lady Josephine to see the falls. Good God, the cursed falls, of all places! The realization that the Earl of Bancroft's youngest daughter had not the least inkling what she was getting herself into had been only slightly less appalling than coming sometime later upon the inauspicious sight of his only offspring, poised in the distance on the brink of annihilation, and Lady Josephine valiantly attempting to talk her out of it.

The denouement, coming, as it had, at the point when he was once more in view of the drama going forth, but yet too far away to be of any use, had been instructive, if nothing else. That Lady Josephine's swoon had quickly struck him as being rather too convenient, not to mention, wholly out of character, had only slightly lessened the unbearable pressure in his chest that had arisen at the sight of the slender figure crumpling in a lifeless heap to the ground, a pressure which had eased with the assurance of his daughter's safety, but had not ceased until he had had recourse to feel Lady Josephine's pulse. The intensity of his relief at discovering a pulse-rate far in excess of what one might reasonably expect in the victim of a swoon had been as revealing to him as it was irrevocably unsettling.

Only the fact that her stratagem had worked to the benefit of his daughter kept him from wringing the lady's neck for what she had put him through. And, now, not content with having placed him in her eternal debt, not to mention having slipped through the formidable defenses that had preserved his heart from a host of other females before her, she proposed to assume his daughter's blame for the whole unhappy affair.

"Enough, my lady," he said cynically. "I daresay you mean well. I'm afraid, however, your efforts at shielding Clarissa are wasted. You cannot honestly expect me to believe that you were responsible for this morning's fiasco."

"I do not entertain any expectations where you are concerned, my lord, honest or otherwise," Josephine did not hesitate to inform him. "You have already made yourself patently clear on that point, have you not? On the other hand, you may be sure that I am not in the habit of lying. As it happens, it was entirely my idea to see the falls. I realize now how foolish it was. Had Clarissa told me beforehand that her mama was often used to come here, you may be certain I should never have insisted."

"Clarissa told you that, did she?" said Ravenaugh, singularly grim-faced. "And what else did my daughter choose to reveal of matters that do not concern you?"

"A great deal that should concern *you*, my lord. I do not pretend to know what lies between you and your daughter, but it does not take a great insight to see that Clarissa feels estranged from your affections. She thinks you do not love her."

"She does, does she? And what do you think?"

"I think you have left her far too long to herself in a house with too many memories. Perhaps you can have no idea how very harmful that can be for a young girl, especially one with a tendency to indulge in romantic fantasies. In time, she may not be able to tell the truth from the fiction she invents."

Ravenaugh regarded her strangely. "She becomes, in fact, an habitual liar, prone to draw in anyone who does not know her well. Clarissa's mother did not make it a practice to come here to the falls, Miss Powell. Eugenie was petrified of heights."

If he had hoped with that announcement to set her off her balance, he was soon to be proved well short of the mark.

"I see," said Josephine, turning to pace a step as she digested that startling piece of information. "Naturally, you cannot be mistaken in such a thing. In which case it would seem there is a great deal that I do not understand."

"You cannot know how relieved I am to hear it," Ravenaugh drawled cynically. "Perhaps you now understand my reluctance, at least, to entrust Clarissa to your care. I am fond of my daughter, Lady Josephine, but I am hardly blind to her singular needs. Her—doctor—warned me. Still, I had hoped she had outgrown her infatuation with these fantasies of hers. My miscalculation almost cost you and Clarissa your lives."

"Dear me," said Josephine, "and now you will make sure that it does not happen again by confining her to Ravenscliff."

Ravenaugh's black eyebrows fairly snapped together over the bridge of his nose. "That would seem the logical solution," he answered. "You do not approve, Lady Josephine?"

"It is hardly my place to offer approval or disapproval. What you do, after all, is hardly any of my affair. Still," she added, knitting her brow in a frown, "it has been my experience that, if something has not worked in the past, it is hardly likely to work in the future no matter how many times it is repeated. In which case, the rational solution would be to try something different. Does it not occur to you, my lord, that she might do much better away from Ravenscliff in the company of other people? If not with me, then perhaps with one of her relations. Clarissa mentioned an aunt in Essex, Lady Eugenie's sister, I believe."

"It does *not,*" said Ravenaugh, amazed that the mettlesome Lady Josephine would still be willing even to contemplate befriending Clarissa after her harrowing adventure. "As to my sister-in-law's taking her, good God, perish the thought. Lady Caroline is dedicated to the cult of nonconformity. I should sooner send my daughter to a school for exotic dancers as consign her to the care of my sister-in-law."

"Really?" Miss Powell's face, Ravenaugh sardonically noted, fairly beamed with sudden interest. "Lady Caroline sounds a fascinating woman. Though I daresay you are in the right of it. A female who espouses freedom from the conventions would hardly be a suitable candidate to look after a young girl about to make her curtsey in society."

"No doubt I am gratified that, at least on that point, you agree with me," observed Ravenaugh dryly. "You might be surprised to learn that, in spite of my frequent absences, I have made every effort to provide for the welfare of my daughter."

"That, I never doubted for an instant, my lord," Josephine assured him. "It is unfortunate, however, that Clarissa does not perfectly comprehend it. Naturally, she is at that difficult age, when one is convinced the sole design of a parent is to make one perfectly miserable. Taken in such a light, I daresay it would be remarkable if she did *not* act out her resentment in small acts of rebellion. Her performance last night in the Music Room would seem to be a perfect example."

"And I suppose her behavior this morning in which she endangered not only herself but you, Lady Josephine, is to be taken as just such another?" demanded Ravenaugh with scant humor. "Next, you will be trying to tell me there is nothing in the least exceptional in her obsession with fantasy."

"It might surprise you to learn that most girls are give to some sort of fancy. I daresay it is not unusual in boys as well. On the other hand, Clarissa's behavior this morning was of an entirely different order. She was deeply affected, I am sure of it—as if she were not acting at all. It is all very puzzling." Josephine frowned, thinking back over the strange events of the morning, beginning with Clarissa's almost frantic insistence that Josephine postpone her departure. "Indeed, the most puzzling thing of all is that she was so utterly convincing. I did not doubt for a moment that she was used to come here often with her mama. Even now, knowing that no mother in her right mind would choose to bring a small child to such a place, I am still finding it difficult to accept that Lady Ravenaugh was never at the falls at all."

There was an odd sort of silence in which Josephine sensed the earl's powerful frame, suddenly tense beside her. She looked up with questioning eyes. Ravenaugh met her glance, his own, glittery hard. "I did not say she was never at the falls."

"Did you not?" Josephine swallowed dryly. How harsh

was his face, bitter with some terrible memory! Josephine folded her hands before her to keep them from going out to him.

"Nor is it strange that Clarissa should be deeply affected. Indeed, it would be strange only if she were not."

He turned away, and, planting his hand against the gnarled trunk of the tree, leaned against it, his gaze distant, unseeing. It took little imagination for Josephine to realize he was seeing the falls again in his mind's eye, as they were at some other time.

Josephine suffered a chill of premonition. Indeed, she knew before he said it.

"Her mother died in that wretched place. She flung herself over the falls to her death on the rocks below." He turned his head to look at her. "Clarissa saw it all. We found her that night, wandering about in the woods in her night clothes. Dazed, frightened. She does not remember any of it. God willing, she never will. And, now, Lady Josephine, I trust you *see* why I will not send Clarissa to you at Harrogate."

Chapter 5

Josephine breathed deeply of the sweet Yorkshire breeze as she vigorously swung her arms in rhythm with her stride. She could not but think perhaps Mrs. Gosset, the housekeeper, was right about one thing—there would seem to be an almost magical healing power about the town on the hill with its airy Two Hundred Acres of sweeping, tree-lined lawns and walks, not to mention the colorful carpet of flowering crocuses, and the pine wood fragrant with marvelously unfamiliar scents. She was not sure she could say the same of the iron and sulphur waters of Tewitt's and St. John's Wells, let alone "The Stinking Spaw," aptly named, though she had stoically downed the prescribed glassful of the stuff once a day. If one placed any credence in the maxim that the benefit of a medicine might be determined in diminishing proportion to the pleasure of its taste, then she doubted not the waters must be a powerful healing agent indeed.

Whatever the case, she had become increasingly aware, since taking up residence at Harrogate ten days earlier, that something wonderful and exciting seemed to be happening to her. She was feeling better, and stronger, she was sure of it. This, she attributed less to any specific beneficial attribute of the town or its waters than to Aunt Reggie's regimen of daily walks, exposure to fresh air and sunshine, and the addition to her diet of a multitude of fresh fruits and vegetables, milk, and herbal tea, of course.

The changes in Josephine, while not dramatic, were yet perceptible. She had put on two or three pounds, her habitual pallor had given way to a translucent ivory tinged with rose, and she had come to the point of being able to walk an entire mile at something more than a leisurely stroll. She had, in fact, that very morning maintained for longer than twenty minutes the long, swinging gait to which her aunt Reggie had introduced her. She was keenly aware of a mounting joy in her accomplishment, when, coming abreast of her aunt, she flung herself into the pace and, gaily calling out, "Catch me if you can," passed the older woman.

Regina, never one to turn down a challenge, especially from "one of her girls," gave an answering shout and lengthened her stride to catch Josephine. The race was on.

Side by side, stride for stride, the two paced beneath the

trees, until, coming no little time later to the edge of the forest, they stumbled at last to a halt, laughing and clinging to one another.

"It really is the most amazing thing," panted Josephine, glowing with the sheer pleasure of the morning's exercise. "I feel as if I might have gone on forever, Aunt Reggie. Indeed, I feel—I feel . . . I don't *know* what I feel, save only that I cannot recall ever having felt quite so marvelously happy!"

Josephine linked her arm in Regina's, and, together, the two women left the woods for the gentle environs of the Valley Gardens.

"Is it always like this? The fresh air, the sunshine, the euphoria? I never want it to end. I want it to go on and on. Indeed, I cannot imagine why I have been coddled and wrapped in soft wool for all these years, when I might have felt like this. I almost believe I shall be well and strong one day. You have made me feel this way, my dearest of aunts."

"But of course you will be well, my dear," Regina declared. "It is only a matter of exercise and sensible eating. If there was anything constitutionally wrong with you, I daresay you have outgrown it long ago. I have always thought it a pity that young girls and women of refinement have come to be treated as delicate creatures unsuited to anything more strenuous than doing needlework or lounging about looking interestingly pale. Is it any wonder that so many succumb to the rigors of childbirth?"

"I daresay it is not," said Josephine, thinking that her sisters, all avid equestrians, had never been prone to lounge about, which was why, no doubt, that they were healthy, vibrant, and strong. "I never thought about it in quite that way. I have, in fact, become so used to the idea that I should never marry or have children that I have never thought about it at all."

"Then perhaps it is time you changed your way of thinking, my dear," Regina replied strangely, pausing at the end of the walk to stare straight ahead.

Josephine and Regina had accounted themselves exceedingly fortunate to have been let a cottage overlooking the Valley Gardens. The park, picturesquely laid out in the natural shelter of a dell with the town partially embracing it, had been a source of never-ending delight to Josephine, who never tired of viewing its sweeping lawns, spreading trees, and, most of all, its profusion of flowerbeds. The cottage itself, a three-story house of dark Yorkshire stone with bay windows facing the gardens in front, stood directly across the street from where the two women had come to a halt.

It was not the cottage, however, that drew Josephine's startled attention, but the chaise and its pair of matched bays that had just pulled up in the street at the front of the house.

Taken wholly unawares, Josephine was quite unprepared for the sudden shock of unmitigated joy that shot through her at the sight of the powerfully built figure of the gentleman, his indecently broad shoulders encased in a many-caped driving coat and his dark, rebellious hair topped by a curly brimmed beaver cocked at a delightfully arrogant angle.

Ravenaugh! Faith, he had come to Harrogate in spite of his conviction that nothing good could come of it, a sentiment that he had made clear to her in those final moments above Ravenscliff; and he had brought Clarissa with him.

What had happened to bring him to such a decision? she wondered. While she had failed utterly to banish the nobleman from her thoughts in the past several days, she had forced herself to accept the fact that she would never see him again. After all, he was a man of resolve, who had made it a rule never to change his mind. Inevitably, her first thought was that it must have something to do with Clarissa. Indeed, she could think of nothing else that would bring the elusive nobleman out of his self-imposed fastness.

Quelling the multitude of questions that sprang to mind, Josephine hurried across the street, Regina following in her wake.

"Jo. Miss Morseby," Clarissa called, waving excitedly. "Father has brought me to see you. We have moved into the cottage that used to be Great Aunt Winifred's. We shall be here for at least a fortnight."

"Clarissa," Josephine exclaimed. "And Ravenaugh. By all that is marvelous. This is indeed a surprise."

The nobleman's head came about, and for an instant it seemed that his dark, piercing gaze lanced straight through her. Josephine's heart gave an unseemly leap, then he turned to give the groom instructions to "walk 'em."

Ravenaugh sprang lightly down from the vehicle. "Not, I hope, an unwelcome one, Lady Josephine," he said, helping Clarissa to dismount.

"You know it could never be that, my lord," Josephine smiled.

"Miss Morseby, a pleasure to see you again."

"Likewise, my lord. Josephine and I were about to have tea. Naturally, you will both join us."

"Yes, please do come in," Josephine added, noting that Mrs. Callaway in the house next door was peering out at them from between a crack in her window curtains and that Widow Pringle and her spinster sister, Lobelia, had paused in their morning stroll to take note of Lady Josephine's callers. Josephine's eyes twinkled up at Ravenaugh. "We seem to be attracting a deal of attention. I should not wish to overstimulate the poor old dears. Too much excitement might send them into palpitations."

"I daresay it would serve them right," declared Regina,

who took a dim view of gossipmongers. "Some people have far too little to do with their time." Turning in disgust, she entered the house, the others following after her.

"I fear Aunt Reggie and I have come in for a deal of speculation since we took up residence," confessed Josephine, as they stepped into a pleasant hall made even more so by green, potted ferns. "It is our walking dresses, you see." Holding her skirts out, she gaily turned before her guests. "I'm afraid they are positively indecent."

The walking dress in question was indeed a daring creation, not because of its bright hue, which was best described as apple green and canary yellow, or even because of its incorporating a gored skirt and bodice in the very newest Gothic style, which allowed the gathered skirt to drape from a very high, narrow waist to a broad base trimmed in Gothic lace. What truly set it off and placed it in the category of "indecent" was the hemline. It was daringly short, reaching a good two inches, in fact, above the ankles to reveal cambric stockings of green and yellow clockwork and green leather half-boots with flat, rounded heels for walking.

Aunt Reggie's costume, while less colorful, being of a sedate blue, was similar in style and length.

Ravenaugh, presented with an enticing glimpse of Lady Josephine's undeniably trim ankles with the suggestion of equally shapely calves above them, was yet more entranced by the glow of the young beauty's complexion. "Positively shocking, my lady," he agreed, with smiling gravity.

"But ever so much more practical," laughed Josephine, a becoming tinge of color invading her cheeks. "One cannot walk freely if one is hampered by overlong skirts that persist in clinging to one's limbs. We had them made up specifically for our daily tramp through the pine woods."

"Well, I, for one, think they are splendid," declared Clarissa in obvious alt.

"I thought perhaps you would," Josephine laughed. "Oh, Mrs. Gosset," she added at the entrance of a middle-aged woman with a kindly aspect and twinkling blue eyes. "We have been honored with a morning call from the Earl of Ravenaugh and his daughter, Lady Clarissa Roth. They will be joining us for tea."

"You picked a fine time for it, m'lord, m'lady," smiled Mrs. Gosset, reaching for Ravenaugh's coat, hat, and gloves and Clarissa's pelisse of rose linen. "I just this instant took a fresh batch of ginger biscuits out'n the oven. Now, you run along, Lady Josephine. I'll show your guests into the parlor while you and Miss Morseby go and freshen up."

"Please," Clarissa pleaded, "say I may go with you. I cannot wait to hear everything that has happened since we last saw you. I daresay it is a lot. You look simply marvelous, Jo."

"How very nice of you to say so. But of course you must come. I promise we shan't be more than a few minutes, my lord," Josephine called to Ravenaugh as she and Clarissa hurried up the staircase after Regina.

"Pray do not hurry on my account," replied Ravenaugh, who was not averse to a few moments alone to collect himself.

Hell and the devil confound it! he cursed to himself upon finding himself alone in the parlor. After having been forced to struggle with his conscience for almost a fortnight, he had achieved at last a measure of peace with his decision not to give rein to emotions that he had neither thought nor desired ever to experience again, only to be brought in the end against his better judgment to make the drive to Harrogate. Nor was that all or the worst of it. No novice in affairs of the heart, he had been made wryly aware with each passing mile that he was experiencing all the unlikely symptoms of a moonstricken cub on the way to a much-anticipated reunion with a female for whom he felt more than a moderate affection.

Still, he had hardly expected, upon laying eyes on Josephine again, that he would suffer a pang of gladness so intense that it had shaken even his formidable reserve. Good God, but she was even more lovely than memory had served! Obviously, counter to his dire expectations, she had blossomed in the healthful environs of Harrogate, a circumstance for which he could only be infinitely grateful.

The devil, he thought, staring grimly out the parlor's bay window on to the park. He had spent the past hour on the road chiding himself for a bloody fool for giving into the compulsion to go against his firm resolve never again to see the enchanting Lady Josephine. It was bad enough his days had been haunted with visions of an angelically lovely countenance cursed with bewitching, otherworldly eyes, which had the perverse tendency to give way to unmitigated imps of laughter whenever he was least expecting it. Even worse, however, his nights had been cut up by the insidious whisperings that it was not uncommon for a man of his age to take a young wife, especially a man who had yet to get himself an heir.

Damn the nights and *damn* his unruly thoughts! There had been a time when he could not see beyond the cursed darkness, he grimly reminded himself. The last thing he wished was to tempt fate a second time. But then, he had never before encountered anyone quite like the Earl of Bancroft's youngest daughter.

He had from the very first been captivated by her extraordinary, fragile beauty. Infinitely worse, however, he had fallen subsequent victim to her gentleness and wit, which, stemming from a deeper source, counted far more heavily with him than a pretty face. In the few hours that he had

been in her remarkable presence, he had been witness to
her seemingly unlimited capacity for understanding, her
generosity and unselfishness, her air of calm good sense
that had made her seem much older than her nineteen
years, and, most captivating of all, her spirited determina-
tion to enjoy life to the fullest in spite of her fragile constitution. Sweet and gentle Josephine, who was yet possessed
of a lamentable tendency to levity. How different from the
tormented young beauty who had been his wife!

With Josephine Powell, he had felt struck with an immediate and overwhelming feeling of empathy, which might
easily have ripened into love.

It might have, that was, if he were foolish enough to
allow it to happen. As tempting as it might seem in the dark
hours of night with a decanter of port at hand, however, the
morning had always served to bring a return to sanity. It
had, that was, until this morning, when he had discovered
Clarissa in close conversation with Adam Saint-Clair, his
cousin.

Ravenaugh's lean jaw hardened. He had hardly been
surprised to discover his cousin, like the proverbial bad
penny, had shown up at Ravenscliff less than a month after
Ravenaugh's own return from the Continent.

Damn Saint-Clair and his cursed hatred of Ravenaugh
and all that the name encompassed! It was nine years since
Eugenie's death. Why should he choose to come back now?

The message from the earl's secretary had given
Ravenaugh fair warning that Saint-Clair had departed
India for England some months past. Ravenaugh's eyes
glittered coldly. There could be only one reason for his
cousin's return—Clarissa, who had always loved Saint-Clair
with what amounted to an unreasoning devotion!

It could hardly have escaped Saint-Clair's notice that
Clarissa was coming of age. No doubt it did not suit his
purposes to see his cousin's only offspring safely married

and away from Ravenscliff. Saint-Clair, not satisfied with having wrecked Ravenaugh's happiness, would not rest until he had destroyed the one thing left to the earl of Eugenia's.

It was perhaps the measure of Ravenaugh's distraction with Lady Josephine that he had almost forgotten the business that had brought him home. Bloody hell! His cousin had caught him unprepared this time. Grimly he vowed it would not happen again.

It had not taken Ravenaugh more than a few moments to deduce that whatever risk he ran in exposing himself to Lady Josephine's irresistible charms was of far less significance than that of allowing his cousin to reinsinuate himself into Clarissa's life and, therefore, by extension, into his own. He knew his cousin and his daughter far too well to do anything so unwise as to openly order Saint-Clair from the house and out of Clarissa's life. Such a maneuver would have served little purpose other than to earn Clarissa's contempt, which was all Saint-Clair required to further turn her against her father. Certainly it would have done little to keep Saint-Clair from seeing Clarissa.

What had been needed was time. A week or two should have been sufficient. By then, all would be ready, his preparations made to rid himself of his cousin's meddling once and for all.

In the meantime, there had been Clarissa to consider, and short of shipping her off to a nunnery, there had seemed but one logical course open to him. Rather than forbid his daughter access to his cousin, it had seemed preferable to distract her with a proposed visit of a few days at Harrogate. While it would not keep Saint-Clair away from Clarissa, Ravenaugh had every hope his daughter would be far too occupied with shopping and various other feminine pursuits to give her kinsman more than the time of day.

As luck would have it, the Waverlys, having elected to forego their customary annual visit to Harrogate, had written to inform Ravenaugh's agent that they would not be letting the cottage, which had once served the earl's aunt as a safe haven from her unhappy existence at Ravenscliff. Though Ravenaugh had not set foot in the place since his aunt's passing, he had maintained for the Waverlys a skeletal staff, which should be sufficient to his needs. He had every expectation that Clarissa would be more often than not with Lady Josephine and Miss Morseby.

It had seemed a good plan at the time. Now he was not so sure. He foresaw no little difficulty in keeping a tight rein on his feelings for the Earl of Bancroft's youngest daughter. Whatever else happened, she must never know that she had captured his lonely heart almost from the first moment he looked down into her smiling, blue-violet eyes. She deserved far better than to be drawn into the final tawdry chapters of a history that should have been ended long ago.

The trill of feminine laughter and the rustle of skirts beyond the parlor door alerted him to the return of the ladies. Schooling his features to reveal nothing of his somber thoughts, he steeled himself to meet the slender beauty who had upset the even tenor of his life and threatened to wreak havoc on his future peace of mind.

"It was all totally unexpected," Clarissa declared as Josephine reached for the doorhandles and slid open the doors. "This morning, out of the blue, Father simply announced we should have a holiday, and here we are."

"Well, I, for one, am very glad that you came," said Josephine, smiling quizzically across the room at the earl. "I daresay you may find the Royal Pump Room a trifle flat, but there is a dance twice a week at the assembly rooms, and the band concerts in the evenings are well worth attending. Aunt Reggie and I never cease to enjoy the various walks through the gardens, and there are some delightful shops, if you care to do some shopping.''

''You may be sure that I shall wish to do everything. Oh, I almost forgot. I brought you a present. Dear, in all the excitement, I must have left it in the carriage.''

''If you mean a certain basket done up in blue ribbons,'' offered Mrs. Gosset, making her entrance with the tea tray, ''your Mr. Ridings was kind enough to leave it with me. I taken it to the kitchens, m'lady. If you like, I can go and fetch it for you.''

''Thank you, Mrs. Gosset, but if you would not mind showing me the way, I should like to go and fetch it myself. It is a very special present. Pray don't wait tea for me, Jo. I shall only be a moment.''

''Well,'' declared Josephine, upon finding herself quite suddenly alone with the earl. ''It seems that there is to be no end of surprises for me this morning. I confess to being consumed with curiosity, my lord. I was under the distinct impression the last time we spoke that you were irrevocably determined against allowing Clarissa to come for a visit.''

''I believe I said I should not send her to visit you,'' Ravenaugh neatly parried. ''Which is not at all the same as bringing her.''

''No, I should say it was an even greater concession on your part,'' Josephine countered, coming in under Ravenaugh's guard. She met his eyes across the room. ''Or perhaps I misunderstood you that night in the library, my lord? No, pray do not answer that. It was rude of me, and I believe I should prefer to be kept in the dark.'' With a calm that she knew to be an utter sham, she busied herself with the tea server. ''You are here,'' she said, filling a dish, ''and I am exceedingly pleased to see you again, for whatever reasons." Smiling, she proffered the cup in its saucer. "If I recall, my lord, you take yours black."

"Your memory is impeccable, my lady," observed Ravenaugh dryly. Accepting the cup, he stood looking down at her. Josephine, returning his look, felt her heart go suddenly still. Then, "Lady Josephine—Josephine," he said at last, "I—"

"Sorry to be late," announced Regina, making a tardy entrance—at a most inopportune moment, to Josephine's way of thinking. "We are most fortunate in having Miss Harcourt and Lady Juliana drop in for a visit, and, look, they have brought their friend, Mr. Michael Lawrence, with them." Regina favored Josephine with a glance pregnant with meaning.

The two fashionably dressed ladies, who were both in their early twenties, swept into the room along with their male companion, a strikingly handsome gentleman of five-and-twenty. Having insinuated himself into Josephine's company on more than one occasion, it had not taken Josephine long to peg Michael Lawrence as a fashionable ne'er-do-well or to realize that, having had the misfortune to be born a younger son, he was on the lookout for an heiress to wed in order that he might live in the lavish manner to which he would like to become accustomed. In spite of her best efforts to convince him that she could look forward to no more than a modest jointure, he had persisted in believing she was a deal plumper in the pocket than was warranted. Michael Lawrence had become what Aunt Reggie was fond of referring to as the proverbial fly in the ointment.

Josephine, who was not in the remotest danger of falling victim to a handsome clothes horse, no matter how pretty his manners, on the other hand, had not been averse to tolerating the gentleman's presence. Having a pretention to dandyism, which was expressed in a preference for lace-bearing cossacks reminiscent of a lady's petticoat, dainty high-heeled shoes, a frothy crop at the neck, and a painted face with beauty marks, the would-be merveilleux was, after all, rather more amusing than the elderly gentlemen who had thus far shown her the favor of their attentions. Clarissa's unexpected arrival, however, would naturally put a different light on things.

An impressionable female not yet out of the schoolroom who had the distinction of being not only the Earl of Ravenaugh's only offspring, but the sole heir to his considerable fortune as well, could not but loom as an irresistible temptation to one of Lawrence's stamp. Even worse, however, Clarissa was bound to find the fair-haired young Adonis, in spite of or perhaps even because of his eccentricities, practically irresistible. A single glance into the earl's ominously bored countenance, furthermore, was enough to inform her that Ravenaugh had already taken Lawrence's measure. Nor did she fool herself into believing he had been given to form a favorable impression. Very likely he was already regretting his decision to allow his daughter into the social sphere of a female who numbered a dandified fortune hunter among her acquaintances.

In this interpretation of events, however, Josephine's unerring insight into people would seem to have failed her. No doubt she would have been greatly surprised and not a little amused, had she been given the faculty of reading Ravenaugh's mind at that moment. A premonition of Clarissa in the arms of the seducer was hardly one to give the earl pause for thought. He, after all, was there as a deterrent to any designs Mr. Lawrence might think to have on his daughter. What had come to plague him, however, was the less than felicitous suspicion that Lady Josephine had fallen prey to the wiles of an adventurer, and with no one to protect her.

The addition of Lady Juliana Brigton and Miss Felicia

Harcourt to what might be conceived as Lady Josephine's cortege of acquaintances was hardly more reassuring. Although their familial connections to the *ton* were of the best, the ladies entertained the dubious distinction of being high-flyers. Had they been males, they undoubtedly would have been numbered among the Carlton set. As females, they had long since been judged outre. They were hardly the sort of associations one would have chosen for a green girl straight out of the North York Moors.

Lady Josephine, however, far from demonstrating the least awareness that she was in fast company, gave every manifestation of one enjoying what must otherwise have been considered an unlikely gathering. The truth was, even before Aunt Reggie had seen fit to warn her that Lady Juliana and Miss Harcourt were free-thinkers, Josephine had, to her delight, already reached the same conclusion. Far from finding fault with Lady Juliana and Miss Harcourt for their eccentricities, she liked them for their originality. They were, besides, exceedingly gay and had a liveliness of manner that she could not but appreciate, reminding her, as it did, of her own, absent sisters.

"Lord Ravenaugh," declared Lady Juliana, a tall, willowy redhead with cool green eyes, "this is a surprise. Lady Josephine never mentioned that she numbered *you* among her acquaintances."

"Indeed, Jo," added Miss Harcourt, a plump blond beauty whose sparkling brown eyes teasingly chided Josephine, "you should have told us you had made such a coup. If you must know, the Earl of Ravenaugh is one of the most sought after gentlemen in London. My mama would have swooned to have his lordship favor me with a morning call, and here he is—in, of all places, Harrogate."

"As I recall, Miss Harcourt, I did call at your mother's house—on more than one occasion," Ravenaugh smoothly countered. "Unfortunately, you were only six or seven at the time. I daresay I made little impression on you."

Miss Harcourt's face instantly brightened. "Oh, but that was to see my Uncle Bertie. I remember now, the two of you were at Oxford together." A shadow flickered in the lovely eyes. "I suppose you heard, my lord. Uncle Bertie fell at Obidos. I—we all miss him dreadfully."

At the sudden catch in Miss Harcourt's voice, Lady Juliana was quick to intervene. "Everyone lost someone in the war. It was all very unfortunate, but, thankfully, it is over now," she said, her smile a trifle brittle. "I, for one, think it is time to cease to wear the willow. I believe, Ravenaugh, that you have not met Mr. Michael Lawrence."

"We have not previously been introduced," Lawrence volunteered, extending a hand resplendent with no less than five rings, "but I have had the privilege of seeing you spar at Jackson's. May I say, my lord, that I have seen few who strip to greater advantage than you in the ring."

"It would seem that you *have* said it, Mr. Lawrence," drawled Ravenaugh with a chilling lack of humor, "whether I should wish it or not."

There was a feminine giggle in attendance with the onset of a suddenly charged silence.

Lawrence drew back, taken off guard. "Well, yes." Nervously he laughed. "I have, haven't I. How very acute of you, really, my lord. I vow I intended no offense."

"No, I am reasonably certain your intention was something entirely different." Setting his cup and saucer on the tray, Ravenaugh coolly addressed his next remark to Josephine. "It has been a pleasure seeing you again, Lady Josephine. I regret that I cannot stay longer."

"No less do I," said Josephine, hurt at his abruptness, but hardly surprised. A man of the old school, he would hardly view with tolerance the introduction of a topic he considered unfit for feminine ears. "I shall at least see you

to the door. Aunt Reggie, if you would, please," she added,
indicating the tea service with a wave of her hand. She
rose to accompany Ravenaugh from the room. "Pray
excuse me, everyone. I shall only be a moment."

"Must you go so soon?" she queried as soon as they
were out of the room. "It is because of Mr. Lawrence's
stupid remark, is it not? It is a pity he has the intelligence
as well as the appearance of a peacock. Indeed, I confess
to being exceedingly vexed at him for driving you away
when you have only just arrived. Could I possibly persuade
you to change your mind if I told you that, having grown
up with three older brothers, I have heard boxing cant
practically all my life and with no perceptible ill effects?"

"Having grown up with three older brothers, did it never
occur to you that Mr. Lawrence, by contrast, is a loose
screw, Miss Powell? And by extension, hardly the sort to
have dangling after you?"

"You may be sure that I cut my eyeteeth no little time
ago," retorted Josephine, amused by his assumption of
authority over her. "I am perfectly aware that Mr. Lawrence
is hanging out for a rich wife, which is why I have few
qualms about enjoying his company. *I* do not fit in that
category. He may not be terribly clever, Ravenaugh, but
he can be amusing. At least grant that I am doing precisely
what you advised me to do. I am having the time of my
life."

"Which is only a polite way of reminding me that I
haven't the least say in *what* you do, is that it?" queried
Ravenaugh with a sardonic curl of the lip.

He was rewarded with a wry gleam of laughter in her
eyes. "I should not have put it so baldly, but, yes, my lord.
That is precisely what it is. And, now, having settled the
matter of Mr. Lawrence, I am reminded that you have not
yet told me why you changed your mind about coming."

His answer, characteristically blunt, was hardly what

Josephine expected. "I am leaving England, Lady Josephine. As soon as I can make all the arrangements."

Josephine faltered in her step. "I see," she said, telling herself that it was no less than she should have expected. Then, smiling somewhat unconvincingly, "How I envy you. Where, if I am not prying, are you going, my lord?"

"The Mediterranean, perhaps. It is to be a sailing cruise of several months' duration. Naturally, I shall be taking Clarissa with me. There are reasons why I thought she would do better away from Ravenscliff until our departure."

"Yes, of course," Josephine replied, assaying a light tone, "she will naturally require some additions to her wardrobe. There are some fine shops here and at least one excellent modiste. Still, I should have thought London or even Yorkshire would have been a more logical choice. A city has a great deal more to offer."

"It does not signify. Clarissa will have the opportunity to expand her wardrobe along the way. I wished her away from Ravenscliff, which is why we are here," said Ravenaugh, shrugging into his great coat. "She does not know yet about our voyage. I have not told her. No one knows, except you, Lady Josephine. I must ask that you keep it that way for the time being."

Josephine tilted her head back to look at him with penetrating eyes. "I am very good at keeping secrets, my lord. Heaven knows I have had a deal of practice, growing up in a household with seven children. Clarissa will not learn of it from me. Still, it is all rather sudden, is it not? Somehow I cannot but think there is more to this than a pleasure cruise." Impulsively, she laid her hand on Ravenaugh's sleeve. "If you are in some sort of trouble, I should hope you would know that I stand ready to be your friend. And Clarissa's. If there is anything I can do—?"

A wry smile twisted at Ravenaugh's lips. The devil, he

thought. Miss Powell had a most damned uncomfortable knack of hitting far too close to the mark. "I fear you are letting your imagination run away with you," he answered smoothly. "I am only following your advice. You did say Clarissa would do better away from Ravenscliff until she is ready to make her curtsey in society. As it happens, I agree with you."

A frown creased Josephine's brow. "That is all there is to it? Are you sure, Ravenaugh?"

"I have told you so. Do you doubt my word, Miss Powell?"

"No, not your word," replied Josephine without hesitation. "But then, you have not given me your word."

It was perhaps fortunate for Ravenaugh that Clarissa chose that moment to make her appearance bearing a basket colorfully bedecked in blue ribbons.

"Here I am at last," she exclaimed, hurrying up to Josephine and the earl. "I am sorry it took me so long. The little darlings got out and we had our hands full catching them." At sight of Ravenaugh in his great coat, his hat and gloves in hand, she faltered to a halt. "We are not going, are we? Not yet, surely, Father. We have only just arrived. We have not even had tea."

"Not 'we,' " Ravenaugh answered. "I, I'm afraid, have a prior engagement. It is only two or three minutes walk to the cottage. I shall leave Ridings to escort you home when you are ready."

"I have a better suggestion," offered Josephine without hesitation. "Why not let Clarissa stay here with us tonight? We were planning to attend the concert this evening in the park and, afterwards, Mrs. Llewellen, a dear soul of impeccable standing in the community, has invited us over for a small impromptu supper and games. We shall send Annabel with Wiggens for whatever Clarissa needs. Naturally, you may feel free to join us whenever you will."

As this was precisely what he had hoped for, Ravenaugh offered no objections. Agreeing that he would see them that evening in the park, he bowed and made his departure, leaving Josephine to stare after him, a speculative frown in her eyes.

"Jo?" queried Clarissa, giving her friend's arm a shake. "Jo, what is it?"

"What—? Oh, it is nothing. I was only woolgathering." Shaking off the feeling that Ravenaugh had not told her everything, Josephine turned at last to Clarissa. "And, now," she said, smiling, "what *do* you have in that basket? I am positively dying of curiosity."

"They are the darlingest things," exclaimed Clarissa, drawing Jo to a bench seat along one wall of the foyer. "And I did so wish to bring you something to remember me by. Please say that you love them."

Josephine, taking the basket and opening the lid, was met with the sight of two pairs of green eyes staring sleepily back at her. "You have brought me two of Miss Priss's kittens," she declared. "Oh, I *do* love them, Clarissa. They are perfectly adorable."

"I call them Snippet and Poppet. They are so delightfully tiny, though I daresay, if they take after their probable sire, they may not always be so." Reaching into the basket, she gently extracted one of the kittens, an orange and white striped ball of fur with a white face and a pink nose, and raised it to her cheek. "Mrs. Gosset was kind enough to give them a dish of cream, and now they are perfectly contented, are you not, my darlings?"

"Then I suggest we have Mrs. Gosset take them back to the kitchens for the time being. As it happens, we have company for tea, and I fear my friends must think me sadly remiss."

"They have, as a matter of fact, sent me to fetch you to them," declared Mr. Lawrence, coming up behind them.

His eyes, Josephine could not help but notice, were fixed with the intentness of a hungry wolf on the Earl of Ravenaugh's only offspring. And little wonder, Josephine thought with a sinking sensation in the pit of her stomach. Lady Clarissa, the kitten nestled against her cheek, was the very personification of youthful beauty and innocence. The devil, she thought, rising to her feet with a sense of having committed herself to a deal more than that for which she had bargained.

"Lady Clarissa Roth," she said, "I believe you have not met Mr. Michael Lawrence."

"I find the very notion of a brass band simply too insipid for words," Miss Harcourt declared not a few moments later as she reached for her fourth ginger biscuit. "They are almost as bad as the absurd excuses for dances held here at the assembly rooms."

"Country dances and the minuet, can you fancy that? I thought Lord Willoughby would succumb to a fit of the vapors when I requested something so daring as a waltz," Lady Juliana gurgled in amusement. "In London, the waltz is practically old hat."

"Yes, but this is not London," Miss Harcourt reminded her bosom friend. "If only it were, you may be sure a concert in the park would be the very last place anyone would even think of going. I fear I shall perish of sheer boredom if something does not happen soon to end our exile. Harrogate is quite the dullest of places."

"No, how can you say so," interjected Mr. Lawrence, his eyes on the youngest member of the assembled company, "when the scenery is so very enchanting?"

Wryly, Josephine observed Clarissa, meeting Mr. Lawrence's glance across the room, blush and lower her eyelashes. "If Harrogate is so little to your taste, Felicia,"

Josephine queried, setting her cup in its saucer, "then what persuaded you to come here at all? I cannot think you are in need of taking the waters."

"Heaven forbid," declared Miss Harcourt. "I should rather perish first. As it happens, I have been prevailed upon by a set of unfortunate circumstances to rusticate for a time in Harrogate."

"You mean Lord Barstowe, your guardian and the keeper of your purse strings, prevailed upon you to come to Harrogate," amended Lady Juliana, laughing at her dearest friend. "And little wonder. He was hardly pleased to have to retrieve your diamond earrings from a cent-per-cent. I did warn you, Felicia."

"Such a dreadful nuisance, it was, too," Miss Harcourt declared with a charming moue of disgust. "But ever so intriguing. Obadiah Hovey was the most delightfully depraved creature one could ever have hoped to imagine. I was ever so disappointed Uncle Percy found everything out before I could deal with the matter myself. I was so looking forward to confronting the wretched creature myself."

"You would have done better to entrust the entire matter to me, my dearest Felicia," Lawrence pointed out. "As it is, you will be fortunate if old Percy ever allows you within a hundred miles of London again."

"Little you could have done about it, my dearest Michael," purred Lady Juliana. "You know you had not a feather to fly with. You never do."

Lawrence's cheeks turned a dusky red at that unwelcome revelation. "That's dashed unfair, Juliana. Can I help it if my father is clutch-fisted?"

"No one can help what his father is," spoke up Clarissa in spirited defense of Mr. Lawrence. "I daresay Mr. Lawrence's heart was in the right place."

"Odd, I was not aware Mr. Lawrence had a heart, my

dear," Lady Juliana murmured sweetly. "But then, no doubt you are in the right of it. Not that it signifies, I'm afraid. Felicia is stuck here for the time being, and so am I, since I have promised to keep her company in exile."

"Be that as it may," Miss Harcourt interjected, "I do not have to submit to attending an alfresco chorale. Juliana and I are off to Knaresborough to see the sights, Jo. We only stopped by to see if you and Miss Moresby would care to join us. Naturally, Lady Clarissa is welcome to come, too. The more, the merrier, after all."

"Could we, Jo?" breathed Clarissa, her face lighting eagerly at so delightful a prospect. "I should like that above all things."

"I'm afraid it is not for me to say, Clarissa," Josephine gently pointed out. "You would naturally have to ask your father. It was kind of Miss Harcourt to offer, but, clearly, it is quite impossible."

"A pity, but of course we understand," said Miss Harcourt, setting her tea cup aside preparatory to rising. "Another time, perhaps. And, now, I daresay we should be going. A pleasure to meet you, Lady Clarissa. Doubtless we shall be seeing you again. Jo, a delight, as always. I must say I am wondering about you. I mean, the Earl of Ravenaugh, after all. Next you will be pulling Prinnie himself out of your pocket."

"I wish you will not be absurd," Josephine protested, laughing, as she walked with Miss Harcourt behind the rest of her departing guests to the foyer. "His lordship was kind enough to render Aunt Reggie and me aid when our coach broke down, and that is all there is to it. Pray do not make more of it than it is."

"As you wish, my dear," smiled Felicia knowingly. Glancing over her shoulder at the others, who had already stepped outside and were conversing on the stoop, she leaned near Josephine and murmured, "You may be sure that Juliana and I shall not spread rumors, but I should not rely on Michael's discretion if I were you. Now that he has seen Lady Clarissa, you will not find it easy to be rid of him. He is a charming rogue, but a man with a single purpose. I should not leave him alone with the earl's daughter for so much as a moment. As fond as I am of Michael, I should not trust him where an heiress is concerned. He is all too likely to carry her off to Gretna Green at the smallest opportunity.''

"You may be sure I shall keep that in mind,'' Josephine returned. "I cannot but wonder, however, how it is that you and Lady Juliana remain safe from Mr. Lawrence's marital ambitions. Either one of you might suit his purposes equally well.''

"Good heavens, no.'' Miss Harcourt gave a merry gurgle of laughter. "The three of us have known one another far too long. He is perfectly aware that we should make his life quite miserable were he married to either one of us. I should keep that in mind if you entertain any hopes where Ravenaugh is concerned. I have never been one to gossip, but I have grown fond of you, Jo, darling. Indeed, I feel compelled to warn you. Rumor has it that the earl's first marriage was anything but happy. Naturally, I do not hold with those who hint that he actually threw her off the cliff, but, where there is smoke, well—*you* know what I mean.''

Before Josephine could formulate a reply to the effect that she knew precisely what Miss Harcourt meant and, furthermore, that it was all a parcel of nonsense, Felicia, giving Josephine a quick pat on the arm, had turned and stepped outside with the others, leaving Josephine to stare in impotent disbelief after her.

Chapter 6

"Faith, Jo," declared Clarissa, wrinkling her nose in disgust. "You cannot really intend to drink that. It smells perfectly dreadful, like something from a bog."

"You may be sure that it tastes even worse than it smells," Josephine informed the other girl with a comical grimace, as they went to join Aunt Reggie, who was already seated outside the Royal Pump Room, an octagonal, glassed building that housed "The Stinking Spaw." "And, yes, I do intend to drink it, just as I have done every morning. It is one of the reasons why I came here, after all."

"Well, if you survive that, I daresay you can survive anything," Clarissa predicted doubtfully. "And you are remarkably improved, so perhaps there is something to be said for it. Oh, look. There is Miss Llewellen. She has just arrived with her mama. Would you mind awfully if I went over to join them?"

"I should not mind in the least. Only, I suggest you do not wander off. You did say your father would meet us here this morning," said Josephine, taking a seat across from Regina.

Forcing herself to drink a swallow of her prescribed dose of mineral water as Clarissa left them to greet a pleasant-faced girl of eighteen, and her mama, a plump matronly woman dressed in pink, she could not but reflect that Ravenaugh had been right about one thing. It was proving more than a little trying playing gooseberry to a school-room miss who displayed a marked tendency toward the self-destructive. It was bad enough that Clarissa had apparently formed an immediate *tendre* for Mr. Michael Lawrence, but in spite of all Josephine's advice to the contrary, the girl had, in the past three days since her arrival at Harrogate, gone out of her way to flaunt it. In addition to slipping off into quiet corners with Lawrence at the slightest opportunity, she had, the previous evening, made a point to stand up with the gentleman no fewer than three times at the dance held in the assembly rooms. In spite of the fact that the earl had been conspicuous by his absence the past few days, indeed, had apparently been making a point of avoiding Josephine, she did not dare to hope he would not eventually hear of it. After all, it was bound to be on everyone's lips this morning.

"At least Ravenaugh can have no objection to Priscilla Llewellen," Josephine observed dryly to Aunt Reggie. "*She* is perfectly unexceptional."

"I did try and warn you, Josephine," Aunt Reggie did not hesitate to remind her. "I should say that Clarissa will eventually outgrow her high spirits, if she does not ruin herself in the process. A pity Mr. Lawrence did not see fit to accompany his friends to Knaresborough. I fear we shall have to devise something to remove Clarissa from Mr. Lawrence's vicinity."

"I daresay it would have to be as far away as the Orient to discourage Mr. Lawrence," Josephine direly predicted. "He is like a bee drawn to honey."

"Or a moth to the flame," amended Regina thoughtfully. "I don't suppose it would do the least good to point out Clarissa is not really our responsibility. Ravenaugh is, after all, her father. A pity he seems determined to remain least seen in the affairs of his daughter."

"He is not ignoring her, Aunt Reggie," Josephine objected. "I told you. He has just returned after several months' absence and is occupied with putting his affairs in order." Just so that he might flee the country again, she added ruefully to herself. Why? she asked, not for the first time since Ravenaugh had confided his plans to her.

Indeed, there was a great deal that troubled her about the earl and his daughter, she reflected. Not that she placed the least credence in Miss Harcourt's whispered innuendos. While she could readily imagine Ravenaugh capable of killing a man in a duel, she did not believe for a minute that he would stoop to murdering his wife, or anyone else, for that matter. It would hardly be in his style, after all. For all his harshness, he was an exceedingly proud man. Such a man would scorn to resort to anything of a vicious or underhanded nature as being beneath him, not to mention counter to his particular code of honor. She would sooner expect pigs to fly than to believe Ravenaugh would cold-bloodedly murder a woman, especially one under his protection, and then calmly lie about it. Even if he had been driven to fling his countess over the cliff in a fit of passion (a possibility that she scouted as being highly unlikely for a man of Ravenaugh's resolute character), he would be far more likely to own up to it and face the consequences with an arrogant indifference to the punishment meted out to him than to play the part of a sneak and a coward.

Still, there was something about Lady Ravenaugh's death that hung like a pall over Ravenscliff and its lord, something that had compelled Ravenaugh to absent himself from his home and his daughter for months at a time; and that something was driving him to leave yet again. Whatever it was, it had had its effect on Clarissa, too. Why else should the child behave like two entirely different people, one of them, sweet and vibrant with joy, and, the other, resentful and rebellious? Josephine thought back to those terrible moments on the cliff, to the bewilderment in Clarissa's eyes. "I don't know why. I never know why," she had said.

That hardly seemed the behavior of a young girl overly given to indulge in fantasies any more than did the curious incident that had occurred on Clarissa's first night in Harrogate.

It was an hour after midnight, and the entire household had long since retired, when Josephine was startled from sleep by a scream that sent her scrambling out of her bed to Clarissa's room, which was next to her own. She had found the girl, tangled in her bedcovers and wrapped in a dream that gave every appearance of being fraught with anguish. Upon starting to wakefulness by Josephine calling her name, she had flung herself, weeping, into the older girl's arms.

"Why, Clarissa, dear," Josephine had exclaimed in startled wonder. "You were dreaming, but you are awake now. Softly, child. You are safe here, I promise."

"What a peagoose you must think me," Clarissa said with a watery hiccough, when, sometime later, the weeping subsided. "I am not usually a watering pot."

"No, of course you are not," replied Josephine, smoothing the tousled hair from the other's girl's forehead. Then, gently, she asked, "Do you wish to tell me about it?"

Clarissa averted her face, but not before Josephine glimpsed the lovely eyes, dark with lingering horror. "It is always the same," the girl said with a shudder. "I am asleep in my bed, when I am awakened by voices lifted in anger. It is Mama and Papa, fighting again, I tell myself. I slip out of bed and down the stairs to the Music Room. The door is ajar, and I look in." She covered her face with her hands. "It is horrible. Mama's face is white. I can see she is frightened. I cannot see Papa's. His back is to me. They are arguing about Cousin Adam. 'I shall kill him, if he has laid a hand on you!' Papa shouts. 'Devon, no!' Mama screams. Papa comes toward the door, and I hide. I am frightened of him, he looks so terribly angry. Then

Mama comes and carries me back to my bed. I-I do not remember what happens after that.''

She had not been telling all the truth, Josephine reflected somberly, staring across the lawn at Clarissa. The girl did remember, Josephine was sure of it. Furthermore, she was very nearly certain everything Ravenaugh had done the past several years was related to whatever it was that Clarissa found too terrible to talk about.

Taken altogether, her odd shifts in behavior, the dream, and the truth Clarissa was not telling would all seem to add up to the behavior of someone who was deeply confused and not a little troubled. And, indeed, how could it be otherwise if, in truth, she had witnessed her mama's terrible death?

In any case, whatever secret Ravenaugh was guarding, Josephine knew in her heart it could never be of a dishonorable nature, which was why she was determined to stand his friend, no matter how many well-meaning souls advised her against it. A Powell, after all, did not make it a habit to abandon a friend in need. And the first order of business was to wean Clarissa away from the trouble she was courting at that very moment, Josephine realized, as she espied the girl's face brighten at the sight of Mr. Lawrence, who, strolling toward the pump room, most surely had not come for the purpose of partaking of "The Stinking Spaw's" loathsome nectar.

"Aunt Reggie—"

"I see him," Regina answered. "I daresay everyone has. I suggest it is time we joined them, before a great deal is made of nothing."

Resisting the urge to pinch her nose while she downed the rest of her daily libation, Josephine gave into a shudder of revulsion before depositing the empty glass on the table before her.

"Done like a real trooper, ma'am," applauded an

amused masculine voice at her elbow. "The waters, like so much that is supposed to be good for us, do not precisely recommend themselves to the palate, I'm afraid."

Startled, Josephine glanced up into the smiling blue eyes of a gentleman, who was strikingly well to look upon, with golden hair and regular, fine-cut features that radiated a warm amicability. Josephine was moved in spite of herself to smile back at him. "Indeed, they are hardly a connoisseur's delight," she agreed, thinking the stranger had not the look of one in need of the salubrious effects of the mineral spring. Not above average height, he was well-knit, deeply tanned, and gave every appearance of being exceptionally fit.

"I beg your pardon," he said in the free and easy manner, which seemed an integral part of the man. "You are undoubtedly wondering who I am and why I should be so forward as to accost two ladies to whom I have not been properly introduced. As it happens, I am not so brash as I might appear. I am Saint-Clair. Doctor Adam Saint-Clair. Lady Clarissa Roth happens to be my cousin. And you are Miss Morseby and Lady Josephine Powell. As Clarissa has told me a great deal about you, I could not resist stopping by to introduce myself."

"We are naturally glad that you did, Dr. Saint-Clair," said Josephine, holding out her hand to him. "It is a pleasure to meet you. I should ask you to join us——" She was about to add they were, however, on the point of leaving, when Saint-Clair, releasing her hand, pulled out a chair.

"I should be happy to," he declared, and seated himself. "I was hoping you would ask. Unfortunately, I can stay only for a moment or two. I was on my way to see a patient, I'm afraid."

Josephine and Regina exchanged helpless glances.

"We were not aware that Clarissa had any family close by,

other than her father, of course," Aunt Reggie volunteered after a moment.

Saint-Clair leaned back in his chair with every evidence of one settling in for a lengthy chat. "As it happens, I have been away until recently. I was, until a short time ago, in the Orient. India, as it happens."

"India. Aunt Reggie spent a good many years there with Colonel Bickerstaff's family. Perhaps you have heard of him?" queried Josephine, quelling the urge to fidget in her chair. Much as she might have enjoyed meeting Ravenaugh's kinsman at any other time, she was at present close to wishing the good doctor to the devil.

"No, I'm afraid not," Saint-Clair smiled with a hint of indulgence. "But then, India covers a vast territory. And I spent most of my time in the interior, doctoring the natives. Where was the colonel stationed, ma'am?"

"He was in the Punjab for a time, then finally Madras," Regina answered shortly. Then, apparently overcoming her instinctive dislike of doctors, she added civilly, "Actually, we seldom knew where we were going to be from one year to the next. Colonel Bickerstaff was moved around a great deal."

"Then you must have become far more extensively acquainted with the country than I. It was all very fascinating, of course. But I am pleased to be home. I have had my fill of foreign lands."

"And so you have returned to England to set up your practice in Harrogate," said Josephine, her worried glance straying to Clarissa, who was standing in close conversation with Mr. Lawrence. The Llewellens had drifted a short distance off to converse with other acquaintances. The devil, Josephine thought. Ravenaugh was promised to join them any moment now for a stroll through the gardens. She would vastly prefer that he did not arrive to discover his daughter for all practical purposes unchaper-

oned in Mr. Lawrence's company. But neither could she wish to draw Saint-Clair's attention to his cousin in the company of an obvious bounder.

"It is my home, Lady Josephine," Saint-Clair rejoined. "I was not aware of how greatly I missed it until I returned to set out my shingle. Then, too, Devon and Clarissa are the closest thing to a family I have left. I am discovering as I grow older that my family ties mean a great deal to me. Indeed, they are more important to me than ever, especially now that I am needed. I'm sure you understand, Lady Josephine. Clarissa tells me you are one of seven children."

"Indeed, I am," replied Josephine, wondering in what way he felt himself most particularly needed and by which of his two cousins—Ravenaugh or Clarissa. "My family means a great deal to me. Have you never married, Doctor Saint-Clair?" Josephine asked politely, trying not to appear distracted at the sight of Clarissa, gazing up at Mr. Lawrence with calf's eyes. Her heart sank as, casting her glance about, she glimpsed in the distance a tall, powerful figure striding toward them along the walk.

"No, never," Saint-Clair was saying with a chuckle. "I have yet to find a woman who would have me. And then, a doctor's life, especially in foreign lands, does not particularly lend itself to domestic tranquillity. I was often called away for days, even weeks, at a time."

"It sounds interesting work, and sometime I should enjoy to hear all that you would care to tell me about it," Josephine offered, hard put to keep the impatience from her voice. Moving as if to rise, she sent a meaningful glance at Aunt Reggie.

"It was fascinating work, as a matter of fact," admitted Saint-Clair, who not only seemed, in his enthusiasm, to be remarkably oblivious to Josephine's less than subtle hint that she was desirous of making her departure, but apparently had forgotten he had a patient somewhere waiting for him. Indeed, it was almost as if the doctor were deliberately detaining them there, Josephine mused, only immediately to dismiss the thought as being quite utterly absurd. "I daresay I learned more about medicine in those nine years than I should ever have hoped to acquire at home. But then, here we do not have swamp fever, poisonous snakes, or any number of exotic diseases, which call for equally exotic cures."

"A circumstance for which we can no doubt be grateful. Well, now," interjected Regina, rising without ceremony, "if you will pardon me, I believe Mrs. Llewellen is most anxious to speak with me. A pleasure to meet you, I'm sure, Doctor Saint-Clair."

"Miss Morseby," said the gentleman, hastily rising half-way out of his chair.

Aunt Regina, however, was already weaving her way through the alfresco setting of tables and people toward Clarissa and her ill-chosen suitor. Josephine, observing her forward progress, only just managed to suppress a sigh of relief. Perhaps there was still a possibility Ravenaugh had yet to spot his only offspring flirting with almost certain disaster, she thought, only, in the next moment, to cast all such vain hopes aside.

"You must excuse my aunt," said Josephine, gazing beyond the doctor's shoulder to Ravenaugh, who had advanced to within a few yards of the outer rim of tables, close enough, in fact, that Josephine could hardly mistake his thunderous expression. "I'm afraid she is of a some-what . . . impulsive nature," she added, her voice trailing off with the sinking realization that the earl was making with firm resolution directly toward his errant daughter.

Saint-Clair, no doubt convinced his cousin had fallen in with rather strange bedfellows indeed, settled back into his chair with a an odd sort of smile. "Not at all, my lady.

I assure you I understand perfectly. I could not be more pleased, as a matter of fact, that my young cousin has found two new friends of your remove. Having had this opportunity to become acquainted with you, I find that I no longer marvel that you would seem to command an unusual influence over both Clarissa and Devon. Although I believe you mean it to be to their benefit, however, as a physician, I must be concerned for your welfare as well as for that of my patient. Clarissa occasions me a deal of worry. I might even go so far as to say she may pose a danger both to herself and to anyone untrained to deal with those suffering from her sort of illness. I feel sure you understand what it is I am trying to say."

Josephine, who had been only half-attending as she steeled herself for what seemed certain to be an unpleasant confrontation between father and daughter, was jolted to full awareness at that remarkable speech. Coming, as it did, from one who professed to be concerned solely for the welfare of his kinsmen, it was curious at the very least. She understood one thing quite clearly. Saint-Clair was warning her away from Clarissa; indeed, it came to her that he had sought her out for the very purpose of scaring her off with a tarradiddle of nonsense. The intriguing question was why?

Indeed, she was so intrigued with the conundrum before her, she quite forgot, for the moment, all about Ravenaugh and Clarissa, not to mention the troublesome Mr. Lawrence. Consequently, she failed to see the earl pause and, with every manifestation of ease, bend to place a buss on Clarissa's cheek, then, straightening, appear to exchange pleasantries with Aunt Regina and Mrs. Llewellen, who demonstrated every evidence of being extraordinarily pleased at so distinguished a condescension. Mr. Lawrence, he did not deign to notice beyond raising his quizzing glass to survey the young jack-a-dandy's frilled neckcloth,

padded breast and corseted waist, not to mention the
beauty patch at the corner of the painted lips, before pro-
ceeding with unmistakable deliberation toward Josephine's table, leaving Mr. Lawrence to stare after the earl's
retreating figure with a distinctly unsettled expression.

"I beg your pardon, Doctor," Josephine said, deliberately misconstruing the content of Saint-Clair's words. "I
fear I do not understand at all. I was not aware Clarissa
was suffering from any sort of illness, let alone one of an
infectious nature that might pose a threat to others. I
daresay Ravenaugh was sadly remiss not to warn me. Or
have you not seen fit to tell him?"

"You may be sure that I have repeatedly warned my
cousin of the peril of allowing Clarissa in the company of
others. I'm afraid he has his own reasons for disregarding
my advice. However, you misunderstand me, Lady Josephine. Clarissa's condition is not contagious."

"Not contagious? I do wish you will make up your mind,
Doctor. First you tell me Clarissa poses a threat both to
herself and to me, and then you say the illness is not of a
communicative nature. Really, I do think you should try
and make yourself clear. Which is it, sir? Is Clarissa a danger
or is she not?"

"She could very well pose a danger, but not from trans-
mitting the disease to another. Diseases of the mind are
not contagious, Lady Josephine. They are, however, very
often inherited."

"I see." Josephine stared at him, as she fought to keep
from laughing in the good doctor's face. Mental disease,
indeed. Saint-Clair's assertions were all patently absurd, or
at least they would have been had they not been fraught
with sinister overtones. Ravenaugh's cousin was not what
he pretended to be. But then, neither was she, she
reflected, favoring the doctor with her best imitation of
charming vapidity. "Dear me, Doctor Saint-Clair," she said

with a becoming flutter of confusion. "What a ninny-hammer you must think me."

"Not at all, my lady," Saint-Clair smiled indulgently. "Naturally you could not have known."

"Oh, but I know now," Josephine observed sweetly. "Indeed, you have made sure of it, have you not? You are saying Clarissa is mentally unbalanced. Dear me. And by extension, I must suppose you believe Ravenaugh similarly afflicted. You did say it was inherited? Or am I to assume it may be traced to Clarissa's mother, poor soul?"

"Ravenaugh might very well have been a victim of madness, Lady Josephine. She was not, however mad—as her physician, I can assure you of that. On the other hand, the late countess, I'm afraid, died under—shall we say, suspicious?—circumstances."

Shall we indeed? thought Josephine, her eyes sparkling dangerously. How dare he point an accusing finger at Ravenaugh behind the earl's back! Josephine felt her normally dormant temper suddenly and irretrievably aroused. "I should say the circumstances, from what I have heard, were extremely suspicious, Doctor Saint-Clair," she declared, dropping any attempt at pretense. "I am certain, on the other hand, that, contrary to what you would seem to intimate, Ravenaugh had nothing to do with his wife's death. His lordship, sir, is neither mad nor a murderer."

Saint-Clair's gaze narrowed sharply on Josephine's countenance, which was significantly no longer befuddled or charmingly vapid, but something else altogether. "You seem very sure, Lady Josephine."

"I am sure, Doctor Saint-Clair," Josephine replied, surprised that her voice should sound calm when she was trembling inside with anger. "I am so far convinced of it that I do not hesitate to tell you I find your allegations and innuendos laughable in the extreme. Indeed, I shall thank you not to bring them up to me again, or I shall be forced to question your motives in doing so. I should most certainly be moved to mention them to your cousin.''

Saint-Clair's face underwent an ugly transformation, quickly masked beneath a veneer of regret. ''Naturally, you must do whatever you feel is right.'' Rising to his feet, he stood looking down at her. ''Perhaps I was wrong to approach you, Miss Powell. Certainly, I regret that you have apparently misinterpreted my motives. I should hope one day you will believe that I was moved by nothing more than a sincere regard for your welfare, not to mention that of my cousins. I have warned you, Miss Powell. It is quite possible that your life is in danger. I cannot make it any clearer than that.''

''Can you not?'' Josephine retorted, coolly. ''Then no doubt I am obliged to you, Doctor. On the other hand, you may cease to worry. If I am in any danger, you may be sure it is not from the Earl of Ravenaugh. He would never do anything so cowardly as to do harm to a female. It simply is not in his nature. I should have thought you, of all people, would know that.''

Josephine felt a shadow loom over her shoulder, even as she saw Saint-Clair suddenly stiffen.

''What, defending me again, Lady Josephine?'' murmured a thrillingly soft masculine voice from behind her. ''I'm afraid, Cousin, I owe you an apology. I should have warned you. 'A faithful friend is a strong defense; and he that hath found such an one hath found a treasure.' ''

''*Ecclesiasticus*,'' declared Josephine, smiling triumphantly up at Ravenaugh. ''It is no such thing, however. I know, if your cousin does not, that you have no need of a defence, my lord. 'Innocence has nothing to dread.' ''

''Racine, my lady. *Phedre*, Act III, if I am not mistaken.'' Saint-Clair smiled coldly. ''Beware that you do not fall victim to the same sort of blind passion that led in that instance to tragic consequences.'' Smoothly, he bowed. ''It has been a distinct pleasure, Lady Josephine. I shall be looking forward to seeing you again. My congratulations, cousin. You have a formidable champion in the lady. Were I you, I should take care nothing happens to her.''

"I shall make sure of it, Cousin," Ravenaugh said with chilling directness. "Indeed, you may depend on it.''

Josephine felt a shiver explore her spine as the men's glances locked and held. Then Saint-Clair smiled fleetingly and, inclining his head, turned on his heel and left.

Josephine breathed a long sigh of relief. "I do not suppose you mean to tell me what that was all about," she commented dryly. "I fear you and your cousin are not precisely on amicable terms.''

"Then you would be mistaken, Lady Josephine," Ravenaugh answered, turning to regard her with unfathomable eyes. "We have been as close as brothers, and, so long as Saint-Clair does nothing to change the status quo, we shall remain for all practical purposes friendly relations. I regret if he said anything to upset you.''

"Oh, nothing to signify," Josephine declared ironically. "Only that he fears for your sanity, not to mention Clarissa's. As a physician, he felt it his duty to warn me that madness apparently runs in your family.''

"Perhaps he is right," said the earl harshly. "I *must* have been mad to allow you to be drawn into this. And a fool to think you would be safe as long as I kept you at a distance. It was regrettably short-sighted of me not to take Clarissa into account. I should have realized Adam would never countenance an influence over her other than his own. For that I shall never forgive myself.''

"I wish you will not be absurd. What is done is done, my lord," Josephine observed practically. "I am now a part of it, that much is clear.''

She did not add that she had not the remotest notion of what she was a part. Indeed, she could only hope that Ravenaugh would see fit to tell her if ever the need arose. At the very least, she thought she had a very good idea not only why Ravenaugh had wished to remove Clarissa from Ravenscliff, but very possibly why he had his mind set on a lengthy voyage in the Mediterranean. Obviously, he was trying to break Saint-Clair's hold over Clarissa, whatever that hold was. She forbore from mentioning that as well, deeming it was not the proper time to push for confidences. Indeed, it was enough for now to know the real reason he had been studiously avoiding her was to keep her from Saint-Clair's notice. That was a deal more comforting than worrying he had unreasonably taken her in adversion.

"It would seem rather pointless now to continue to keep me at arm's length," she said instead. "In which case, I do not hesitate to bring up a matter that Regina and I have had under discussion. Perhaps, my lord, we may be able to kill two birds with one stone, so to speak."

Ravenaugh, who had yet to completely recover from the cold clamp of rage that had gripped his vitals at sight of his cousin in the company of Lady Josephine, turned to regard her with hooded eyes. "Two birds, my lady?" he queried, marveling at her calm composure. Only moments before, she had seemed an avenging tigress out to protect her own.

"Dr. Saint-Clair and Mr. Lawrence, my lord," Josephine answered with a conspiratorial grin. "Two birds of a feather, it would appear, and both with designs on your daughter. It has occurred to me, and Aunt Reggie agrees, that a sight-seeing tour might be in order. Besides, my month is almost half over, and I have yet to see Knaresborough. What do you say, my lord? It would give us a few days away from Mr. Lawrence and your cousin. That should at least be worth something."

It would, in fact, be worth a great deal more to him than she could possibly imagine, reflected Ravenaugh, chiding himself for a fool to even consider anything so clearly unthinkable, but at what price to her or himself? At the very least, two or three days in Lady Josephine's company would put a serious strain even on his formidable powers of self-restraint. And yet, what other choice had he? She had been right about one thing. She was a part of the whole wretched business now, and she would be better off with him to watch over her than off on her own without the least notion of the danger she was courting. Hell and the devil confound it! The truth was he found himself in a damnable coil.

"Well, my lord?" queried Josephine, waiting.

"I suggest, my lady," he said with a wry twist of the lips, "that we leave as soon as possible—*before* Clarissa can have the opportunity to inform Mr. Lawrence of our plans. We shall keep it as a surprise until the very last moment. Shall we say immediately after luncheon? Will that give you time enough to pack?"

Josephine rose from the table. "More than enough time, my lord. I daresay my aunt and I shall travel lightly, if it means we should be rid of Mr. Lawrence for a while. And now, if everything is settled, I shall tell Aunt Reggie that I am suffering the sudden onset of a headache and must return home at once. I shall leave it to you to extract Clarissa from Mr. Lawrence."

"Josephine," Ravenaugh said, as she turned to go.

Josephine, startled to hear her name without a title before it on his lips, stopped and looked back at the earl. Her heart sank at sight of the hard cast of his manly features. "My lord?"

"About Saint-Clair," he said grimly. "In future, I shall thank you not to come so nobly to my defense. It was generous, perhaps, but exceedingly unwise. Unfortunately, it is not in my power to change what has happened. If I were your father, I should order you to return to your marvelous Greensward with all haste. In lieu of that, I can only hope you will be more cautious in future. Beware of Saint-Clair. Promise me you will never allow yourself to be alone with him."

"Very well, I promise. Was there anything else, my lord?" She waited for the wry twist of his lips. Poor, dear Ravenaugh, she thought. He simply could not accept that she was not a child, but a fully grown woman with a wholly logical mind. Naturally, it would make little sense to place herself at the mercy of a man who had already shown himself to be of a devious nature, especially when she had not the benefit of her father or brothers to protect her. Far from ever wishing to be alone with him, she would be perfectly content never again to have to lay eyes on Dr. Adam Saint-Clair.

"I am obliged, Lady Josephine," Ravenaugh said quietly at last. "It would seem you are one of those rare creatures—a woman of sense."

"You are mistaken, my lord," Josephine did not hesitate to inform him with an imp of laughter in her marvelous eyes. "Women of sense are not in the least rare. If they were, you may be sure there would be few households efficiently run or children who did not grow up to be wholly uncivilized. A woman's world is filled with mundane tasks to which few men would deign to apply themselves, considering them too far beneath them. Women, therefore, are of necessity sensible creatures. Their world, after all, demands it of them. What you have found rare, my lord, is a woman who readily agrees with you."

"Hornet," pronounced Ravenaugh with obvious feeling.

"Not at all, my lord." Josephine slid open with a flourish her green parasol made gay with Egyptian fringing around the bottom. "It is only the truth." Ravenaugh, having been landed a facer, was next treated to a sublime smile of affection, as Josephine settled the parasol handle against her shoulder. "And, now, if there is nothing more," she added before he could offer a rebuttal, "I shall wish you a good day, my lord, with the expectation of seeing you around two with Clarissa."

The devil, thought Ravenaugh, watching in sardonic amusement as Lady Josephine made her way gracefully through the crowd to Clarissa and Aunt Regina. Lady Josephine Powell had not the least notion just how singular she was.

"I had not to resort to persuasion at all, Aunt Reggie. Ravenaugh was perfectly amenable to the idea," Josephine assured her aunt some little time later as the two women with Annabel's help hurried with their packing. "I daresay he saw the wisdom in spending some time with Clarissa. Now, if only we could find someone to serve to distract Clarissa from Mr. Lawrence. A young man with a strong masculine appeal and a sensible head on his shoulders who would not be prone to have the wool pulled over his eyes. I daresay our troubles with Clarissa would be over."

"Unfortunately," Regina observed dryly, "Harrogate would seem to be woefully lacking in young, healthy male specimens not on the look-out for a wealthy wife. It is, by its very nature, prone to attract the very opposite sort."

"You are right, of course," agreed Josephine, handing Annabel a pair of sturdy brown half-boots and flannel drawers in case they should go out walking in the aftermath of an afternoon shower. "Which is why I most particularly wished to give Knaresborough a look. I daresay there might be any number of likely possibilities in a town noted for its scenic attractions, not to mention fishing, hiking, and a number of historical oddities."

"If you find any," said Aunt Reggie dryly, "males, that is, I suggest you reserve one for yourself. Need I remind you that Lady Clarissa Roth is not the only eligible young beauty who would benefit from a change of scenery? It would not hurt if a certain grim-faced nobleman saw Lady Josephine Powell in the company of a handsome young admirer or two."

"Do you really think so, Aunt Reggie?" queried Josephine, pausing to consider. It had never occurred to her that what Ravenaugh might need in order to see her as an attractive female was an interested third party. "I confess I am very near to giving up all hope of ever breaking through his lordship's formidable defences. It is all so very frustrating. I have been so *sure* that he likes me—in spite of the fact he is nobly resolved not to show it merely because I have the misfortune to be young enough to be his daughter. You can have no idea how very frustrating it is to be considered too young to know what is good for one or, worse, too young to know one's own heart. In that respect, I feel ages older than Ravenaugh, who refuses to realize that between two kindred souls, age is of little significance."

"Then I suggest, my dearest Jo, that it is up to you to *make* him see it," Aunt Reggie declared with an odd sort of vehemence. "Perhaps it is time you ceased to be logical and instead gave in to the promptings of your own heart before it is too late. If you do not, you may very well end up like me—a middle-aged spinster with a whole lifetime of regrets."

Josephine, taken aback at such an admission from Regina, stared at the older woman. "Forgive me, dearest aunt," she said quietly. "Except for wondering at one time if you perhaps had a *tendre* for Ravenaugh, I was not aware you had any regrets. You have always seemed remarkably well contented with your life."

"A *tendre* for Ravenaugh? Good heavens, what gave you that unlikely notion?" exclaimed Regina, considerably startled.

"Well, you did seem uncommonly persistent in urging me to stay longer at Ravenscliff. And the earl is, after all, your contemporary. It did not seem in the least inconceivable that you might have formed an attraction to him."

Regina gave vent to what sounded like a very unladylike snort. "I have never heard anything so absurd. It occurred to me almost at once that you and his lordship were remarkably well suited to one another. I thought it a shame you were in such a hurry to fling away your chance with him."

"Are you sure, Aunt Reggie?" Josephine said doubtfully. "I have been wanting to ask you about it for ever so long."

"But of course I am sure," Regina stolidly affirmed. "I could never lose my heart to the Earl of Ravenaugh, when I lost it years ago to Colonel Bickerstaff, now could I?"

"Colonel Bickerstaff!" Josephine exclaimed, taken off guard. "But I thought—"

"That I was dedicated to a career of being someone's governess?" Reggie gave vent to a short laugh. "I'm afraid I am not so high-minded as that, my dearest Jo. After Mrs. Bickerstaff died, the colonel was quite utterly devastated. I arrived to take my post as governess to find the household in a sad state of affairs. The girls were far too young to be without a mother, and I'm afraid I did not hesitate to do what I could to make up for it. In the process, I quite lost my heart to them—all of them, the colonel included. He never knew, of course. I simply could not bring myself to tell him. I was, after all, the governess. It would hardly have been proper to put myself in the way of my employer. I daresay the poor dear would have been quite dreadfully shocked, and with good reason. Nevertheless, I have since found myself wishing I had been far less concerned with the proprieties and a deal more determined to grasp at my chance at happiness, no matter what the consequences. Does that shock you, Jo? I confess it does me."

"No, Aunt," murmured Josephine. "Nothing you do could ever shock me. Why did you never tell me?"

"There hardly seemed any point. The last thing I should wish is for you to feel sorry for me. I only tell you now because I see you making the same mistakes I did. If you love Ravenaugh, then let nothing stop you, Jo. Go after him. Use all the feminine wiles at your command. I daresay you are more than a match for any man, and Ravenaugh, after all, is already in love with you."

It was no doubt fortunate, in the wake of that startling pronouncement, that Mrs. Gosset chose just that moment to scratch at the door. Certainly, Josephine was in no case to find a suitable answer for her aunt. It was disturbing enough that Aunt Reggie had assumed Josephine was in love with Ravenaugh, but the very notion that the reverse was also true was just too much for her to contemplate all in a single moment.

"Yes, Mrs. Gosset?" she managed, feeling her blood hot in her cheeks, as if the housekeeper had caught her in the act of some childish indiscretion. "What is it?"

"You have a visitor, m'lady. A gentleman who insists you will be more than happy to see him. He wouldn't leave his card. Said as how he wished it to be a surprise."

Josephine's first lowering thought, that it was Saint-Clair come to further attempt to pull the wool over her eyes, served to calm her agitated state. Immediately, then, it came to her that Saint-Clair would have little reason to call on her so soon after their meeting at the Royal Pump Room. Everything, after all, had already been said. Then who?

Unaccountably, she felt her heart quicken.

"I shall come down directly, Mrs. Gosset. Thank you," she said, smoothing her skirts and giving her curls a pat.

"Well?" she queried of her aunt. "Shall we go and see this mysterious gentleman?"

Josephine was not at all certain what, or rather whom, she expected upon sliding open the door to the parlor. Certainly it was not a tall young man with wonderfully broad shoulders, a slim waist, and stubbornly straight blond hair.

A glad cry welled up in her throat, as the gentleman turned to regard her with merry blue eyes remarkably similar to her own.

"Timothy! It is you!"

One corner of the handsome lips rose in a dearly familiar lop-sided grin. "I shan't deny it, but, good God, Jo, is it really you?"

"Oh, yes. Yes. Don't you know me?" The next instant she had flung herself, laughing and weeping all at the same time, in her brother's arms. "Timothy. Timothy, you cannot know how glad I am to see you. What are you doing here? How did you know where to find me? Have you been to see Mama and Papa? How is Papa? You must tell me everything. Where is Tom? Surely he came with you?"

An odd sort of pain twisted somewhere deep inside her as she felt her brother go suddenly still.

"Timothy?" she queried, drawing away. "Pray tell me Tom is all right?"

"Now don't get all in a stir. Tom was wounded. At the Battle of New Orleans. You should have seen him, Jo. The mad fool charged the barricades at the head of his men. It took two shots to bring him down."

"Two shots—?" Josephine felt the blood drain from her face, and suddenly the room seemed to tilt and whirl.

"Here, now," she heard Timothy gasp in alarm.

"Jo, dear," exclaimed Aunt Reggie.

Even as she felt her knees threatening to give way beneath her, Josephine was aware of the door opening and of Mrs. Gosset announcing the arrival of callers.

Ravenaugh's voice rang out, harsh and commanding. "Josephine! What the devil——!"

"I-I'm all right," she said. There were footsteps. Some-one—Ravenaugh—gripped her, pulled her into the strength of his arms. "No, really," she protested.

"I say, sir. Who the devil are you to barge in on my sister and——"

"Ravenaugh. You are her brother? What the deuce did you say to her to throw her into a quake?"

"I am *not* in a quake," interrupted Josephine.

"No, of course you are not," agreed Ravenaugh sooth-ingly. "You are only as white as a sheet. What did this young jackanapes tell you to knock the wind from your sails?"

Timothy Powell, who found little to recommend in being referred to as a jackanapes, drew indignantly up. "I beg your pardon. I was telling her about our brother Tom's having been wounded. Not that it is any business of yours. She is my sister——"

"Then you should know better than to drop something like that on her without warning," coolly observed Ravenaugh.

"This is not the time to stand around talking," spoke up Aunt Reggie. "Josephine has sustained a shock. If you would help her to the sofa, my lord."

"Right, as always, Miss Morseby. Yes, that is better. Mrs. Gosset, fetch the smelling salts, if you will."

"No. No smelling salts." Josephine, seated on the sofa with Ravenaugh's arm around her, tried weakly to push herself up, only to be firmly pulled back again. "I shall be fine. Please. Only tell me. Tom. Is he—is he——? Please say he is not dead."

Timothy clasped her fluttering hand. "Dash it all, sis. Is that what all the fuss is about? Tom is alive. It was touch and go for a long while, and the cursed sea voyage was little help. But I daresay he will be almost as good as new now that he has Mama to look after him. I left him at home, Jo, at Greensward. He'll be there, waiting for you when you return."

"Thank God," breathed Josephine, considerably distracted. "When you said Tom was shot, two bullets, you said. I thought . . . It doesn't matter, now, what I thought. Only, what do you mean, *almost* as good as new?"

Timothy's eyes darkened, and he glanced away. "Tom's leg was crushed rather badly in the fall, Jo. He was forced to sell out of the regiment. It looks as if he may be something of a cripple."

"Oh, but he is alive," Josephine exclaimed, "and that is all that matters. But never mind that now." Josephine, feeling sick and not a little dizzy, drew a long, steadying breath. "I must beg your pardon, everyone, for being such a gaby. Indeed, I have been sadly remiss. I have yet to introduce to you Timothy, my brother." Holding her brother's hand, she glanced up into Ravenaugh's harsh countenance. "I believe you have already met my dear friend, the Earl of Ravenaugh," she said, keenly aware that she still resided in the sustaining circle of Ravenaugh's arm. "I daresay you remember Mama's sister, Aunt Reggie. And that very attractive young woman who appears just now to have eyes too big for her face is the earl's daughter, Lady Clarissa Roth. Clarissa, dear, come here and say hello to Captain Timothy Powell, my brother."

"My lord," murmured that young lady, displaying an unwonted shyness as she dipped a curtsey before Timothy Powell, who was staring into her liquid brown eyes with every appearance of a man mortally stricken by what amounted to a sublime revelation.

Chapter 7

Knaresborough, rising from the banks of the River Nidd, clung picturesquely to the steep side of a river gorge, while the ancient ruins of Knaresborough Castle, destroyed by the Roundheads in 1646, watched over it. It was Wednesday, market day, and the little town was already teeming with farmers and artisans hawking their wares when Josephine and Aunt Reggie made their way downstairs to the common room of the Half Moon Inn. There they were to join the rest of their party for a proposed tour of the town, which was to culminate with a visit to Mother Shipton's Cave and The Petrifying Well.

"I am most anxious to stop in the local chemist's shop for a bottle of lavender water," declared Aunt Reggie. "It is supposed to be quite excellent. They make it on the premises, you know, according to a secret recipe which has been in their possession for countless generations."

"We shall make that our first stop, then, Aunt," replied Josephine, her heart warming at the sight of Timothy, looking exceptionally tall and handsome in buff unmentionables and a morning coat of bottle green Superfine. How strange to realize Tom was not with him! Where there was one twin, there had always been the other for as long as she could remember.

"I say, sis, it is about time you and Aunt Reggie showed yourselves," called out Timothy gaily, espying the two women on the stairway. "I was beginning to think we should have to send someone up to roust you out of bed."

"Pooh," Josephine retorted. "Aunt Reggie and I have

been up since dawn. We have already had our morning constitutional, as a matter of fact. We went to the viaduct and back along the loveliest riverside walk imaginable."

"No doubt that explains the roses in your cheeks. Egad, Jo. You've grown into a real beauty while I've been away. Who would ever have thought our little Josephine would one day put even Florence in the shade, what, Aunt Reggie?"

"Unfortunately, I have not seen Florence since she was an infant and consequently cannot be a judge in the matter. However, I should not have thought there would ever have been any question but what Jo would grow into a beauty," replied Regina confidently.

"Careful," Josephine laughed. "The two of you will turn my head with your flattery. You know very well I could never compare to Florence, Timothy. It is sweet of you to say so, however."

"Sweet, nothing. It's the truth. I daresay you have only to ask Ravenaugh. His lordship, for all he tries to hide it, looks at you as if he might eat you."

Josephine blushed rosily, to her dismay. "Nonsense, he does no such thing. I notice you, however, gaze at Lady Clarissa as if she were a bowl of plump strawberries smothered in cream."

"Brat," commented Timothy, giving her his lop-sided grin. "You always did see too much. I admit Lady Clarissa fairly knocked me off my pins. I depend on you to put in a good word for me, Jo, old girl. It would not hurt to have the inside track with the lady before the rest of the pack discovers her next spring in London."

"Be careful, dearest Timothy. She is only seventeen. I daresay she may lead you on a merry chase. And you are not, I'm afraid, her only suitor."

"No? But then I am the only one here at present. You may be sure I shan't let the grass grow under my feet. If you ask me," he winked, "you would do well to follow my example."

"Your example? Whatever do you mean?" Josephine laughed, startled.

"I think you know. Ravenaugh may not be young anymore—"

"I beg your pardon," Josephine interjected, "he is hardly old, Timothy. He is not even middle-aged."

"—but he has the reputation for being a man," continued her brother as if she had not even spoken. "I'll wager you did not know he spent the war as an aide to Wellington himself. Not one of the sort who fetch and carry, mind you, but a point man in all the filthiest fighting. He went in first to gather intelligence. The lads still talk about him. He was Wellington's Unstoppable Colonel."

"That, I can well believe," Josephine said feelingly. "He is a man of no little resolution. I cannot see what that has to do with me, however."

"Come on, sis, it's plain as a pikestaff. You like him, now, just a little, do you not?"

"I like Ravenaugh very much, Timothy," Josephine admitted with aplomb. "I told you, he is my very dear friend."

Timothy grinned conspiratorially. "I think he might be more than that, if you only examine your feelings. I daresay it is none of my affair, sis, but the truth is you could do a lot worse than Ravenaugh."

"You are right, it is none of your affair. On the other hand, it has already occurred to me that a woman could find no better man than the Earl of Ravenaugh. Not that it signifies. Ravenaugh has already made it plain he is not interested in anything but the most platonic of relationships. Where is he, by the way? I should have thought he and Clarissa would have put in an appearance by now."

"Oh, but they have. Lady Clarissa expressed a desire to

add a few items to our picnic luncheon. She and Ravenaugh have gone out to see what they can discover in the market square. I am to take you to meet them. If you are ready . . .''

"I am all eagerness," declared Josephine, experiencing an unexpected pang of gladness at Timothy's assurance that Ravenaugh was even now waiting for them. She had half-expected the maddeningly elusive earl to find some excuse to cry off from the day's outing. "We can stop off at the chemist's shop along the way, Aunt Reggie, if that is all right."

"Whatever is expedient," Aunt Reggie replied, obviously pleased at the prospect.

The Old Chemist Shop in the market square appeared much as it must have done in 1720 when it was first opened, Josephine decided as, leaving Timothy outside to watch for Clarissa and the earl, she and Regina stepped into the murky interior and were met with the tingling scents of camphor and eucalyptus along with aromatic bitters. Bottles of various powders, elixirs, oils, and other intriguing substances were arranged on wooden shelves lining the wall behind a counter that housed a balance and scales and a mortar and pestle, not to mention a jar of licorice sticks.

While Regina waited at the counter to request a bottle of lavender water, Josephine amused herself by wandering along the shelves and glassed cases displaying sachets, soaps, bottled scents, smelling salts, incense sticks and candles, among other curiosities designed for various and sundry uses. Consequently, she did not at first notice the gentleman emerge from the back of the shop and, espying her, pause momentarily as though recovering from a shock of surprise. Whatever the cause of his hesitation, it was quickly hidden behind a smiling front, as he made deliberately toward Josephine.

"Lady Josephine," he exclaimed, coming up to her, "this is a surprise. Here to see the local points of interest, are you?"

Josephine, who could think of any number of people she would rather have encountered than Doctor Adam Saint-Clair, was quick to hide her dismay upon looking up to find herself face to face with Ravenaugh's cousin.

"As a matter of fact, yes, Doctor Saint-Clair," she said, thinking it was an unhappy coincidence that should have brought them together. "And you, sir? Is that why you are here, or do you include residents of Knaresborough among your patients?"

"A little of both, ma'am," Saint-Clair admitted, slipping a small packet into his coat pocket. "I never tire of the scenery and therefore count it as a pleasure when I am called to Knaresborough. If it is just you and your aunt, perhaps you would allow me to serve as your guide. I am well-acquainted with all the local attractions."

"How very kind of you to offer," replied Josephine, who did not believe in the least that it was any feeling of altruism that motivated Saint-Clair, but something altogether different. "As it happens, my brother Timothy has agreed to play escort. He is just outside, and since I see Aunt Reggie has completed her purchases, I'm afraid I shall have to ask you to excuse me. I cannot wish to keep my brother waiting too long." Josephine coolly extended her hand. "A pleasure to see you again, Doctor."

"Surely you do not mean to dismiss me so soon, Lady Josephine," Saint-Clair objected smoothly, pressing her hand before releasing it. "At least allow me to see you and your aunt to the door."

Josephine, short of being openly rude, had little choice but to let Saint-Clair escort her across the room to Aunt

Regina, who was eyeing Ravenaugh's cousin with scarcely concealed disfavor. Any hope she might have had that a meeting between Ravenaugh and Saint-Clair might yet be avoided was dashed as soon as they emerged from the shop.

"Cousin Adam!" piped Clarissa's voice the moment they stepped, blinking, into the sunshine. "I did not expect to see *you* here. How simply splendid. We are on our way to tour the castle, and, afterwards, we are going to have a picnic above the viaduct. Please do say you will join us."

Josephine's heart sank as she met Ravenaugh's hooded eyes.

"As it happens, I have finished my business and am therefore at your disposal," Saint-Clair responded cheerily. "What could be better, after all, than a family outing?"

"What, indeed," drawled Ravenaugh, meeting his cousin's glance with the look of one coming down with an advanced case of ennui. Josephine, however, was not fooled. Behind the facade of boredom, Ravenaugh was a deal less than pleased at the prospect of having his cousin join them. "It is, at the very least, a timely coincidence. What, by the way, brings you to Knaresborough, Adam?"

"The purchase of some medicinal compounds. I often come to the Old Chemist Shop for that purpose. I certainly never expected to run into you or Lady Josephine and her aunt. And this, I must presume," he added, turning affably to the tall young stranger, favoring Saint-Clair with a coolly appraising glance, "is Lady Josephine's brother. There is a marked family resemblance, I believe."

"All the Powells favor one another, except for our sister Lucy," Josephine spoke up. "Doctor Adam Saint-Clair, I should like you to meet Captain Timothy Powell, my brother."

"Your servant, sir," said Timothy, meeting the doctor's handclasp with a strong one of his own.

"Likewise, I'm sure, Captain," smiled Saint-Clair. "Well, now. I daresay Lady Josephine and my young cousin, here, are eager to see the castle and its infamous prisons in which, I might add, it is recorded not a few unfortunates suffered slow agonizing deaths. You are neither of you, I hope, faint of heart."

"As it happens, I have already seen such a prison in Lathrop Castle near my home," replied Josephine, little caring for Saint-Clair's patronizing manner. "I am not faint of heart, but nor am I particularly eager at the prospect of seeing another. They are shameful, wretched places in which no one would even think to confine an animal. I am, however, looking forward to seeing the town. The inn keeper was telling me that, besides the ancient walkways, it is riddled with secret passages, used most recently, it is rumored, by owlers in the smuggling of contraband wool."

"I doubt that very much," scoffed Saint-Clair. "I should say, in fact, it little more than a Banbury story designed to tickle the fancy of naive travelers. Even if such secret passages did exist and one could discover them, it would not seem very wise, would it? Why, we should very likely find ourselves breaking into private homes and shops. I daresay you would incur the displeasure of not a few of Knaresborough's leading residents."

"Well, then, Lady Clarissa, if I may have the honor?" said Timothy. Gallantly relieving her of the basket she was carrying, he offered her his arm with a flourish. "I suggest we proceed to the castle. The last thing we should wish on a lovely day like today is to incite the wrath of The Gentlemen, or the pillars of the community, as the case may be. I shall permit nothing to spoil what promises to be a splendid outing with three beautiful ladies."

Clarissa, clearly unused to receiving the flattering notice of a young, handsome gentleman, who far from being a fop or a dandy, was both virile and decidedly masculine, blushed prettily. "Indeed, sir, that would be a pity," she murmured, dazzling Timothy Powell, had she but known it, with the sweetness of her smile.

If Clarissa was unaware of her devastating effect on Timothy, however, Josephine was quite certain Saint-Clair had not failed to notice it. As the doctor's eyes came to rest on her brother, Josephine inexplicably felt a cold touch of fear.

The leisurely walk up the tree-shaded streets revealed an intriguing glimpse of a maze of cobbled alleys, running behind and between buildings. In spite of Saint-Clair's assurances to the contrary, Josephine thought they might easily have led to any number of secret passages. Indeed, she could not but suffer a delicious feeling that beneath its sleepy exterior, the town was steeped in mystery. She was made to feel an added sense of time-frozen antiquity as the small party came at last to the stark remains of Knaresborough Castle.

Timothy and Clarissa immediately evinced an eagerness to see the infamous prisons, upon which Saint-Clair graciously offered his services as guide. Aunt Regina, who entertained an instinctive distrust of doctors in general and of Saint-Clair most in particular, professed what Josephine considered an unlikely interest in moldering dungeons and declared her intent to go on the subterranean tour, which left Ravenaugh and Josephine to explore what remained of the castle above ground.

Josephine, who was intimately acquainted with Lathrop Castle, belonging, as it did, to her brother-in-law, the Duke of Lathrop, could not help but feel the sprawling remains of the once great fortress overlooking the town of Knaresborough left something to be desired. Nevertheless, she had to admit that an aura of past magnificence yet clung to the seemingly indestructible twin towers of the main gate, which had been left standing in the wake of the Roundheads' victorious assault. Nor could she deny that she felt a delectable tingling at the nape of her neck as she and Ravenaugh stood alone in what had once served as the King's Chamber.

"Do you feel it, my lord?" she asked, her voice instinctively hushed. "It is as if the life that once was here lives on in that distant past, sending echoes forward in time. I daresay it is the shades of those people, talking and eating and going about the business of living. I feel almost as if I might reach out and touch them."

" 'I can call spirits from the vasty deep'?" drawled Ravenaugh, smiling whimsically down at her.

"Yes, but like Hotspur, I cannot make them come to me. Still, I seem to feel them, as though they are part of the stones that make up these walls—as if so long as a single stone remains, they will not fade utterly from this plane."

"You are a romantic, Lady Josephine," Ravenaugh declared in cynical amusement.

"And you are not, I suppose," Josephine countered, running a hand over the cold stonework of a window embrasure.

Ravenaugh's eyes glittered darkly. "I have no affection for shades, if that is what you mean. I should prefer the dead remain buried and, if not forgotten, then at least left to fade in peace."

"And are they not buried, my lord?" queried Josephine softly, staring out over the ruined bailey to the twin towers guarding the fallen gate. When he did not immediately answer, she turned to look at him. "Are they not in peace?"

"At peace? I daresay they can never be in peace so long as the living continue to resurrect them, to feed on their memories like bloody vultures. Do I shock you, Miss Powell?" he said, his smile mocking her.

"I think perhaps *sadden* is a better term," Josephine replied gravely. "I should wish the dead did not trouble you."

He laughed at that, a harsh sound that reverberated through the ancient, moldering chamber. "Believe me, your pity is misplaced. Did you think I have been wearing the willow all these years for my dead countess? That is what we are talking about, is it not? The tragic death of Eugenie."

"I think that such a passing must always leave scars, especially if it is a terrible death of one who was loved." Josephine probed his harsh features with eyes he must have found galling to meet. "You did love her? Clarissa said you were childhood sweethearts."

A shadow flickered across the hard countenance. "Yes, I loved her."

Josephine bit her lip as he turned away to lean, looking out, with his hands on the window sill.

"All who knew her loved Eugenie. How could they not? She was a rare creature of sunlight and laughter. She had that singular quality of imparting joy to others. One had only to look at her—" His voice stopped, the muscle leaping along the hard line of his jaw. "All that changed, however, when my uncle was so disobliging as to pass on, leaving me the title. When we took up residence at Ravenscliff, *she* changed, like a wren, caged and robbed of its will to sing."

"Lady Ravenaugh was unhappy at Ravenscliff? But why?" queried Josephine, surprised somehow. It had never occurred to her that the greystone manor on the cliffs should have been the source of the young beauty's discontent.

"I have come to wonder if anyone could be truly happy

in that cursed pile. Strangely enough, I think Eugenie might have been, if . . . But, no matter. She evinced every pleasure at living in the house which had seen me grow to manhood. The house, which, if not for an unkind quirk of fate, should have gone to my cousin Adam.''

"Adam! But how—?" She knew, of course, before he answered.

Ravenaugh glanced at her, his look cynically amused. "My uncle's wife was barren. Adam was the son of one of my uncle's several mistresses, acknowledged and taken to be reared by his father. I was seven and Adam only a year older when my parents died of fever within months of one another. My aunt and uncle took me in. Ironic, is it not? Adam and I grew up like brothers.''

"Yes, I suppose it is ironic," agreed Josephine, her heart going out to Ravenaugh. He had loved Adam. That much was plain. And yet, how hard it must have been for both of them—Adam, the earl's by-blow, who could never be his father's heir, and Devon Roth, the nephew, with all the rights that should otherwise have accrued to the earl's only living son! And yet, at one time they had been closer than brothers. Ravenaugh had said so only the previous day at the Royal Pump Room. The death of the earl must have been like a wedge driven between the cousins. And then Devon, the new Earl of Ravenaugh, had brought home his young, beautiful countess and their daughter.

What bitter gall that must have been to Adam Saint-Clair, who could not even claim his father's name, let alone his title!

"What happened, my lord?" Josephine asked quietly. "What drove Lady Ravenaugh to take her own life?"

Josephine's breath caught as Ravenaugh came around to impale her with glittering eyes. "You saw her likeness in the Music Room. You must have wondered what she was thinking as she sat there, playing her blasted harp.

The devil knows I have lain awake at nights pondering that very question. But then, she had ceased to confide in me long before Saint-Clair talked me into having the cursed painting done. You must have heard the rumors by now, the innuendoes. Good God, you saw her eyes. The joy was gone out of her, along with whatever warmth she might once have felt for me, long before she threw herself over the falls. The devil take her for that. She carried the answer to the question of why she should have done it with her to her grave.''

''Perhaps not, my lord,'' Josephine said, refusing to flinch before his steely gaze. ''In any mysterious happening there are always clues, signs, if you will, that point to a resolution, if one is only able to spot them. You said Lady Ravenaugh changed. How did she change? Humor me, my lord,'' she added at sight of the earl's cynical disbelief. ''I beg you. Lady Ravenaugh was subject to extremes in mood, was she not? One moment almost desperately gay, and the next just as desperately unhappy?''

Silently Ravenaugh cursed. How could she possibly have known that? The impossible child was far too sagacious for his own peace of mind. Worse, he was keenly aware she would not stop until she had the whole of it. Still, he had gone this far. And soon it would hardly matter any more. Strange how bloody easy it was to talk to the irrepressible Lady Josephine.

''Brava, my lady, you are quite right. Eugenie was given to extremes in mood. Worse, she demonstrated an almost morbid fear of leaving Clarissa in the care of her nurse. She formed an obsession for slipping out of her room at night to look in on the child asleep in her bed. Unfortunately, that was not all she came to fear. She was afraid of me. Did you guess that, Lady Josephine? She shrank if I came near. The devil, she *trembled* at my touch. In the end, I was all too aware that she loathed the very sight of me.

Perhaps," he said cynically, "you should take your cue from her. I daresay Adam was right to warn you. You should be afraid of me. There is a good chance I shall bring you to harm in the end."

"Now you are being absurd, my lord," Josephine retorted. "I am not in the least afraid of you. And if Lady Ravenaugh appeared to hold you in dread, it was very likely because of some secret she was keeping from you, something she was afraid to have you find out. Everything you have told me points to a woman who felt herself trapped in a quandary. A woman does not cease to love overnight, Ravenaugh, unless there is a very good reason. You had not, had you, taken to drinking and, while in a drunken rage, formed the habit of striking or browbeating your wife?"

Josephine nearly flinched at the fierce leap of his eyes. "Good God, you have an odd notion of my character if that is what you think," declared Ravenaugh with obvious feeling. "The fact is, until I met you, my lady, I have never been in the least tempted to browbeat a woman, in my cups or not. Nor am I prone to drunken rages. Contrary to the popular belief, I never raised a hand against Eugenie."

"Quite so, my lord," declared Josephine with an unmistakable air of triumph. "I never for the moment thought that you had. Indeed, you are far too logical-minded ever to give into fits of irrationality. Which, besides proving my point, leads me to suspect that Lady Ravenaugh, far from loathing you, loved you more than you could ever possibly have imagined. I believe she was, in fact, trying to protect you."

"Protect me!" Ravenaugh's eyebrows fairly snapped together over the bridge of his nose. "Now you are letting your imagination run away with you. Good God. Protect me from what?"

"From yourself, perhaps," Josephine replied, absently

tapping a forefinger to her lips as she contemplated the possibilities. "Or from someone else. Or perhaps merely from something she could not wish you to know for any number of reasons. I am neither a fortune-teller nor a crystal-gazer. I cannot say what secret she was keeping from you. As a woman, however, I can tell you that she displayed all the symptoms of a female who was both troubled and gravely frightened. No doubt it was because she loved you and Clarissa that she could not find it in herself to divulge her secret to you. Do you not see, my dearest lord?" she said, yielding to the impulse to touch her palm to the side of his face. "Lady Ravenaugh was never afraid *of* you. She was afraid *for* you. I suggest, therefore, that you stop blaming yourself for what happened. It really was not your fault."

"Was it not?"

Josephine's heart gave a leap as Ravenaugh's fingers closed about her wrist and, dragging her hand down between them, held it captive there.

"You are remarkably sure of yourself, Lady Josephine."

"If I am, my lord, it is because I have come to know you. If Lady Ravenaugh was all that you say she was, she would never have ceased to love you. How could she? You are one of those rare men of honor who combine strength with compassion. Any woman would count herself fortunate to be loved by you."

Ravenaugh's fingers tightened on her wrist. "And you, my girl, are a rare combination of naivete and brashness if that is what you believe. I told you before I am not noted for any kindliness in my nature, but for something quite different."

"Good God, I never said compassion was your only character trait," Josephine did not hesitate to point out. "You are stubborn and bullheaded, not to mention top-lofty and arrogant. I daresay you drink too much and probably gamble as well. And you have an irritating habit of assuming that because I am young and a female that I am a child to be bullied and protected from what you imagine to be my own foolhardiness. Well, I am not a child, Lord Ravenaugh. I am a woman fully capable of knowing my own heart and mind. And if you were not so determined to save me from my own folly, you would not waste our time alone ranting at me. You would kiss me.''

"Impudent baggage," growled Ravenaugh. His marvelous eyes leaped with something besides startled amazement at that wholly unexpected conclusion to her deductive reasoning.

"Very likely, my lord," agreed Josephine, lifting her free hand to the back of his neck. Brazenly, she leaned against his broad, powerful chest. "On the other hand, I am advised by my brother that I should not allow the grass to grow under my feet, and you, after all, are planning to leave England. I'm afraid I cannot afford to pay heed to the proprieties. Are you going to kiss me or not?"

"It would serve you right if I ravished you," declared Ravenaugh with a savage lack of humor. Good God, she had not the sense of an infant.

Josephine, to whom such a possibility did not loom nearly so dire as he clearly intended it to, responded by tilting her head back in order to afford him an unimpeded assault on her lips. "I could not agree with you more, my lord," she had the gall to inform him. "However, for the present I shall be content with nothing more strenuous than a simple kiss. Indeed, I fear we haven't time for anything else."

"Jade," he retorted, hard pressed not to give into temptation. "If I did not know better, I should think you were trying to compromise me."

In answer to that observation, Josephine deliberately raised herself up on tiptoe. "Perhaps you do not know me so well as you imagine," she said, thrilling to the unwitting leap of his lean, strong body. Her otherworldly eyes smiled up at him. "Kiss me, my dearest lord. I promise it will not hurt you."

Presented with the almost irresistible inducement of Lady Josephine's lips within a bare two inches of his own, Ravenaugh only just managed to stifle a groan. She could not know what she was doing to him or realize the consequences if he gave into her sweet allure. Indeed, only the bitter certainty that an assault on those lovely lips would be his utter undoing prevented him from crushing her to him and teaching her a lesson in love she would never forget.

"You are a beautiful, alluring young woman, Lady Josephine," he said grimly. Reaching up, he pulled her arm down from around his neck. "Rather than kiss you, however, I shall very likely turn you over my knee if you do not behave yourself."

Josephine settled back on her heels with a disappointed sigh. "My poor, dear Ravenaugh," she murmured, shaking her head in perplexity. "What *am* I to do with you?"

"You have not been listening, you impossible child," countered the earl, framing her face with the palms of his hands. "You are to do nothing with me. You will make your curtsey in Society and find yourself a younger man. Believe me, my dear, you deserve someone better than I."

"For a man of reason, you are unreasonably thick-headed," Josephine retorted, as close as she had ever come to utterly losing her patience with him. "If you were not so blinded by whatever it is that brought you back to Ravenscliff only to drive you away again, you would see that there cannot possibly be anyone better suited to me than you. Furthermore, you may be certain of one thing, my lord. I shall never give up on you so long as there is the smallest hope that you will be made to see it. My singlemost vice, I'm afraid, is that I can be exceedingly stubborn.''

As Ravenaugh had already been given a fair inkling of just how stubborn Lady Josephine could be, it was perhaps fortunate that he was prevented from having to formulate an answer to that provocatively offered challenge by a gurgle of laughter and the sound of approaching footsteps. Reluctantly he dropped his hands and turned away from Josephine—just in time to meet the arrival of Clarissa and Saint-Clair, the picnic basket on his arm.

"Ah, Devon," murmured Saint-Clair, his gaze specula-tive as it went from Josephine to Ravenaugh and back again. "And Lady Josephine. Still just where we left you, are you? What, I wonder, can you find to fascinate in this unadorned rubble?"

Ravenaugh stiffened. Furiously, Josephine felt the blood rush to her cheeks. No doubt the doctor had glimpsed Ravenaugh move hastily away from her. Certainly there was little doubt that he sensed the undercurrent of tension running rife in the room. The devil, she thought, amused at her shocking lack of morals. She did not care a whit what Saint-Clair might have seen or sensed.

"Jo," exclaimed Clarissa, apparently seeing nothing untoward in her father's rigid stance or Josephine's height-ened color. "You really ought to have come with us. Cousin Adam practically chilled our blood with his tales of the prisoners who have perished in that horrid place. Not that he needed to elaborate overmuch," she added with a nervous gurgle of laughter. "It was enough to see the wretched cells and imagine finding oneself entombed there without even so much as the sunlight to give one comfort. Faith, one shudders to think of it."

"Then let us not think of it," declared Timothy, who, with Aunt Reggie, had come up behind the girl. His glance rested pointedly on Saint-Clair. "Your cousin paints too vivid a picture. Besides, this is a demmed depressing place. What we need is fresh air and sunlight. I say, did someone mention a picnic luncheon? I find I am devilishly sharp set.''

With the exception of Saint-Clair, who, claiming he had a patient to see, surprised everyone by begging off, the immediate consensus of opinion was to retreat at once from the old stone fortress to the rather more pleasant surrounds of the shaded woods along the river. Josephine, having sensed something amiss in her brother's mood, fell into step beside Timothy.

"Well, brother dear?" she queried softly. "What happened to twist your tail?"

For once, Timothy did not offer up his endearingly boyish grin. "Nothing," he said shortly. "Only, this Saint-Clair has a peculiar notion of what is proper entertainment for a young, impressionable female. He made Lucy's stories sound in comparison like nursery tales. If Aunt Reggie and I had not been there to make light of him, I hate to think the impression he would have made on Lady Clarissa."

Josephine frowned. "Beware of him, Timothy. I do not trust his intentions toward either you or Clarissa."

"You needn't worry about me, Jo," Timothy scoffed. "I trust him even less where you are concerned, however. He has a funny way of looking at you. I do not suppose it would do the least good to suggest *you* go home where you would be at a safe distance from all of this—whatever it is that is going on. If Ravenaugh cares at all, he will come after you."

"I wish you will not be absurd," Josephine retorted with a comical grimace. "You may be sure Ravenaugh can be depended on to do no such thing. And you are quite right. There is not the smallest chance I shall leave. Not, now, when I have decided to take your earlier advice to heart. Besides, what could possibly happen to me? If Saint-Clair wants to spread stories about me in a silly attempt to ruin my reputation, I promise I could not care less. In a fortnight I shall very likely be back at Greensward, where nothing he says can possibly matter.''

Josephine, who seldom if ever ate heartily, found that the company, minus Saint-Clair, and the morning's exercise along with the alfresco setting in a meadow overlooking the high bridge and the River Nidd had lent her an unusually keen appetite. Even a small helping of pickled pigs' feet, which normally held little appeal, afforded her palate a piquant pleasure, as did the kidney pie, tart cheese, and saffron bread. In lieu of the marchpane and chocolate covered cherries Clarissa favored, Josephine chose to complete her repast from her aunt's contributions of preserved peaches, fresh carrots, celery, boiled eggs (all garnered from the kitchens at the inn), and a few sips from her own special blend of herbal tea, which Aunt Reggie had labeled so as not to confuse it with her own.

It was, consequently, to the Stone's Ginger Wine, which Timothy had caused to be added to the substantial picnic basket and to a small libation of which Josephine had consented solely out of a wish to preserve the conviviality of the gathering, that she attributed the peculiar light-headedness that beset her shortly after the meal was finished.

Determined that nothing should spoil the day's outing, she said nothing of her peculiar malady. Indeed, she did not even consider crying off from the proposed excursion to Mother Shipton's Cave and the Petrifying Well, both of which lay only a few minutes' walk from town. Nevertheless, she could not but be grateful that Ravenaugh, who had been eyeing her with a hint of disapproval, insisted that they wait until his carriage could be summoned.

"I am aware that you will insist you are perfectly capable of walking any number of miles, Lady Josephine," he stated coolly. "However, you have already had a deal of exercise today. It occurs to me that there is little point in overtaxing your strength."

"Ravenaugh is right, sis," Timothy agreed with a conspiratorial grin. "Now that I look at you, I daresay you could do with a little rest. In the meantime, if Aunt Reggie and Lady Clarissa are agreeable, I suggest we walk on ahead. I hear the Long Walk through Sir Henry Slingsby's forest is exceptionally lovely this time of year, and, since the inn is on the way, we can send Ridings to you with the carriage."

"It would seem that I am to be given little choice in the matter," Josephine replied, glad enough to have the others go on ahead. At least if she were to grow worse rather than better, she would not be the cause of ruining their afternoon. "Pray enjoy your walk. We shall see you at the cave."

It was to occur to her only when she found herself alone once again with Ravenaugh that perhaps she had miscalculated. Hardly had the others departed, than she was made instantly and keenly aware of Ravenaugh's eyes on her.

"Very well, my lord," she sighed, wishing she had not to engage in a verbal exchange when she was not feeling at all the thing at the moment. "There is something you wish to say to me. Pray do not be afraid to open the budget. Only be gentle. As it happens, I fear I am not at all accustomed to drinking wine, even Stone's Ginger Wine. It appears to have made me a trifle dizzy. But then, you knew that, did you not? I daresay that is why you have elected to send for the carriage."

Ravenaugh, uttering a curse, caught her by the arms as she swayed on her feet. "Repellent brat. I wondered, when you did not see fit to put up an argument. Did it never once occur to you to tell us you were not up to trig? The blasted cave can wait for another day."

Josephine, who could only feel grateful to have Ravenaugh's strength to sustain her, smiled wanly up at him. "I have found, my dearest lord, that putting things off to another day can lead to a whole lifetime of missed opportunities. I haven't so many days left of my holiday that I can afford to waste even one, I promise you. Besides, I am already feeling better. I do hope you are not going to insist on taking me back to the inn. Not now, Ravenaugh, when I am not in the least up to arguing you out of it."

"For now, you will rest, impossible child," Ravenaugh growled. "We shall see what is best to do when the carriage arrives."

"I told you I am not a child," Josephine said snappishly.

"And you will undoubtedly keep telling me," Ravenaugh countered. "I shall, in fact, depend on you to do so."

"Abominable man," Josephine retorted, choking on a burble of laughter. "How very detestable you are."

"Excellent," applauded Ravenaugh. "At last we are making progress. I have been trying to convince you I am not the paragon you think I am since our unfortunate first encounter."

"It was not in the least unfortunate," Josephine did not hesitate to correct him. "And as it happens, I like abominable men. At least they are never boring."

Ravenaugh, helping her to a fallen log, curtly ordered her to sit while he gathered up the remains of the picnic lunch. Bitterly he cursed himself for a bloody fool. He should have insisted at once that she return to the inn. Still, if she were only feeling the effects of the wine, perhaps there would be little harm in waiting.

When some minutes later Ridings drove up with the carriage, Josephine was feeling somewhat improved. Indeed, other than a dull headache and a firm resolve never again to indulge in even so much as a sip of wine, she seemed to have come through her momentary setback with few ill effects.

"There, you see, my lord," she said, her smile neverthe-less brighter than she was actually feeling. "All I needed was a little rest. I am perfectly ready to join the others."

Ravenaugh, eyeing her doubtfully, could not deny that she had lost the pallor of complexion that had triggered his initial alarm. When she demonstrated that she was steady on her feet as well, he consented, albeit with reserva-tions, to drive her to the cave.

The rest of the afternoon passed happily enough, with Josephine continuing to improve in both spirits and color. She delighted in the Petrifying Well, whose waters cascaded over the entrance to Mother Shipton's Cave, and even went so far as to offer up her locket to see it turned to stone before her very eyes. The cave, which had seen the birth of the prophetess over three hundred years earlier, was both roomy and dry. Josephine, gazing out through the curtain of water at the stream and woods, could not but smile as she glimpsed Timothy and Clarissa, their hands clasped as they gazed into one another's eyes, obviously lost to the world around them. If nothing else, she told herself, at least they appeared a promising match.

She was not nearly so hopeful where Ravenaugh was concerned. Any headway she might have made that morn-ing in the castle, she doubted not had been set back by her silly indisposition. Really, it was too bad she had had to have a bout of dizziness just when she was so sure she was on the road to improvement. What man, after all, would want to saddle himself with a wife who was of a sickly disposition? The fact that the maddening earl had seemed to withdraw into an impenetrable shell on the drive back to the Half Moon Inn would seem ample proof that

Ravenaugh did not. Indeed, Josephine doubted not she had wasted her wish at Mother Shipton's Wishing Well.

Her sleep that night was anything but fortifying. Restless, she batted her pillows and turned in her bed until well into the night only to fall into an exhausted slumber troubled by a disturbing nightmare in which the wall of her bedchamber opened up to admit a dark, enshrouded figure who came to hover over her in her bed. She awakened with a start, her mouth dry and her limbs entangled in the covers.

Feeling foolish, she reached for the glass of herbal elixir her aunt had left by her bedside the evening before and drank thirstily.

With a sigh she lay back and tried not to think of a certain nobleman with dark, unfathomable eyes, who, she was quite certain, had utterly and irrevocably captured her heart. Curse the man's stubbornness she thought. Then a sudden spasm of pain left her retching and gasping for air, and she was thrust into a nightmare from which there seemed to be no escape.

Chapter 8

"It has been three days, Captain," announced a solemn voice somewhere over Josephine's head, "without any noticeable improvement. If anything, your sister's condition has deteriorated. I truly regret there seems little more I can do for her, save counsel you to send for her mother and father."

"You may be certain they have been notified. But I'm demmed if I shall tell them there is no hope. My sister is going to come out of this. I daresay what we *need* is another doctor."

Timothy's heated retort brought a small, fretful frown to Josephine's brow. It was not at all like her brother to be rude. Powells might be forceful, even boisterous, but they were never uncivil. She told herself she really had ought to open her eyes and discover what had got him in such a huff, but somehow she simply could not find the strength. Indeed, the effort to do so contributed not a little to the headache with which she had been plagued for a seeming eternity of sickness and pain.

"You will of course do whatever you think is right," came the doctor's reply in sympathetic tones. "I am sorry, Captain. Truly, I am. In cases such as these, however, there is little that can be done. I daresay from what you have said Lady Josephine has never been very strong."

Josephine, who, even in her drifting state, could not but feel a twinge of resentment at that pronouncement from the lips of a complete stranger, could not but feel somewhat vindicated at her brother's instantaneous leap to her defence.

"The devil you do," declared Timothy in no uncertain terms. "The truth is, you know nothing about her. By God, she is stronger than either one of us. She has had to be, just to survive all you bloody doctors. And now I shall bid you good day, Dr. Withercombe. No doubt this will compensate you for your trouble."

Dear Timothy, thought Josephine, feeling a ridiculous tear slip from beneath her eyelid. Strange that she had never before realized that he felt that way about her. She was distracted, then, by the clink of coins exchanging hands, upon which the doctor coughed, presumably to clear his throat.

"You are naturally upset, Captain. I do understand,

believe me. If you should change your mind, you know where to find me.''

There was the sound of footsteps, then Timothy's voice, gruff with apology. ''Doctor Withercombe. I beg you will forget anything I might have said just then. I fear I am not myself at the moment. I know Jo would wish me to thank you for everything you have tried to do.''

''Think nothing of it, Captain. I only wish I could have done more. Goodbye, sir.''

Retreating footsteps and the creak of door hinges told Josephine that she was alone again. With the ensuing silence, she experienced a decided sense of relief. Now perhaps she would be allowed to go back to drifting aimlessly in a weightless expanse of darkness. It was a deal better than fighting the nausea, the horrid retching and the merciless pain. At the moment she could not think of a single reason why she should wish to return to the hideous nightmare of living.

Hardly had that tendril of thought wafted through her reeling consciousness than the door opened and closed again. She heard a light, strangely thrilling step approach her bed. No doubt it was only her customary nocturnal visitor who played a part in the confusion of dreams she had been having, she told herself, drifting disinterestedly off again.

A substantial weight sinking down on the edge of her bed, however, was hardly in the usual style of her dream phantom. In the norm he did no more than stand over her bed before retreating, to vanish seemingly into thin air. Certainly, the figment of her imagination had never clasped her hand with flesh and blood fingers or brushed the sweat-dampened hair from her forehead with infinite gentleness. Intrigued in spite of herself, Josephine found herself waiting for what was to happen next.

Certainly the last thing she expected was to feel the

featherlight brush of lips against hers or, then, to hear her name whispered softly in her ear.

"Josephine. Josephine, wake up. It is time you came back to us."

It was like slipping from a nightmare into a dream. She opened her eyes to Ravenaugh, leaning over her. Only it was a Ravenaugh she had never seen before. Careworn, his eyes hollow from lack of sleep, he had not the look of the impervious nobleman who had coolly resisted her advances in the King's Chamber at Knaresborough Castle.

"Josephine." The dark eyes, shadowed with weariness, lit with a sudden, swift light that seemed meant, somehow, for her alone. Ever so gently, he ran his hand over her hair. "Welcome back, my lady. You have had us worried. How are you feeling?"

Josephine stared back at him as she struggled to comprehend. "You kissed me," she whispered. "I did not dream it?"

The wry smile, dearly familiar, tugged at the corners of his mouth. Ravenaugh shook his head. "It was not a dream. You have been ill, my darling girl. But you will get better now."

Her eyes reflected the wonder of but one indisputable fact, even as her hand lifted tentatively to touch the side of his face. "You *are* real flesh and blood, unlike the phantom who comes to my room at night. You did kiss me, Ravenaugh. It was never . . . a dream."

"Josephine? Jo, darling . . ."

It was all she had the strength for. As he felt her hand begin to slide down his face, Ravenaugh caught her wrist and held it. Helplessly, he watched her eyelids drift down over her eyes, felt her slipping away from him.

"That's right, you rest now," he said, his voice rough. "Only don't go too far away. I expect you to come back to us again. Do you hear, you impossible girl? I insist you come back again. You've an odd notion of my character if you think I shall allow you to fling away what is left of your holiday."

Becoming aware of the rustle of skirts at the far side of the room, he laid Josephine's hand carefully at her side. "She was awake for a moment. She spoke to me quite clearly." His brow darkened as he contemplated her still face against the pillows. "She said a strange thing. Something about a phantom visitor who comes to her in the night."

Aunt Reggie, having risen from the cot that had been set up in the dressing room, wearily shook her head. "She was delirious, I'm afraid. Either Annabel or I have been in that chair every night since she fell ill," she said, indicating an armchair near the bed. "Even when we doze off, we should know if anyone came through that door. The hinges are loud enough to wake the dead."

Ravenaugh glanced consideringly from Regina to the door. "You are right, of course. Still, I wonder." Standing, he ran his fingers wearily through his hair. "What the devil ails her, Miss Morseby? You have been a student of Oriental healing. Surely you must have some idea. Only a few days ago, I should have sworn she was well on her way to being as healthy as any girl her age. She has seemed so strong, until this."

Regina hesitated, her glance going to Josephine. "As it happens, I have seen symptoms like these before," she said carefully. "In an Indian prince, who, having the misfortune to be his father's favorite, unhappily stood in the way of another's ambitions. If I did not know better I should think Jo was suffering the ill effects of some foreign substance being systematically introduced into her body. A substance with the properties to simulate a degenerative illness. It would have to be very carefully done, of course, in order to avoid the suspicion of a too sudden demise."

Ravenaugh's head came around, his eyes suddenly intent. "What, precisely, are you saying, Miss Morseby? That you think Lady Josephine is being poisoned?"

Deliberately, Regina folded her hands before her. "It was my first suspicion, I admit, my lord. However, I simply do not see how it could have been done. I have taken the precaution of tasting whatever comes into this room—the broth, the water, even the medicine left by the doctor. Josephine has not been alone since the morning Annabel discovered her, sick in her bed. And then there are the questions of who would wish to do her harm and why. My niece, by all accounts, has led an extremely secluded life. Who would wish to do such a thing?"

"A madman perhaps." Ravenaugh studied Regina with inscrutable eyes. "Or the offspring of one?"

Regina's gaze never wavered from the earl's. "I place as little credence in your cousin's insinuations and allegations as did Josephine, my lord," she firmly replied. "You will admit I have had no little experience with young girls. It is my considered opinion that Lady Clarissa is no more capable of deliberately poisoning someone than am I. As for yourself, I hope you will pardon my bluntness, your lordship, but it is obvious to me that you hold my niece in no little affection. It would never occur to me that you would ever harm her."

A look of perfect understanding passed between Ravenaugh and Regina. "Thank you, Miss Morseby. You are obviously a woman of great common sense. Which is why I do not hesitate to put forward a suggestion that could be considered highly improper."

"You intend to watch over her at night," Regina stated flatly. "Here, in this room."

"With your permission." A cold glitter came to Ravenaugh's eyes. "I have a curiosity to see this phantom who can apparently materialize at will with no one the wiser.''

Ravenaugh, understandably, was not alone in wishing to resolve the mystery of Josephine's phantom visitor, if it did not exist solely in Josephine's delirious imaginings. When apprised of the earl's intent to stand guard in the sickroom, Timothy was immediately moved to protest that his sister's welfare rested with himself.

''I appreciate your concern, my lord,'' he declared. ''However, if anyone is to stand guard over my sister, it will naturally be I.''

''I should never dispute your right to do so, Captain,'' Ravenaugh coolly agreed. ''On the other hand, as a soldier, you will concede that it is essential for a sentry to remain constantly alert. If your sister is to be properly protected, we should relieve one another at reasonable intervals. I suggest, therefore, that we draw lots to see who will stand the first watch.''

Timothy, unable to deny the rationale of Ravenaugh's argument, had to be satisfied with drawing the first watch. He was to be consoled for his diminished role as his sister's sole protector by the circumstance of having Lady Clarissa as an unexpected companion. The young beauty, observing that Josephine's illness was hardly a danger to her, insisted on taking her turn sitting with the patient after the evening meal until bedtime.

''How is she?'' softly murmured Clarissa, entering and crossing to Timothy, who stood looking down at his sister in the bed.

''I thought for a while that she looked more peaceful somehow, almost as if she were sleeping normally.'' Wearily, he shook his head. ''Now, I am no longer sure. I fear she has only grown weaker.''

Clarissa's hand went earnestly out to him. "She will be better, I know it. I spoke with Cousin Adam today. He will be happy to come and look at her, if you like. He is a splendid doctor. Surely, there is something he could do for her."

"No." The reply came out perhaps more tersely than he intended. Seeing Clarissa draw back, the captain repeated more quietly, "No, but thank you. No more doctors for now. Perhaps later, if she does no better. Aunt Reggie is doing all that can be done for her at present." A smile softened his bleak features. "Thank you for coming," he said. "It is good of you to sit with her."

Clarissa gave a flutter of a hand. "No, I-I wanted to come. I have felt so helpless. I'm glad Miss Morseby let me relieve her for a while. The poor dear looks dreadfully pulled."

"She tries not to show it, but she is worried." The helpless look returned to the captain's eyes. "I hardly know what to think of this notion of hers that someone is poisoning Jo. It hardly makes sense, when you think about it. Who in heaven's name could profit by it? Jo, who never hurt a fly. Who could possibly hold her in such aversion as to wish to cut her stick for her?"

"I daresay there is no one who could. Very likely it is not poison at all, but only some food she ate," Clarissa offered hopefully. "Something, perhaps, that simply did not agree with her. I knew a kitchen maid who became dreadfully ill if she ever ingested onions. It does happen you know."

"Yes, it does," smiled Timothy, who did not in the least believe his sister's strange malady could be so simply explained. Perhaps Dr. Withercombe was right, he thought somberly. Perhaps it was putrefaction of the liver or a weakening heart. God knew, Josephine had always been of a sickly disposition. And yet, she had not had the look of a girl on the edge of a sharp decline only four days before. She had looked healthier than he had ever seen her before.

"Well," said Clarissa, glancing around her when the silence had begun to stretch uncomfortably. "Miss Morseby suggested I might read to your sister. She thinks perhaps it will help if Jo knows someone is with her. It is her hope it might somehow serve as an anchor to keep Jo from . . ." She stopped, mortified at what she had been about to say.

"Slipping away?" Timothy smiled gravely and took her hand. "I think Aunt Reggie's is an excellent idea. I daresay Jo would like very much to hear you read to her."

Shyly, Clarissa smiled back at him as he led her to the arm chair. "I was not sure what she might like. I brought something Miss Llewellen was kind enough to lend to me. It is called *The Lady in Waiting: or the Skeleton in the Castle Dungeon* by Miss Lucinda Evalina." Clarissa drew up at sight of the startled gleam of humor in Captain Powell's extraordinarily blue eyes. "I hear she is all the rage in London," she added defensively, "though perhaps it is not the sort of thing Jo is used to reading."

Timothy threw back his head and laughed. The girl stared at him as though entranced. The care momentarily lifted from his manly features transformed him into the dashing officer who had charmed her from the very first moment she laid eyes on him. Indeed, she thought she had never seen anyone so handsome.

"On the contrary, Lady Clarissa," Timothy was quick to reassure her. "The truth is you could not have chosen anything Jo would like better. Lucinda Evalina is undeniably her favorite author. She is, in fact, our oldest sister Lucy."

"Your sister. I did not know," Clarissa exclaimed, her lovely face lighting up with sudden understanding. "But how simply splendid. All the world is trying to guess Lucinda Evalina's identity. How I envy you your family.''

Timothy, who, far too occupied with pursuing the nomadic life of a king's soldier, had never before been remotely in the petticoat line, could not but be struck by the young beauty's extraordinarily sweet innocence. Indeed, gazing down from his considerable height at the vibrant blush on the girl's cheeks, he was quite positive there had never been nor ever could be again anyone so utterly enchanting as Lady Clarissa Roth. ''And now you are one of only a dozen or so who know the truth,'' he said, ''that she is, in fact, the Duchess of Lathrop.''

''Oh, you may be sure I shall not let the cat out of the bag. I am very good at keeping secrets. After all, whom would I tell? I never see anyone at Ravenscliff.''

Impulsively, Timothy squeezed her hand. ''You may tell whomever you will. Lucy would not mind in the least. I feel reasonably certain she would take no little delight in signing her name in your book for you if you wished.''

''I do wish it. Indeed, I should like it above all things, save, perhaps to meet her one day.''

''Then, you may be sure I shall be glad to introduce you to her when you arrive in London. You may expect an invitation to one of her parties. I have yet to be home to attend one myself, but I understand they are all the rage.''

''You are ever so kind, sir,'' declared Clarissa, her eyes shining up at him with such devastating effect that the captain was hard put not to kiss her then and there on the lips.

Indeed, only his overriding sense of honor, which must ever prevent him from taking advantage of a young, single female who had generously come to sit with his sister in her time of illness, gave him the strength to draw back from almost irresistible temptation. ''Not at all, Lady Clarissa. It would be my pleasure. And I shall enjoy hearing you read.

Indeed, I shall be just over there," he said, indicating a straight-backed chair set in a corner hidden in deep shadows.

Clarissa smiled and, taking her seat in the chair, opened her copy of Lucy's book and began to read. "The night was dark with portent too horrible to contemplate, as a lone rider raced across the moors only moments ahead of her relentless pursuers. . . ."

Ravenaugh, arriving at midnight to relieve Timothy at his post, found the young captain in a singularly distracted mood.

"I have nothing to report, save that she is the same," whispered the young man gloomily. "Lady Clarissa read to her, but whether she heard or not . . ." He swallowed and shook his head. "Perhaps the doctor was right. Perhaps I should send for our mother. Egad, it is not as if Mama did not already have her hands full with Papa and now Tom. And yet, she would wish to be here if she knew how serious it is with Jo. The devil, Ravenaugh. She could not bear it to lose our little Jo, I know she could not."

Ravenaugh's hand firmly gripped the captain's shoulder. "She will not lose her. Your sister is far too stubborn to give up the fight now. She will rally. Depend on it."

Timothy nodded, clearly unconvinced. At last with a curt nod, he left Ravenaugh to watch with Aunt Reggie.

It was a strange vigil—Regina in the armchair, reading by the light of a single, shaded lamp, the still form of the girl in the bed, and Ravenaugh watching from the shadows. Ravenaugh forced himself to dismiss the notion that it had all the qualities of a wake. Grimly he reminded himself that at last he had the means to save the girl—if only it was not already too late!

Josephine's nocturnal visitor would come; Ravenaugh

did not doubt it for a moment. And when he did come, it would be Adam. Ravenaugh was sure of it. Miss Morseby had made a great deal clear to Ravenaugh the moment she suggested the true nature of Josephine's illness.

The earl's mouth thinned to a hard line. Things had changed indeed if Adam could cold-bloodedly murder an innocent girl. But then, his cousin would seem the only logical choice. As a doctor, Adam had knowledge of any number of substances that might give the appearance of a degenerative disorder, and he had the ready means of obtaining them. Then, too, the day of their excursion to Knaresborough Castle, Adam had had access as well to the picnic basket in which had resided a container with an herbal drink clearly indicated for Josephine. The basket had been in Adam's possession when he arrived at the King's Chamber, and Lady Josephine had first fallen ill immediately after finishing her meal. It might have the look of coincidence, but Ravenaugh knew his cousin too well to dismiss it, especially in light of Adam's earlier attempt to turn the fiercely loyal Josephine against her "very dear friend." It was not the sort of failure Adam was prone to take lightly.

Ravenaugh smiled mirthlessly at the memory of Josephine's spirited defense of him. He could not recall that anyone had ever stood up for him, especially against Adam or with such unshakable conviction. Certainly, no one had when they were boys growing up together—Adam, the earl's golden-haired boy, who could do no wrong, and Devon, the unwanted usurper. How ironic that Adam had, in those days, been his only friend and confidante!

Those days, however, were long past, he reminded himself. Grimly he steeled himself against the memories. If Adam had caused his sweet Josephine's suffering, then nothing in this world could save him. Not ever again.

The clock on the mantel, striking the half-hour past

three, roused Ravenaugh from his somber reverie. In the yellow glow of the light, Josephine's face shone, pale and still, against the pillows. A mirthless smile tugged at the earl's lips at the quiet rasp of breathing. Miss Morseby sat with her chin on her chest, asleep. Stiffly, Ravenaugh rose from his chair and stretched weary muscles. The phantom would not show himself this night, he told himself, a bleak mood descending over him at the thought. With an explanation for what ailed his darling girl, he had had some hope, no matter how dismal, to which to cling. More importantly, there had been something he could do other than stand helplessly by and watch Josephine fade away before his eyes.

The devil. He would rather fight in a dozen battles than be faced with doing nothing!

A whisper of sound froze him where he stood, his eyes fixed and staring. Suddenly a cold smile spread thinly across his lips.

The phantom's puzzling ability to appear and disappear without having recourse to the door was not a mystery at all, he realized. The answer had been before him all the time, but he had been too preoccupied with other things to make note of it. Josephine herself had told him, told them all; and Adam had, in his own way, confirmed it.

Josephine said the inn keeper had informed her the town was riddled with secret passages, and Adam had scoffed at the idea. Ravenaugh should have known then that Saint-Clair might have his reasons for discouraging any further interest in that particular subject. He was here, now, in Lady Josephine's room, and he had entered through a secret, sliding panel in the wall.

Ravenaugh watched as the shadowy figure, draped to the ankles in a hooded cloak paused to make certain Miss Morseby was indeed asleep, then stole noiselessly to the bed to stand gazing down at Josephine. A cold rage started in the pit of Ravenaugh's belly as a stealthy hand reached out to the glass on the bedside table. The poison dropped into the liquid contained in the glass—the barley-water Aunt Regina gave to her niece to drink to soothe the girl's unsettled stomach.

Good God, it was little wonder that Josephine weakened a little more with each new day! The villain was the devil incarnate, intent on killing his victim by slow, agonizing degrees. But it would end now, this very night. Ravenaugh steeled himself to confront his cousin.

The evil business accomplished, the figure turned. The lamplight played over the face beneath the hood.

Ravenaugh froze, recognition a hard fist in his belly.

Clarissa!

Chapter 9

A rain was falling as Ravenaugh carried Josephine, snugly wrapped in a quilt, out on to the sun porch overlooking Mrs. Gosset's cottage garden and, laying her carefully down on a chaise longue, arranged a pillow at her back.

"There," breathed Josephine, savoring the rain-perfumed air along with the musky scent of potted nasturtiums set out on the porch. "I told you I should be perfectly fine out here. Pray do not look so disapproving, my lord. I really could not bear another moment as a shut-in. Besides, I am ever so much better. You might as well accept the fact that I am quite determined to be out walking again before many more days have passed."

"Accept it?" Ravenaugh, reaching down to pick up a kitten that was vigorously attacking the tassel on one of

his shiny black Hessians, lightly dropped the orange ball
of fur in Josephine's lap. "Frankly, my girl, I expect you
to be up and dancing at the assembly rooms. Your brother
was telling me you are to have your stay at Harrogate
extended. Three more weeks is it?"

Josephine, who was not in the least fooled by the earl's
show of sang-froid, smiled fondly up at him. "Yes, three
whole weeks, and you may be sure I do not intend to waste
them lounging about in bed. I have had a fortnight to
recuperate from my mysterious malady. In my book, that
is quite enough."

Ravenaugh leaned his hands against the porch railing.
"You are, in fact, a medical wonder. Dr. Withercombe, I
believe, views your recovery something in the light of a
miracle. A mere fortnight ago he had given up all hope
for you."

A bare fortnight, he repeated silently to himself, staring
out into the rain. Could it truly have been only two weeks
ago that he discovered the identity of the phantom poi-
soner? Two weeks since he had followed her through that
damnable secret passage into the alleyway that led to an
empty house behind the Half Moon Inn? It seemed like
a bloody eternity since he had confronted her—Clarissa,
wearing her nightdress beneath the black hooded cloak,
his own sweet girl, his daughter!

Even now his blood ran cold at the memory. She had
indeed worn the appearance of a phantom, a lifeless ghost
of the child who so resembled her dead mama that she
had been for far too long both his joy and his bitter
torment. Good God, she had stared at him with blind eyes,
the eyes of a sleep-walker, and she had not known him!

His hands tightened on the rail with the memory, just
as they had tightened that night on his daughter's arms,
hurting her.

"*Why*, Clarissa? *Talk* to me! What the devil have you done?"

It was only then, as he shook her out of her mindless stupor, that he realized she had been indeed in a state of sleep, or something damnably close to it. Her eyes coming alive with fright had stared at him without comprehension.

"Papa? Papa, what—?"

He had not seen in her face the cunning of a cold-blooded killer, but the confusion of a frightened child—*his* child, who had awakened in a strange place without the least knowledge of how she had come to be there. Casting all other considerations aside, he clasped her to him in his arms.

"Softly," he crooned, his eyes grim as he held her and stroked her hair, just as he had done once before—that night in the woods, when he had found her wandering alone and dazed with the shock of the terrible thing she had witnessed. "It is all right, Clarissa. You have been walking in your sleep, that is all. But you are awake now, *enfant.* Everything will be all right, I promise."

Even the words had seemed a mockery as he scooped her up in his arms and carried her back to her room. There, he tucked her safely in her bed. He could only be grateful the abigail had not awakened to discover her mistress gone in the night. With Clarissa attended to, he had wasted little time making his way back to Josephine.

The secret passage, a narrow, windowless corridor, running between the rooms at the back of the inn, had probably originally been designed to allow the servants access to the kitchens. Very likely the sliding panels to the chambers had been added later, during the Civil War, to provide escape routes for the Royalist sympathizers, who quite conceivably had met in secret there. After all, Knaresborough Castle had fallen to the Roundheads only two years after the Royalist defeat at the Battle of Marston Moor.

He had returned to find Regina yet asleep and Josephine so still that he had momentarily been gripped by an icy fear. His glance flew to the half-empty glass by the bedside. By all appearances, it had not been touched. Grimly, he dashed its tainted contents into the grate and replaced it with a new glass, half-filled from the pitcher of barley-water Regina kept for that purpose.

At last he had returned to his post in the shadows to watch over Josephine while she slept, in the morning to report no occurrence of any untoward events in the night.

That had been the beginning of the despicable lie. It had been a simple matter to disable the mechanism that operated the sliding panel in Clarissa's room. Upon extracting a promise from Clarissa to keep their little adventure a secret between themselves, he had had little difficulty persuading his daughter that it was best to lock her in at night. After all, she had been not a little frightened to suddenly find herself in a strange place and with no memory of how she happened to be there. The rest had been a matter of waiting and watching over Josephine each night through the long, dark hours with only his thoughts to keep him company.

His joy in beholding the patient steadily improve from that night forward had been tempered only by the terrible knowledge he carried with him that Clarissa, in the grip of madness, had been the cause of Josephine's suffering and near demise!

It was bitter gall to him that he had failed both of them, just as he had failed Eugenie. But, no more. Another fortnight would see the last of the cursed breed of Roths on the yacht, sailing away from England, away from Josephine. The Earl of Bancroft's youngest daughter would be safe, then, and Clarissa would have the help she needed.

A blur of pain clouded his vision. Clarissa would be made

well again. His rage had brought her to this. By God, he would not rest until she was made well again!

Josephine's voice, gently quizzing, brought him out of his somber reverie. "You seem very far away, my lord," she observed. "You know, you really do not have to keep me company. You have already done far more than I should have any right to ask of you. And I shall be fine out here, I promise. Timothy will be home soon if I need a strong arm to help me back inside."

Have to keep her company! Good God. He could only hope she never knew how he had come to look for the smallest excuse to be near her, to drink in her gentle loveliness and see that she was indeed alive and growing stronger with every hour. Every moment away from her was bitter torment. Only so long as she was in his sight could he be certain his sweet Josephine was safe from the evil he had brought upon her. She must *never* learn that, or know how thoroughly she filled the emptiness that had been so long a part of him. Soon the whole wretched business would be over, and he would remove himself from her life forever.

Ravenaugh turned. "Trying to rid yourself of me, Lady Josephine?" he quizzed her even as he steeled himself to meet her too-discerning eyes. "And just when you had me believing you enjoyed having me around."

"If I have done that, my lord," she replied, her grave smile twisting at his insides, "then I have accomplished far more than I had come to think possible. Thus far you have been singularly stubborn in resisting my every effort to win your confidence. Do you not think you could trust me just a little, my dearest Ravenaugh? I promise I am a very good listener."

Coming to sit beside her on the edge of the chaise longue, Ravenaugh smiled his wonderfully wry smile, which never failed to do strange things to her heart. "Trust you, my lady?'' he said, taking her hand in his. "I have already revealed more to you about myself than I have to any other person alive. I daresay I should not have to say a word, and you would still know me far better than is good for my peace of mind. What, precisely, would you have me tell you?''

"Whatever it is that has cast a shadow over your brow, my lord,'' Josephine managed to reply firmly in spite of the tingling jolts of electricity that seemed to shoot up her arm from the warmth of his fingers curling about hers. Really, it was most disconcerting. Indeed, she wished he would not run his thumb over the back of her hand in such a manner as to threaten to scatter her thoughts just when she most wished to convey to him the decision to which she had come over the past two weeks while she lay helpless in her bed. With an effort she gathered both her thoughts and her courage. "I am no longer ill or delirious, Ravenaugh. I can see perfectly well you are troubled. If you are worried about me, you may cease to do so. Certainly my health need not concern you. I am well on the road to recovery. And if it is that you think I place too great store in what happened in Knaresborough, then you may dismiss that from your mind as well. I have always known I should never marry or have children, so you may feel perfectly safe in that regard. No doubt it will surprise you to learn the most I have ever hoped for is that we might be friends.''

"Little termagant,'' murmured Ravenaugh, wondering at this sudden start of hers. Not marry. Only a short time ago, she had seemed determined to bring him up to scratch. "I was under the impression we were fast friends, you and I.''

"Are we?'' Josephine countered, swallowing dryly. Resolutely, she refused to give into the distracting emotions aroused by his nearness, not the least of which was a melting sensation in the pit of her stomach. Deliberately, she probed his marvelous dark eyes with hers. "Friends share their troubles. They do not shut one another out. Friends trust one another to help."

"Do they?" Ravenaugh's lip curled cynically. Egad, how beautiful she was, and how frail in appearance! Her skin was a pale, translucent ivory against which her eyes shone like great starry pools, unfathomable and infinitely lovely. He experienced an unwitting pang, like a knife thrust to his heart, at the thought of how near they had come to losing her. "A lovely sentiment, but unfortunately that is not always the way of it. Sometimes there are secrets not even a friend may know."

The answering retort on the tip of her tongue, died, unspoken; indeed, Josephine's heart seemed to stop, as Ravenaugh lifted her hand and, holding her with his eyes, deliberately pressed her palm to his lips. "Tell me why you have suddenly determined you will not marry. Not only is the idea absurd, but you will pardon me if I say it sounds suspiciously like self-pity. Strange, I should not have thought that was in your style, my friend."

"No more than it is in your style to bully me," countered Josephine, trying ineffectually to pull her hand away. The devil take him. It was not enough that the merest touch of his hand was sufficient to render her perilously close to giving into a fit of the vapors, but he must choose now, when she was not in the least up to snuff, to batter her already tenuous defenses with a tenderness that was wholly unexpected. Really, it was too bad of him. Aware of a growing ache somewhere in the vicinity of her breastbone, she resolutely steeled herself to go on. "I told you, my lord, that I am a creature of logic. I might have fooled myself into believing for a short time that I should be strong enough to be someone's wife, but I know now that it was only wishful thinking. This last bout of illness is ample proof, is it not?''

She was hardly prepared for the steely flash of his eyes or for the bleak shadow that flickered briefly across the hard planes of his face, like a ripple of emotion in a mask.

"Pray do not look at me like that, Ravenaugh. I do not view spinsterhood as the end of the world. I assure you I am perfectly reconciled to playing the role of auntie to my nephews and nieces. At least in that capacity, I shall always feel useful. I do wish, however—''

She stopped, mortified to find a lump had risen in her throat and that her voice had been on the point of breaking. Enough, Josephine Powell, she told herself sternly. It would be a fine thing to disgrace herself in front of a man who had just accused her of feeling sorry for herself. Really, she must get a grip on herself.

"What do you wish?" The words, dropping in the silence, and Ravenaugh's fingers gripping her hand brought her back to the present.

"What—?" Distracted, Josephine glanced up at Ravenaugh. A blush stained her cheeks as it came to her how absurd it would sound to voice it out loud. If only he would not look at her so with those compellingly dark, unreadable eyes that made her wish to fling her arms about his neck. Detesting her cowardice, she lowered her eyes to Poppet, who lay sprawled on his back across her lap in kittenish abandonment. "Nothing really, only that I might dance just once at a ball. It is a silly, childish thing, I own. Nothing I should ever have told anyone about in the norm.'' She smiled whimsically, her gaze bemused, distant. "Since I was a little girl, I have pictured myself in a beautiful ball gown. I am dancing the waltz in the arms of a man who finds me incredibly attractive. I am as light as a feather on my feet, and my gown swirls about my limbs like liquid silk.'' Laughing a little, she dropped her eyes and tickled

Poppet on his belly. "I suppose it is every little girl's dream. I, however, am not a little girl any more. What a silly fool you must think me."

The muscle leaped along the lean line of Ravenaugh's jaw. She had not the least notion what he thought of her or her girlish fantasies. How young she looked, and how grave. By all rights she should be dancing the waltz every night with a host of moonstricken young admirers. And one day she would; he knew it, if she did not. One day the fantasy would be a reality, if he had not taken that from her, too.

"Allow me to decide what I find foolish," he said harshly, fighting the urge to kiss the sadness from her lips and brow. "As it happens, Clarissa's eighteenth birthday is little more than a fortnight away, and I have been wondering how best to celebrate the occasion. If what you say is true, it would seem a ball is in order. Naturally, I shall depend on you and Miss Morseby to help Clarissa choose a suitable gown. As for yourself—"

Josephine silenced him with the tips of her fingers pressed lightly to his lips. "Pray do not say it," she said warningly. "I have a ball gown. A perfectly lovely dress, as a matter of fact." She paused, a frown wrinkling her brow. "You needn't do this, Ravenaugh, not for my sake. Indeed, I wish you will not."

"Did I say it was for your sake?" queried Ravenaugh with uplifted eyebrows.

"You did not have to, my lord." Josephine's voice faltered, then grew firm with resolve. "I thought, or at least I have been expecting that you would be going away soon. You did tell me you were leaving England. Do not think I am not perfectly aware you have stayed this long only because I was ill. And now you have come up with the absurd notion of flinging a ball so that I might dance the waltz. It really is not necessary, Ravenaugh."

"On the contrary, it would seem patently necessary. You did say it was every girl's wish, did you not? What better gift could I give my daughter than the fulfillment of a dream?" Squeezing her hand, he relinquished it and stood. "And now you must get well. I shall be depending on you for the first waltz."

"I'm afraid that will not be possible, my lord," Josephine demurred, her smile failing to reach her eyes. "That one, after all, should go to Clarissa, should it not?"

"Now you are being absurd," Ravenaugh said, flicking her lightly on the tip of her nose with a careless forefinger. "The promenade, undoubtedly, but hardly the waltz. You cannot expect me to believe the man in your fantasy was your father?"

"No, I do not suppose I should," agreed Josephine, for once unable to respond to his humor. "Very well, my dear friend. I shall be well enough to dance the waltz with you, I promise."

A farewell waltz. And then she would go home with Timothy, thought Josephine, laying her head back against the pillow. Home to Greensward and Mama and Papa, and Tom, of course. Timothy would be returning to his regiment, no doubt, but Lucy and Phillip would soon be home with the children, and Francie and Harry were to be back sometime in July or August. Greensward would come alive again, if only for a few weeks. And then everything would go back to the way it was, the way it would always be.

Well, she had had her glorious grand adventure, and with that she would have to be satisfied, she told herself, only immediately to wonder how she would ever learn to live with the dreadful feeling of hollowness, the emptiness of a life without Ravenaugh. How ironic that her one glimpse at happiness should have proven little more than a fragile wisp of a dream.

* * *

The days following Ravenaugh's decision to give Clarissa
a birthday ball were not to be tranquil ones for Josephine.
The knowledge that the earl was soon to be leaving and
that very likely she would never see him again weighed
heavily upon her. Furthermore, the fact that she was still
weak from her recent illness made it all too tempting to
languish in bed. Each morning, under Regina's watchful
eye, she forced herself to rise and dress and go through
at least the semblance of her normal routine, but her heart
simply was not in it.

Regina, a keen observer, could hardly fail to note that,
despite the brave front her niece presented to the world,
Josephine was far from her usual self. Her marked tendency to drift into lengthy silences, her eyes distant and
contemplative, were not in the least like the Jo Regina
had come to know. There was a distinct air of sadness
about the child in such moments that had never been
there before. Even Timothy was given to remark that their
Jo seemed uncommonly low in spirits. It was as if that part
of her that had always burned like a bright beacon of
enduring hope had been dimmed, irrevocably perhaps, by
her most recent bout with illness. And, indeed, Regina
had only to see her with Ravenaugh to know the reason
why.

It was in the way Josephine looked at him whenever
she thought she was unobserved, like someone storing
memories for a bleak and barren future. The girl had
decided to give him up. Where was Josephine's fighting
mettle? fretted her aunt. Not that Ravenaugh was one whit
better. The maddening nobleman gave every manifestation
of a man encased in stone. If Regina had not already been
given to see behind the earl's careful front, she might have

thought he was wholly impervious to her niece. Clearly, they were both making a mull of it.

At last, troubled at the girl's failure to gain in spirits as she had in health, Regina determined to take matters into her own hands. Indeed, she all but dragged Josephine out one morning for a stroll in the gardens.

"You will accomplish nothing sitting around brooding over things," declared that worthy, fetching Josephine a straw bonnet and a pelisse. "It is a perfectly glorious day. A little exercise will put the roses back in your cheeks if it does nothing else."

"I am not brooding, Aunt Reggie," Josephine demurred, sorely wishing Regina would leave her be. "Whatever should I have to brood about?"

"As if it were not as plain as the nose on your face," said Aunt Reggie. Firmly she led Josephine out of the house. "Hasn't his lordship enough problems without having to watch you, moping about as if you had not a spark of life left in you? And after he nigh wore himself to the nub, worrying about you all the time you lay ill? You should be ashamed of yourself Josephine Louise Powell. The man is eating his heart out over you."

Josephine, suffering a sharp pang in the region of her heart, hastily averted her face from her aunt. "I wish you will not be absurd, Aunt Reggie," she objected, close to wishing her well-meaning kinswoman to the devil. "Even if he did care, just a little, it can no longer signify. I have had plenty of time to think about it these past weeks, after all, and I realize now that I shall never marry anyone. Do you not see, my dearest of aunts? Nothing has changed really. I shall always be faced with the prospect of falling ill at the least little thing. I have come to accept that. I shall even eventually learn all over again to live with it, if not with contentment, then at least with a certain equanimity. I

will not, however, burden Ravenaugh or any other man
with a sickly wife.''

Regina uttered what sounded very like an unladylike
snort. ''A hideous prospect, indeed. For shame. I never
thought to hear such mush from you, Josephine Powell.
It is high time you stopped playing the martyr and started
using that head of yours. Has it never once occurred to
you that there was something just a bit havey-cavey about
this mysterious illness of yours?''

''No, of course not,'' Josephine retorted. ''Why should
it? I was ill, just as I often am. What could there possibly
be queer in that?''

''Nothing,'' agreed Regina, eyeing her niece with a sapient air. ''Which is why it almost worked. Only think, Jo,
dear. Does it not occur to you that it came upon you most
peculiarly suddenly at a time when you were in better
health than you have ever been before? Why, if it had been
your heart or your liver, do you think you would be up
walking around this minute? Personally, I find it more
than a little curious that you should have demonstrated a
remarkable recovery almost from the moment Ravenaugh
and Timothy took it upon themselves to stand guard in
your room.''

Josephine suffered a cold clamp of premonition.
''Ravenaugh was there?'' she queried in an odd voice. ''In
my room?''

''Every night from midnight to dawn. Try as I might, my
dear, I *would* nod off.'' Regina gave vent to a sigh. ''I'm
afraid I am not so young as I was used to be. Many is the
time when I stood watch all night over the girls in camp.
Now, I cannot even stay awake to keep my own flesh and
blood safe from a single intruder.''

''Intruder?'' Josephine caught Regina's arm. ''What
intruder?''

Regina, glad at last to see a spark of interest in her

niece's eyes, replied in no uncertain terms. "Your nocturnal phantom, Jo, dear. The one you kept mumbling about
in your delirium. The man who, I believe, was trying to
poison you."

"Poison me! Good God, what are you saying?" Josephine stared incredulously at her aunt. "You *saw* him? You
saw a man come into the room and stand over me while
I lay in my bed?"

"Well, I never actually saw him. None of us did," Regina
reluctantly admitted. "But I do not for a moment doubt
in his existence or his purpose in sneaking into that room.
He was slipping you poison in your barley-water, I am
certain of that. As soon as the fiend, whoever he is, became
aware that you were being closely guarded, he ceased to
come, and you began almost at once to improve. In my
mind, that is proof enough that your illness was not due
to any natural causes."

Josephine turned away, a shadow of uncertainty clouding
the purity of her brow. "I don't know, Aunt Reggie," she
said slowly. "It is all so very difficult to believe. Perhaps
my getting well was only coincidental. Certainly, I should
require something more tangible to make me believe someone was trying deliberately to cut my stick for me." Resolutely, Josephine shook her head. "No, dearest Aunt, it is
all simply too preposterous."

"On the contrary," declared Regina, a curious gleam
in her eye. "It is not in the least preposterous. I, after all,
have never been one to accept anything at face value.
When I began to suspect you were suffering the effects of
poison, I made every attempt to protect you. If I failed in
that, I at least managed to discover something of no little
consequence. I know how the deed was accomplished."

Feeling a wave of sickness wash over her, Josephine
listened to her aunt apprise her of the manner in which
a thorough search of the room at the inn had revealed

the secret of the hidden panel. It was one thing to wish to experience a harrowing adventure to relieve the monotony of one's life. It was quite another to realize someone had actually set about to cold-bloodedly put a period to one's existence. Why? she wondered. Who could think so ill of her as to wish to see her dead?

Almost immediately an image of Adam Saint-Clair at Knaresborough Castle leaped to mind. Indeed, she was chillingly reminded of the look in the doctor's eyes the moment he had come upon Ravenaugh and her in the King's Chamber. She felt again what she had felt then. The earl's cousin, far from wishing her well, had given every appearance of one who entertained a thorough loathing of her.

If Saint-Clair *was* the phantom who had come to her in the dark of night, he had executed his malicious plot with the cunning of a madman. And if it had been he, might not that explain Ravenaugh's brooding reticence?

Ravenaugh, too, had guessed the truth about his cousin. She knew it instantly, just as she knew Saint-Clair was responsible for her own near demise. It was hardly any wonder that Ravenaugh had found it impossible to share his dark secret with her. She did not doubt that he had taken all the blame for what had happened to her on himself! It would be so very like him.

The thought, far from giving her comfort, filled her with an unwonted anger. How dared he keep the truth from her! Surely he must have seen what it was doing to her. And, still, he had allowed her to go on believing her illness was due to her fragile constitution. Oh, it really was too bad of him. Indeed, it suddenly struck her that it was, in fact, wholly illogical and, therefore, utterly out of character.

Ravenaugh would never have felt compelled to protect his cousin in such a manner. He would be far more likely to call Saint-Clair out and deliver the man the thrashing of his life than keep such an evil secret to himself. There must be some other reason for his silence, something that went far deeper than his kinship with the cousin who had betrayed him.

Clearly there was still a great deal she did not understand. She understood enough, however, to realize everything Ravenaugh had done the past few weeks had been to protect her. Might he not be protecting someone else as well? Not Saint-Clair, she told herself, but Clarissa, over whom Saint-Clair wielded an unwholesome influence?

In spite of herself, Josephine arrived home feeling a deal better for her outing. Indeed, it was as though a cloud had been lifted from her. What a fool she had been to waste time feeling sorry for herself, when Ravenaugh had needed her clear-headed and rational! She felt a pang at the knowledge that all the time he had been bearing this terrible burden alone, but not anymore, she vowed, a hard little gleam in her eye. If Ravenaugh could not bring himself to confide in her, she must simply help him without his knowledge. Somehow she would come up with a way to prove his cousin's villainy. Indeed, she already had a germ of an idea. It required only a little research. A note, in fact, to the proprietor of the Old Chemist Shop in Knaresborough should set things in motion, a note which she would compose without a moment's delay.

Hardly had she divested herself of her bonnet and pelisse, however, than she was met by the sight of Timothy, waiting for her in the parlor, a Timothy that she could not recall ever having seen before. Dressed in riding garb, he paced restlessly, while, in time with each step, he smartly tapped the top of one of his military long boots with his riding crop. Obviously, he had just returned from his morning ride with Clarissa, and from the looks of him,

things were not at all as they should be. The poor dear
was positively grim-faced.

"I am leaving, Jo," he announced, almost before she
had time to ring for the tea tray. "The truth is I never
meant to stay longer than a day or two to see how you
went on. Now that you are feeling more the thing, I feel
it is time I rejoined the regiment."

"Of course if you must report back now, then you must,"
calmly agreed Josephine, as, thoughtfully, she studied her
brother's gloomy profile. "Still, it is all rather sudden, is it
not? I thought you were looking forward to Lady Clarissa's
ball."

"I am a soldier, not some bloody demmed dancing master," Timothy declared with unwonted vehemence. "I
daresay Lady Clarissa and her ball will do famously without
me."

"I see," said Josephine, who did indeed have more than
a glimmer of an idea as to what had inspired her brother's
sudden yearning for the regiment. "Let me guess. You and
Clarissa have had a falling out. It must have been something
quite serious. I should not in the norm have expected *you*
to run in the face of adversity."

She watched expectantly, the angry flush of anger, followed by the endearingly wry, grimacing smile. "The devil,
Jo. No *man* could say that to my face."

"Fortunately, however, I am not a man. I am your sister,
and I am waiting for you to climb down off your high horse
and tell me what happened between you and Clarissa."

In a fit of exasperation, Timothy ran his fingers through
his hair. "Demmed if I know. One moment we were doing
famously, and the next she was wishing me at Jericho. It
was all because of that demmed coxcomb, Lawrence. A
bounder if ever I saw one."

"And you, naturally, saw fit to warn her away from him.

Oh, Timothy, how could you? Clearly, you have a great deal to learn about women.''

"Women? Lady Clarissa is hardly a woman. She is a contrary kid of a girl who would do better with a firm hand at the reins. If it is Lawrence she wants, then I bloody well wish her well of him.''

"Then she will have him, and it will be entirely your own fault, Timothy Powell,'' Josephine said sternly. "You know as well as I that Lawrence would not hesitate to throw a sack over her head and carry her off to Gretna Green. Is that what you want?''

"Oh, Jo,'' groaned Timothy, dropping down all at once on the sofa. "You always did have a way of cutting to the heart of a matter. Lady Clarissa is as sweet and innocent as an angel. I'd bloody well call Lawrence out before I should let anything like that happen to her.''

"And then you would be forced to flee the country, your career in ruins,'' Josephine did not hesitate to remind him. "Why, you would break Mama's heart, and all because you did not stop to think. If you wish to save Clarissa from Lawrence, you will have to do a deal better than that.''

"What can I do, Jo? I know I have made a mull of it. I daresay she will not deign to so much as look at me again, and who could blame her. I behaved like a boor.''

He looked so utterly forlorn and dejected that Josephine's heart went instantly out to him. "You will not run, Timothy Powell, that much is certain. For Clarissa's sake you will stand and take your medicine. I suggest you practice holding on to your temper and concentrate instead on presenting Clarissa with a strong, manly front. It would not hurt if you could manage to be at the very least civil to Mr. Lawrence when Clarissa is about.''

"Civil! Good God, to Lawrence? I should sooner make up to a polecat.''

"Then pray go and do so at once and kindly spare me

your megrims," said Josephine calmly. "If you do not
intend to listen to my advice, then there would seem little
point in taking up any more of my time, now would there."

She had so much the look of their mother as she pronounced this judgment, that Timothy was startled into
laughter. "Egad, Jo, you do have a way about you. I beg
your pardon, it would appear I was talking when I should
have been listening. Why, precisely, should I play nice to
Mr. Lawrence?"

"If you wished a green colt to go through a gate, would
you bully or coax him?" Josephine answered, apparently
irrelevantly.

"I should coax him, of course," declared Timothy with
an impatient wave of the hand. "Any fool knows that. A
spirited animal must be allowed to overcome its fear, else
it will balk from that moment on at every gate it comes to.
Papa taught us that practically before we were out of leading strings."

"Yes, of course, he did," agreed Josephine, who had
been considerably older before she was allowed even within
hailing distance of a horse. "Then tell me, when you draw
a fish to the lure, do you do so by waving your arms and
shouting or flinging sticks into the water to drive the creature to it?"

"Egad, Jo, if that is what you think, then you do not
know the first thing about fishing," declared Timothy,
who, an inveterate angler, was clearly astounded at so
incredible a notion. "Why, you would drive every fish
within a hundred yards into hiding if you did any such
thing. Why the devil do you think it is called a 'lure'?"

"Because, I should think," replied Josephine with a
sober mien, "it is meant to attract the fish's notice and
then, having captured its fancy, entice it further to strike
at the bait."

Timothy eyed her warily, suspecting, no doubt, a trap

in the making. "Essentially you are in the right of it. There is a deal more to it than that, however. It requires a deal of skill and not a little patience to successfully lure a fish to the bait."

"Does it, indeed?"

"I suspect you know very well it does," Timothy declared. "You could not be a Powell and not know it. What the devil does any of this have to do with Clarissa?"

"All in good time, Timothy, dear. Now, let me understand you." Josephine, pressing the side of an index finger to her lips, took a turn about the room. "You would coax a green colt in order to avoid making it skittish, and to catch a fish, you would resort to endless patience and skill to entice it to take the bait. A woman, on the other hand, you would boss and bully and dictate to, as if she had not a brain in her head, let alone a mind and will of her own. I find that curious. Can it be that Papa has been seriously misled in his notions of rearing children? I cannot think of a single instance in which he bossed or bullied any of us girls, or you boys, for that matter, can you?"

Timothy, who had been properly led down the garden path, stared at his youngest sister as if struck by divine revelation. "The devil, Jo. You know very well I cannot. I daresay you could have taught even Papa a thing or two. You might just have said straight out what you had in mind instead of knocking me over the head with it."

"You do, however, get the point, do you not? I suggest, if you do not wish Clarissa to bolt, you should try patience and tact to win her over. You may be sure any attempt to dictate to her will result in precisely what happened today. The one sure way to disarm her is to pretend to approve her choice of companions, even if he is a fop and dandy. Oh, and Timothy, it would not hurt to let her see you in your regimentals—say at Clarissa's ball tomorrow night. I assure you the contrast between you in uniform and Lawrence in all his finery will prove an irresistible lure."

"The devil, why did I not think of that?" Timothy, springing to his feet, picked Josephine up and danced her around the room. "You, little sister, are a genius. Demmed if I don't think it will work."

"Think what will work?" queried Aunt Reggie, smiling quizzically as she came into the room.

"You tell her, Jo. I must be off. A prior engagement, you know. Take care of our girl, Aunt Reggie. She's a positive genius."

"Well, and what was that all about?" Regina said in no little bemusement, as Timothy, pausing only long enough to give his aunt a sound buss on the cheek, exited out the door.

"I believe it is called 'love,' " replied Josephine, as if that explained everything.

Some thirty minutes later, Josephine, sitting at the secretary in her room, finished reading over the note she had just composed. Satisfied with its contents, she folded the paper and sealed it with wax. Then summoning Wiggens to her, she placed the missive in his hand and, instructing him to wait for a reply, sent him on his way.

The tersely written answer she received after little more than an hour of nervous pacing in her room was enough to send her immediately in search of her Aunt Regina.

"Tell me, dearest aunt," she said, upon encountering her in the cottage garden cultivating some herbs she had planted among the vegetables with Mrs. Gosset's permission, "everything you know about *Humulus lupulus,* or, more specifically, Cannabaceae."

"Hops?" said Regina, glancing up in surprise. "It has been used in the brewing of beer since the ninth century and is known to have a sedative effect. I myself use it in my sleeping potion. Why do you ask?"

"First tell me about *Papaveraceae*," Josephine insisted.

"Poppies? Why, they are grown extensively in the Orient and are the basis of laudanum. The green pods of the fruit and the sap from the stems can be extremely dangerous. I am sure you are aware of their narcotic effect."

"And *Solanaceae?*"

"Good heavens, Jo, where did you come up with that one?"

"Please, just tell me what it is, Aunt Reggie. All shall be made clear to you directly."

"It has many common names, chief among them jimsonweed, mad apple, sacred datura, and devil's trumpet. It has been reportedly used in witchcraft through the centuries. In India, it was employed by thieves, who used it to incapacitate their victims. Even though it is employed in medicines to treat a wide variety of ailments, including the falling sickness, hysteria, and various forms of madness, it is extremely dangerous, Jo. I do not recommend that you have anything to do with it."

"I'm afraid it is too late for that, Aunt Reggie," Josephine said strangely. "If I am not mistaken, I have already been made intimately familiar with its painful effects. And you, my dearest of aunts, may cease to trouble yourself about your inability to stay awake at nights. I believe you were administered a sleeping potion not unlike the one you make up yourself."

Chapter 10

"Pray be sensible, Jo," exclaimed Aunt Reggie in no little consternation. "You *must* tell Ravenaugh. Or Timothy, surely. When Saint-Clair learns a female has written the chemist's shop inquiring about his purchases, he is bound to put two and two together. He will know instantly it was you." In her earnestness, she grasped Josephine's hands in both her own. "Jo, we already know of what he is capable. Surely you must realize you are in the gravest peril of your life."

"I do realize it, Aunt Reggie, and you may be sure I shall take every precaution." Pulling away, Josephine paced fitfully along a row of purple and pink irises. At last she came around, her head up, as she faced her aunt over the motherwort and garlic. "I do not wish to tell Ravenaugh just yet. Or Timothy either, for that matter. Heavens, there is no telling what my brother might do, and I have Mama and Papa to consider. They nearly lost Tom. I shall not place Timothy in danger, too."

"Then tell Ravenaugh, without delay," Regina insisted.

"I cannot! Oh, do you not see, Aunt? It would be a fine thing if he took it into his head to call Saint-Clair out, just when he and Clarissa are finally showing signs of working out their differences. Surely, it would not hurt to put it off for just a little while longer. The ball is tomorrow night, and after that he and Clarissa will—"

She stopped, aware that she had been on the point of saying Ravenaugh and Clarissa would be leaving England.

"He and Clarissa will what?" demanded Regina, eyeing her niece with patent disapproval.

"Will have the ball behind them," Josephine finished somewhat lamely. "Really, Aunt Reggie, it would be a shame to spoil it for them, and I shall be perfectly safe here in the house. If I do go out, I shall be sure and take Wiggens or Timothy with me. Even Saint-Clair would not dare to try anything in a public place with one of them to protect me. Everything will be all right, you will see. Please promise me you will say nothing about this to anyone."

Regina bit her tongue to keep from voicing any number of objections that leaped to her mind, not the least of which was that a madman capable of calculated murder was not at all to be trusted not to kill them all in their beds. She could see at a glance, however, that it would do little good to remonstrate with Josephine. The girl could be uncommonly stubborn when she chose to be. But then, she consoled herself, at least Josephine was no longer sunk in a quagmire of despondency. Almost anything was better than seeing the child utterly dispirited.

"Oh, very well. I promise to say nothing until after the ball. But then, you *will* tell Ravenaugh," Regina warned. "Or I most certainly shall. Is that understood, Jo?"

"I understand perfectly," smiled Josephine, giving Regina a sound buss on the cheek. "I understand you are the very dearest of aunts."

Josephine, true to her word, remained inside the rest of the morning, contenting herself with pretending to read and catch up on her correspondence, when she would much have preferred to go out for a walk in Valley Gardens or do anything that would distract her from her thoughts. She sorely missed Ravenaugh's daily visit. Indeed, more than once she found herself listening for his light, thrilling step. Ravenaugh, however, had left Harrogate that afternoon with Clarissa for Ravenscliff to see to the final preparations for the ball, and Timothy, unable to stand being cooped up, had taken himself off without explanation.

Josephine, having reread for the fifth time the opening paragraph of Sir Walter Scott's *Guy Mannering* without having registered so much as a single word, was wishing for any sort of diversion when the rattle of carriage wheels and the jingle of harness at the front of the house drew her to her window. She looked out upon the arrival of a magnificent coach, bearing a coat of arms and drawn by a team of matched bays, all of which she recognized immediately as belonging to the Earl of Ravenaugh.

It was not the Earl of Ravenaugh, however, who descended from the coach. Nor was the fashionably dressed female whom the gentleman turned to assist to the ground Lady Clarissa. With a wild leap of joy and not a little surprise, Josephine recognized her mama and papa. Furthermore, if she was not mistaken, the gentleman still seated in the coach was none other than her brother, Tom!

It was Ravenaugh's doing, she realized all in a heartbeat. He had not only sent for the Earl and Countess of Bancroft to be with their daughter at her very first ball, but he had despatched his very own travelling coach to convey them. A myriad of emotions engulfed her as she hastened down the stairs to greet them, not the least of which were a dawning appreciation of how greatly she had been wishing to have her mama with her the past several days and a dull ache as it came to her precisely why Ravenaugh should have gone to all the trouble.

Clearly the nobleman's generosity was surpassed only by his thoughtfulness. Indeed, she could not but be perfectly aware his purpose had been to provide her with the support and no doubt the protection of her family upon the circumstance of his own imminent departure.

That knowledge, far from rendering her comfort, came very near to shattering her already tenuous defenses. Hardly had she flung her arms about her mother than Josephine felt herself on the verge of disgracing herself with a wholly uncharacteristic shed of tears.

"Why, Jo, darling," exclaimed her mama, considerably taken aback at so emotive a greeting from her normally calm and collected daughter. "My poor child, what is it?"

"It-it is nothing, really, Mama," Josephine said with a watery laugh. "I am just so very happy to see you and-and Papa."

"I was wondering when you would find time to notice your old papa," said Bancroft, holding out his uninjured arm to embrace Josephine. "How is my girl?"

"I am much better now, Papa," Josephine assured him. Careful of his arm in the sling across his chest, she stepped into his warm embrace. "And I have been having a simply splendid time in spite of-of—well, of everything."

"I, for one, am exceedingly curious to hear about the 'everything,' " observed a dearly familiar voice, which brought Josephine quickly around.

"Tom!" Beholding her brother, considerably altered since last she had seen him, but standing on his own two feet with only the assistance of a cane, threatened to break down the last of her reserves. "Tom, how—how *good* it is to—see you!"

"The devil, Jo," said Tom, clasping her to him with an arm about her shoulders. "Ravenaugh wrote you had been having a rather sad time of it. And here I find you, all grown up and a diamond of the first water. By heaven, Jo, I hardly recognize you."

"I am the same Jo you have always known," objected Josephine, smiling up into his worn features. How pale he was, and thin! And yet somehow the same Thomas, grown older, it was true, but still with the same bright courage in his smile, the same gleam of mischief in his eyes so like Timothy's.

"Timothy is away at the moment, but Aunt Reggie is here," Josephine was saying as she ushered them all inside. "I cannot wait to hear all about your travels."

It was to be some time, however, before Josephine caught up on all the news. Hardly had they all gotten settled in the parlor with a tea tray and a cold collation of meats and various cheeses for nuncheon than Mrs. Gosset entered to announce Lady Juliana and Miss Harcourt, who had just arrived back in Harrogate after an extended shopping spree in York.

"No, please do not get up on our account," said Lady Juliana, espying Tom, reaching for his cane.

"Perhaps we should not stay, Jo," Miss Harcourt added. "I fear we have interrupted a family gathering."

"Nonsense," said Lady Bancroft. "We are happy to meet Josephine's friends. Please, do come in and join us."

Josephine quickly made the introductions all around. "Tom is just home from America," she added for the benefit of Lady Juliana, who had been unobtrusively studying Tom. "He fought under General Packenham in the Battle for New Orleans. Lady Juliana's brother was with Colonel Beckwith in the Peninsular Campaign."

"Was he," said Tom with unfeigned interest. "Then I daresay he made the march to Talavera. A harrowing experience, that. The march is legendary among the regiments."

"My brother fell at Talavera," Lady Juliana said quietly.

A gleam of sudden understanding passed over Tom's face. "A lot of brave lads fell at Talavera. I am sorry."

Lady Juliana lifted her head and smiled resolutely. "There is no need to be. He was doing what he most wanted to do. I daresay there was not a day in his life that he did not wish to be a soldier. And, you, sir, shall you be rejoining your regiment one day soon?"

"I'm afraid my soldiering days were finished by an American sharpshooter," replied Tom without so much as a trace of bitterness. "A rugged lot, those Americans," he added reflectively. "I've half a mind to go back there one day and try my luck at forging a place of my own out of that wild, wonderful land. I daresay it would suit me a deal better than would the law or the clergy."

"Tom," exclaimed Emmaline. "I had no idea you had any such thing in mind. Good heavens—America. You never mentioned it before."

"No need to get all in a pother, Emmaline. I think it sounds a splendid notion for a young man with an adventurous spirit," pronounced Bancroft in a voice of reason. "I daresay it might prove a marvelous opportunity for the lad. Something to shoot for at any rate," he added with a meaningful look at Emmaline.

"Besides, Mama," interjected Josephine, who had not failed to interpret the meaning behind that glance between her mama and papa, "it is not as if Tom is leaving today." Indeed, she thought, observing the manner in which Lady Juliana was looking at Tom, any number of things might happen in the interim to change his mind about taking up residence away from England.

Timothy, arriving at the cottage to discover a sizeable portion of his family present, served as a welcome diversion from the serious mood that had fallen over the company. The impromptu gathering took on an immediate festive air marked by a deal of laughter and merriment.

Consequently, the afternoon had progressed toward evening before Emmaline at last had the opportunity to talk to her youngest daughter alone. Lady Juliana and Miss Harcourt had long since departed, having given their assurances that they were looking forward to seeing everyone

at Ravenscliff for the ball. Leaving her husband and sons
in a lively debate on the merits of the Arabian versus the
English Thoroughbred and her sister Regina overseeing
the preparation of their rooms for the night, the countess
led Josephine out on to the sun porch.

"Ah, this is much better," pronounced Emmaline,
breathing in the evening breeze scented with roses. "Come
and sit with me, Jo, dear. You look tired after all the
excitement."

"I suppose I am, a little," Josephine confessed, taking
a seat beside her mama on the porch swing. "I shall never
be able to thank Ravenaugh enough for this latest of his
many kindnesses. A pity he could not be here to enjoy it
with us. I daresay he has not experienced anything to
compare with a Powell family gathering."

"Has he not?" murmured Emmaline, watching the subtle play of emotion on her daughter's face.

"He was made an orphan at a very young age and taken
to be reared in his uncle's home with his cousin, who was
only a few months older. I think it was not a very happy
arrangement. Certainly, he never knew what it was to grow
up in a large, exceedingly boisterous family. I believe he
has not known much of joy in his life, which is a shame.
For if you must know, he is the kindest, most gentle of
men."

"You are quite fond of his lordship," ventured her
mama, who had already more than an inkling in which
quarter the wind lay. "And little wonder. His correspondence to us during your illness demonstrated a most
thoughtful disposition. Indeed, I should never have been
able to countenance remaining home had we not had his
letters to sustain us."

"His letters?" Josephine turned startled eyes on Emmaline. "Mama, he wrote to you?"

"But of course, dear. Surely you must have known. He

wrote us regularly even after you were clearly out of danger. Such wonderfully encouraging letters, full of assurances that you would soon be up and about again. You can have no idea what a comfort they were to us, especially as Tom was in no case to be left alone at the time.''

"I did not know. He never told me," Josephine said slowly, as she digested this newest evidence of Ravenaugh's kindness. Then, "But how very like him," she declared in tones of sudden enlightenment and, bolting to her feet, began to pace as she unburdened herself of a whole range of feelings that had been begging for expression for no little time. "He is the most infuriatingly secretive, hopelessly noncommunicative man who ever lived. Furthermore, he is stubborn, managing, thick-skulled, and shortsighted. And if all that were not enough, he simply cannot bring himself to trust in anyone. He let me go on believing I was ill because of my fragile constitution, when he knew perfectly well it was nothing of the kind, and all because of his stupid sense of guilt! Oh, how I should like to have him here that I might give him a piece of my mind. Not that it would do the least good. He will never be brought to realize that I am not a child, but a woman who could make him exceedingly happy if only he were not too pigheaded to see it. It would serve him right if I did just what he is always advising me to do and utterly gave up on him. The hopeless idiot. I daresay I shall be happy he is leaving England with Clarissa after the ball. And, indeed, I should be, if only I did not love him so!" At last, dropping down on her knees before Emmaline, she laid her head in her mama's lap. "Oh, Mama, what am I to do?" she whispered brokenly. "I have no wish to live without him."

Ravenaugh, the following morning, was to further demonstrate his thoughtfulness by sending his chaise in addition to his coach to conduct the Powell contingent to Ravenscliff, which allowed all but the trunks and baggage, relegated to the ancient Powell travel coach, to ride in luxurious comfort.

Josephine exchanged a tearful farewell with Mrs. Gosset, who expressed the hope that Lady Josephine and Miss Morseby would see fit to return the following year to Harrogate. "I do wish you well, my lady, with his lordship. He seems a fine man, not at all what is said of him."

"He has been a dear friend, Mrs. Gosset," said Josephine, wondering if everyone in Harrogate knew she had lost her heart to the maddeningly elusive nobleman. "And you have been more than kind to us all. Thank you and goodbye."

How different was the drive to Ravenscliff from that first eventful visit so long ago, it now seemed. Could it only have been two months? Josephine marveled. She had lived more and suffered more in those two months than she had in all the previous years of her existence. And yet how soon it was to be over, her sweet dream of love and home and family. Tomorrow she would have her long wished-for waltz, and then she would bid farewell forever to Ravenaugh.

At least, Josephine consoled herself, he and Clarissa would soon be safe from Saint-Clair's evil manipulations. She felt only pity for the doctor. How twisted with hate he must be! But then, it could not have been easy for him, growing up as the earl's by-blow, denied even a place in Society. Perhaps had the fates been kinder, he might have been a good, even a generous man. Unwittingly she shivered. What could he possibly have thought to gain in killing her?

She had not been a threat to him. She could not have claimed more than a passing acquaintanceship with him. It would seem to make little sense. But then, she supposed madmen were not supposed to make sense to anyone but themselves. Soon it would not matter anymore. She would be back at Greensward, and she could not think he would have cause to follow her there.

As the small cavalcade came at last to the gorge and its plunging waterfall, she dismissed Saint-Clair from her mind in favor of other, more immediate emotions, not the least of which was the remembered terror of beholding Clarissa poised on the brink of the precipice. What part had that episode played in the mystery surrounding Ravenscliff? she wondered. Then the manor rising from the cliffs on the far side of the bridge elicited a chorus of admiration from the Powells, who were seeing it for the very first time, and she steeled herself to meet Ravenaugh in front of her family.

She was not in the least sure she would not betray herself to her brother Tom's hawk eyes or her Papa's astute powers of observation. The last thing she could wish was to make a blushing fool of herself in front of everyone.

She need not have worried. Ravenaugh, striding across the great domed hall to greet them, formed the cynosure of attention. Bancroft, who knew a man when he saw one and who had guessed a deal more about the earl from the nobleman's correspondences, extended a ready hand in greeting, while Tom, suspecting the "everything" that Josephine had yet to confide in him had a great deal to do with the earl, appeared to be reserving judgment. No doubt Lady Emmaline, who had been made privy to a deal more than the others, gave the strong masculine features the closest scrutiny, a circumstance that Ravenaugh did not fail to note with a faint, sardonic twist of the lips .

"Welcome to Ravenscliff, Lady Bancroft," he drawled, bowing over the countess's hand. "I believe I should have known you anywhere. Your daughter favors you."

"All of our children were fortunate to inherit Emmaline's fair looks," proudly declared Bancroft, "save for our Lucy, who is a throwback to my Irish grandmama. A great beauty in her day, Grandmama."

"You have a lovely home here, my lord Ravenaugh," observed Emmaline as she allowed Phelps to help her out of her pelisse. "I should say the setting is most particularly breathtaking. It is, in fact, precisely as Josephine described it in her letters."

"A storybook palace, only draughty no matter what the season," smiled Josephine reminiscently. "I am glad to be here again."

"You are always welcome at Ravenscliff," murmured Ravenaugh, his gimlet-eyed glance having the disconcerting effect of seeming to make her heart turn over beneath her breast. "Your journey, I trust, was uneventful."

"Thanks in large part to your thoughtfulness, my lord," observed Josephine. Hoping her heart was not in her eyes, she made herself look straightly into his dark orbs. "I can never thank you enough for all your many kindnesses. Bringing Mama and Papa and Tom to me was a deal more than I should ever have expected from one who disclaims any tendencies to generosity."

"Indeed, my lord," Regina interjected, a meaningful gleam in the look she bent upon his lordship, "you have outdone yourself this time."

"It was the least I could do for friends, Miss Morseby," returned the earl, remembering the former governess's unshakable belief in himself and Clarissa. How misplaced had been that faith!

Perhaps fortunately for the earl, Clarissa chose just that moment to appear at the head of the stairs. "Jo!" she cried. "Jo, you are here!"

She was hurrying down the stairs in her excitement,

when her eager glance fell on Timothy Powell's tall, masculine figure. Abruptly she slowed to a more seemly pace.

"Jo," she said, going straight up to clasp Josephine's hands. "I thought you would never arrive. And this must be your father, the earl, and Lady Bancroft, your mama." Releasing Josephine's hands, the girl dropped a graceful curtsey. "I have been so looking forward to meeting you, my lord, my lady." She rose, then, and, pointedly ignoring Timothy, turned her dazzling smile on Tom. "I know you must be Captain Thomas Powell. Jo has told me so much about you. Welcome, sir, and everyone, to Ravenscliff."

In all the bustle of unpacking and settling in, not to mention hearing all about Clarissa's contributions toward the decorating of the ball room and Emmaline's insistence that her daughter rest for an hour or two, Josephine was not to see Ravenaugh again before it was time to dress for the evening's entertainments.

Consequently, she was unaware that Emmaline, after wishing her daughter a peaceful repose, set deliberately out to waylay their host.

Coming on Ravenaugh as he was on the point of leaving his study, she did not hesitate to make known her wish to have a moment alone with him.

"I rather thought that you might, my lady," replied Ravenaugh, who, a keen judge of character, could not have failed to comprehend a great deal about the countess from the first moment he laid eyes on her, not the least of which was that she was a lady of quality in the truest sense of the word. More importantly, she was Josephine's mama. He did not doubt that her purpose in seeking him out was to discover his intentions toward her daughter or that she fully intended to point out the obvious unsuitability of so unlikely a match. He, after all, was Ravenaugh, a man, who, besides being considerably older than she could possibly wish for one of Josephine's tender years, was rumored to have, at the very least, driven his wife to her death. The discussion, at least, promised not to last longer than it took for him to assure her he had no intentions at all toward her daughter.

"May I offer you some refreshment, Lady Bancroft?" he asked, when she was seated in one of the two leather-upholstered wing chairs, facing one another before the Adams fireplace. "I'm afraid I haven't any ratafia. Some sherry, perhaps?"

"I should enjoy a glass of sherry, my lord," replied Emmaline, folding her hands in her lap with perfect composure.

If she realized she had surprised him with her response, she gave no indication of it. It came to Ravenaugh, as he poured two glasses of sherry, that Josephine had not come by her formidable strength of character purely by chance. If anything, she was her mama's daughter.

"And, now," said Ravenaugh, handing Emmaline her sherry before taking the seat across from her, "how may I be of service to you?"

Emmaline, studying the earl over the rim of the glass, took a sip of sherry. "You may begin, my lord," she said, settling the glass in the palm of her hand in her lap, "by telling me why you are determined to break my daughter's heart."

Ravenaugh, who had been expecting something rather of a different order, was understandably taken off guard. Having just imbibed a swig of sherry, he was, in fact, hard put not to disgrace himself by choking.

"Forgive me. I realize this must seem all rather sudden to you," continued Emmaline, correctly interpreting the pained expression in her host's watering eyes. "Indeed, you may be certain I meant it to be. For if you must know, there is nothing so effective as the element of surprise in bringing out someone's true feelings in what I fully understand to be a delicate matter. You do not have to tell me that you love her. If it had not been in every word you wrote to us, I should have known it as soon as I saw you look at her. It must follow, then, that you envision some impediment to marrying her. It is that which I have come to hear, my lord."

"I should think it would be obvious, my lady," replied Ravenaugh, having recovered both his breath and his equilibrium. "I am neither a callow youth nor a moonstricken cub. I am a man of eight-and-thirty, a widower with a daughter almost of an age with Josephine." Setting aside the glass of sherry, Ravenaugh unfolded his long length from the chair. Deliberately, he crossed to the fireplace to stand with his elbow propped against the mantelpiece, his head bent as he stared into the fire. "Your daughter, Lady Bancroft, is a beautiful, vibrant young woman. She deserves someone better than a man twice her age. A man, moreover, who has a less than exemplary history behind him."

"I see," said Emmaline, studying Ravenaugh's uncompromising back. "My daughter's happiness is to be sacrificed for a principle. No doubt some would think that a noble act. I, however, consider it selfish and irresponsible."

Ravenaugh's head came up, his glance searching on Emmaline's. "I begin to see," he observed dryly, "from whence comes your daughter's unique outlook on life. Her mother is a remarkable woman. On the other hand, selfish and irresponsible or not, I shall be doing Josephine a favor by leaving her to marry some man more deserving of her."

"No matter that she loves *you?*" queried Emmaline, watching him as she calmly sipped her sherry. "So much so, in fact, that she has professed that she has no wish to live without you?''

Emmaline's reward for that betrayal of her daughter's confidence was a swift blur of pain across the nobleman's harsh countenance, quickly masked behind a cynical front. "She is young. I daresay she believes she is in love now, but she will get over it. If I have learned nothing else from my disreputable past, it is that time is the cure for everything.''

"Time, on the other hand, is not always enough. From what Josephine has told me of your history, I should say you, of all people, should know just how uncertain life is in reality. I wonder if you have stopped to consider how very rare it is for two people to experience such a love as I believe you and Josephine have for one another. It is not something, Lord Ravenaugh, to be flung lightly away for a principle of questionable merit.''

"Perhaps not, Lady Bancroft," Ravenaugh returned. "But then, there are many kinds of love, and love is not always the only consideration. Sometimes a man must weigh duty to others above all else. I regret, ma'am, that I cannot answer you any more plainly than that.''

"I see." Emmaline studied him for a long moment. Ravenaugh, watching her weigh his words, was acutely reminded of Josephine in this very room. "Are you certain, my lord," she said at last, "that this duty of which you speak necessitates sacrificing whatever chance at happiness the two of you might have? I beg you will think carefully before you answer. I have watched over Josephine all her life, never knowing from one year to the next if I might lose her. If I am to see her heart broken, I should like to know it was for a very good reason.''

Ravenaugh met her gaze steadily. "I'm afraid, Countess, that the relative merit of my reasons does not signify. The truth is they are inescapable. I have no choice, but to follow the course that was set for me before I ever met your daughter.''

He saw Emmaline accept his pronouncement. At last, deliberately setting the glass aside, the countess stood. "Then I am sorry for you both. Still, I shall wish the best for you, Ravenaugh," she said, extending her hand to him. "And know my blessings go with you."

She smiled gravely as Ravenaugh released her hand, then, turning, walked to the door.

"Countess."

Emmaline paused.

"I should never intentionally do anything to hurt Josephine. How could I? I do not expect you to believe me. However, it has always been my sincerest hope to spare your daughter."

Emmaline turned her head to look him straightly in the eye. "But I do believe you, my lord," she said simply. "More's the pity." Then, turning, she let herself out the door.

Josephine, staring at her reflection in the ormolu looking glass, felt as if she were caught up in a dream. Certainly she had never looked so well, she decided. But then, she had never before had her hair arranged in a fashionable coiffure by Clara, her mama's abigail, who was an absolute wizard at the art of turning out a fashionably dressed lady. Nor had she ever before worn a gown of ivory satin with seed pearls sewn into a bodice that, having off-the-shoulder puffed sleeves, revealed an inordinate expanse of bare back, neck, shoulders, and bosom. As if to call attention to that fact, the diamond pendant, which her mama had lent her, caught the lamplight with a sparkle. Bemused, Josephine tilted her head to catch the flash of the pendant's matching diamond earrings in her lobes. The diamond tiara that graced her curls had been her great grandmama's and was her papa's contribution to transforming her into a storybook princess.

Josephine smiled gravely at the thought. She had never wished to be a princess, in a storybook or otherwise. She certainly had never asked to be in love. Indeed, if this was love she was feeling, she could very well have done without it. But then, unrequited love must of necessity be different from that which was fulfilled, she reflected logically. The emotions that made one sick at one's stomach with yearning were at least in the latter case resolved so that one could go on about one's life.

Drawing on her limerick gloves, she had just turned away from the looking glass and was looking for the ivory-stick folding fan wrapped in tissue and ribbons that she meant as a gift for Clarissa, when, giving a brief knock on the door, Clarissa burst into the room.

"Jo, how beautiful you are!" she exclaimed. "Just wait until Papa sees you. I daresay his eyes will pop out."

"I shall take that as the very highest of compliments," replied Josephine, laughing. "Come. Let me see you." Drawing the other girl up beside her, she turned so that they were looking at their reflections, side by side, in the looking glass. "There. I daresay there will not be another female to outshine us. I almost feel sorry for Timothy and Thomas. You, my dear girl, are about to dazzle my poor unsuspecting brothers."

And, indeed, Clarissa, in pale rose sarcenet, her dark curls piled on top of her head, was extraordinarily lovely. The very simplicity of her gown and the single strand of pearls about her slender neck along with the pearl drops at her ears could not have been improved upon. Like a rose bud on the point of blossoming, she embodied youth and beauty and innocence.

Josephine, by contrast, was ivory perfection, save for her

eyes. They shone like blue-violet pools—glimmering, deep, and infinitely mysterious. For the first time it came to her what it might mean to be a woman with a woman's power.

Suddenly her head came up, her eyes sparkling dangerously. Perhaps, she thought, it was time Ravenaugh was given an inkling of it, too. She was a Powell, after all, and Powells were not accustomed to giving up in a fight.

Neither girl noticed the small twist of paper that fell from Clarissa's bodice to the floor as the girl gave a gay pirouette about the room; and the ivory-stick folding fan wrapped in tissue and ribbons lay where it was, forgotten, as Clarissa pulled Josephine to the door.

Arm in arm, the two girls made their way downstairs.

Chapter 11

Dinner, preceding the ball was an unusually intimate affair. In addition to Clarissa, Ravenaugh, and the Powell contingent, there were only Miss Harcourt, Lady Juliana, Mr. Lawrence, and Mr., Mrs., and Miss Llewellen in attendance. It was an exceptionally festive meal.

Clarissa, clearly in alt at being the guest of honor on the occasion of her birthday, appeared to sparkle with vitality and not a little of the devil. Seated at the foot of the table, with Lawrence on one side and Timothy on the other, she seemed determined to pit one beau against the other.

Timothy, on the other hand, Josephine could not but note with both pride and amusement, would appear to be equally determined to maintain an imperturbable front before the imperious young beauty and her fancy-dressed

swain. No doubt her brother could comfort himself with
the undeniable fact that his tall, masculine figure showed to
distinct advantage in red and blue regimentals. Certainly,
Lawrence, in spite of the sartorial splendor of his collar,
which aspired to truly stupendous heights, or the singular-
ity of his neckcloth, which lent the impression his head,
rather than depending on a neck to hold it up, rested
solely on the voluminous linen folds of cloth, could not
hold a candle to the handsome young captain. If not even
Lawrence's cossacks, trimmed in ribbons and lace, or his
face, painted and patched, could surpass Captain Timothy
Powell's compellingly military presence, neither could his
barbed wit breach the young officer's civility or shake his
cool unassailability.

Timothy was clearly a soldier on a mission.

If Timothy seemed impervious to Lady Clarissa's sparkling allure, on the other hand, Josephine could not but
note that Thomas appeared quietly enamored of Lady
Juliana's cool wit and sophisticated charm. Josephine had
liked the red-haired beauty before for her originality of
thought; she liked her even more, now, for her disregard
of Thomas's infirmity. Lady Juliana not only gave every
impression of one wholly indifferent to the fact that Josephine's brother was a cripple, but appeared distinctly aware
of him as a man.

In spite of the diversion afforded her by her brothers,
however, Josephine was most acutely aware that there was
one man who outshone all the others both in the quiet
elegance of his dress and in the undeniable charm of his
manner.

Ravenaugh, attired in black evening dress, remarkable
for the perfect fit of the double breasted coat, white mar-
cella waistcoat, and black pantaloons, which, having been
made fashionable by Beau Brummell, particularly suited
the earl's strong air of masculinity, had never looked more

handsome. He had, furthermore, seated Lady Emmaline
and Josephine in the places of honor, one on either side
of him at the head of the table, so that Josephine was in
a uniquely advantageous position to observe him as he
entertained them with *on dits* from London, Paris, Lisbon,
and Madrid. Josephine, who had already had occasion to
see him at his most engaging, watched, fascinated, as he
worked the same spell on Emmaline. Or perhaps the effect
was reciprocal. Josephine's papa had been wont to say, if
Emmaline had not preferred the life of rearing a family
in the country, she could have taken her place in London
at any time as one of the Town's leading hostesses. Seeing
her now, with Ravenaugh, Josephine did not doubt it for
a moment. And if she, herself, might seem in comparison
a trifle provincial, Josephine did not mind. She could only
be proud that Emmaline was her mother and pleased that
two people she dearly loved gave every appearance of a
mutual regard for another.

Had Josephine but known it, her own quiet humor and
ready laughter, not to mention her extraordinary beauty,
worked far greater to her advantage than an entire reper-
toire of fashionable small talk might have done. Ravenaugh, who was keenly aware of it, knew the devastating
effect she was having on him. Indeed, he could not but
think that, after this, he would find it a deal harder to be
a man. Still, he could not regret it. He would have endured
far more to see Josephine, vibrant and beautiful, as she
was on this, their last night together.

It was not until the sweetmeats and jellies had been
sampled and the ladies had risen from the table to leave
the men to their cigars and brandy that Josephine was
reminded of Clarissa's birthday gift, left, forgotten, on the

dressing table. Telling her mama that she would be only a minute, Josephine hurried up the stairs to her room.

Snatching up the birthday gift, she turned to leave, when her glance rested on a folded paper on the floor. She bent to pick it up.

She saw almost at once that it was a note done in a twist. Unfolding it, she was made immediately aware that, addressed to "C," it was a reminder of a meeting that was to take place in the rose garden at midnight. It was signed only "Your devoted M."

Josephine's heart sank. It required very little reasoning to deduce the "C" stood for Clarissa, in which case the "M" could be none other than Michael Lawrence. No doubt Clarissa had dropped the note when she was in the room earlier. Surely Clarissa did not mean to keep such an assignation and on this night of all nights! Clearly, Lawrence, realizing he had a formidable rival in Timothy Powell and, further, that Ravenaugh would never countenance a match between his daughter and a penniless ne'er-do-well, had determined it was time he made his play for the heiress. Very likely he had a curricle and pair ready and waiting for the chance to whisk Clarissa off at a moment's notice to Gretna Green.

Faith, it did not bear thinking on, fumed Josephine. Just when it appeared Clarissa was coming to be on amicable terms with her father, to have this happen. Judging from her previous experiences with the girl, Josephine would not have put it past Clarissa to pull just such a harebrained stunt for the sole purpose of vexing her father. But then, Josephine meant to make sure Ravenaugh never got wind of it. If she could not talk some sense into the girl, Josephine would not hesitate to elicit Timothy's aid to prevent Clarissa from keeping her assignation with Lawrence.

Intending to corner the girl at once, Josephine wasted

little time rejoining the ladies in the withdrawing room. Crossing straight to Clarissa, who was sitting with Miss Llewellen, she presented the gift, saying, "Many happy returns of the day, Clarissa, dear."

Clarissa, clapping her hands together in delight, hardly had the look of a female scheming to elope, reflected Josephine dryly. Fairly ripping the tissue away, she appeared at the moment little more than an eager child.

"Jo, it is lovely," exclaimed the girl, obviously delighted with the exquisitely hand-painted velum mount on ivory sticks. "And it goes perfectly with my gown." Slipping the strap over her wrist, she beamed up at Josephine. "I do love it, Jo. Thank you ever so much."

"You are quite welcome." Josephine was on the point of adding that she would like to have a word with Clarissa in private, when the door, opening, heralded the arrival of the gentlemen. As Timothy and Lawrence wasted little time taking up positions on either side of Clarissa, Josephine was forced to content herself with waiting for another opportunity to have the girl to herself.

That opportunity did not present itself before the ball began, and, afterwards, it was utterly impossible to draw the girl away from the bevy of admirers who clustered around her. Clarissa was, after all, not only exceedingly well to look up, but she was also the Earl of Ravenaugh's only daughter and therefore heir to a considerable fortune. Undoubtedly, not of a few of the young bloods in attendance at the earl's ball were keenly aware of the opportunity afforded them to make an impression on the heiress before she officially entered, with her come-out in London the following Season, the lists of marriageable females.

Josephine had no better luck with Timothy, who, appearing to be holding his own not only with Clarissa, but with any number of the other females present, had yet to think of his sister, sitting on the sidelines with her mother.

Josephine, herself, was not to be allowed to remain a wallflower for very long. Hardly had the promenade ended, than the strains of a waltz filled the air. Experiencing a sudden and immediate presentiment, she glanced up—and was rewarded with the sight of Ravenaugh's tall, elegant figure striding toward her with cool deliberation, his intent unmistakable not only to her, but to everyone in the ballroom.

She experienced a mingling of emotions, chief of which were a thrill of pride that he would deliberately single her out for his attentions in front of the three hundred guests present, and an unwitting flutter of her heart at the thought that soon she would be waltzing in the arms of the man of whom she had always dreamed, but never expected to meet. Rebelliously, she quelled the small, persistent voice that whispered that this would be her only dance with Ravenaugh or that somehow she must make the next moments last a lifetime. Whatever came would come. She would not spoil the moment by thinking ahead.

Then Ravenaugh had come to a halt before her.

"Lady Josephine."

Josephine smiled gravely up at him. "My lord?"

"I believe I have the honor of this dance."

"Indeed, my lord, I have been looking forward to it." Placing her hand in his waiting palm, she stood.

It was just as she had always dreamed it would be—the lilting strains of the waltz, the man gazing down at her as if he had eyes only for her, the sense that everyone in the room was looking at them alone—and yet how different from anything she had ever imagined. Surely, nothing could have prepared her for the shock of feeling Ravenaugh's strong masculine arm slip around her waist or his long, supple fingers lightly envelop her hand. How small

and fragile she felt next to his powerful frame! And yet
how secure in his embrace! She had never experienced
anything remotely like that before, certainly not when she
had practiced the waltz with her oldest brother William,
who had taught her her steps when she was only twelve.
It occurred to her that she must be sadly lacking in morals.
Shamelessly, she wished that he might hold her more
closely!

Then Ravenaugh lifted her into the movement of the
dance, and Josephine had the most peculiar sensation of
floating away into a marvelous place where time was a
whirling rhythm of motion. She felt marvelously weightless,
magically tireless, as if she might have lived on forever in
the dance, forever locked in Ravenaugh's embrace. They
did not speak. They did not have to; their eyes, exchanging
an endless embrace, said it all.

The music came to an end, and Josephine, still in the
grips of the dream, stared, uncomprehendingly, as Ravenaugh, holding her with his eyes, raised both of her hands
to his lips. Then with a vague sense of unreality she became
aware that time had stopped and that Ravenaugh was leading her back to her mama.

After her single waltz with Ravenaugh, Josephine was
not to be left alone either to savor the fulfillment of a
dream or to mourn its fleeting nature. She could not but
find it ironic that Ravenaugh, in singling her out for his
attentions, had made her an instant success. But then, that
had undoubtedly been his intention all along, she told
herself, as she found herself surrounded by gentlemen
imploring her for the favor of a dance. While she did not
fool herself into believing she would have attracted such
flattering notice had it not been for Ravenaugh, she could
not but find the unexpected circumstance of her popular-

ity appealed to something distinctly feminine in her. She enjoyed the illusion of being thought beautiful and charming, and she found she liked dancing even more than she had imagined.

No doubt she would have been surprised to learn she had caught the attention of a large number of the male contingent before ever Ravenaugh signaled his approval of her. Certainly she would have scoffed had anyone told her that, having been found to be not the least high in the instep, but, on the contrary, refreshingly unaffected and possessed of unexceptional manners, she had been judged by males and females alike as not only a diamond of the first water, but an Incomparable and an Original.

For a while Josephine quite forgot herself in the novelty of twirling about the dance floor and engaging in light repartee with any number of attractive gentlemen. And if she found herself more than once looking over the crowded dance floor for a tall, languorous figure in black evening clothes, she did manage to enjoy herself. She derived so much pleasure, in fact, dancing the reel with a retired colonel of the Royal Horseguards, that for a quarter of an hour, she quite forgot all about Clarissa and the time.

The arrival of the supper dance jolted her to a belated awareness that the hour of Clarissa's tryst with Lawrence was already upon her. With a sinking sensation in the pit of her stomach, she searched the crowd for Clarissa—in vain. Neither Lawrence nor the girl was anywhere to be found. Even worse, Timothy, too, it seemed, had vanished into thin air.

Faith, what a fool she had been to think Ravenaugh could be kept in the dark! Clearly she must tell him now. Indeed, she had already put it off too long. But where the devil was he?

Josephine, startled by the light touch of a hand on her

arm and a feminine voice pronouncing her name, nearly jumped.

"Why, Jo, dear. What is it?" Miss Harcourt exclaimed in instant concern.

"Faith you startled me," breathed Josephine, a hand over her heart. "But never mind. I need a favor of you, Felicia."

"Why, anything, Jo. You know that." Seeing Josephine extract a small twist of paper from one of her gloves, Miss Harcourt smiled knowingly. "Indeed, my dear, I should be happy to help you. Only say what I must do."

"Find Ravenaugh for me. Give him this and tell him he is needed at once in the rose garden. Please, no questions. There isn't time to explain. It is, however, extremely important that you find his lordship without delay."

"But of course, Jo. I shall do so at once. But where are you going?" Miss Harcourt called after Josephine's retreating form.

"I shall be waiting in the garden. Hurry, Felicia," Josephine admonished over her shoulder. "Before it is too late."

Josephine, slipping out the French windows, which led out on to the terrace, could not but reflect that she had very likely just ruined her reputation and probably compromised Ravenaugh in the process. Miss Harcourt obviously believed Josephine had summoned the earl to the garden for a tryst. Better Josephine's reputation than Clarissa's, however, and, if Ravenaugh felt compelled to make it right with Josephine by insisting on offering for her, then so be it. She would deal with that problem if and when it should arise. She had other, far more pressing, concerns at the moment.

She would never forgive herself if she was too late to save Clarissa from Lawrence. And where in heaven's name was Timothy? Had he followed Clarissa? Good God, either

Timothy or Lawrence might be lying somewhere hurt this very minute, or worse—one of them might be dead! And it would be all her fault. Faith, it did not bear thinking on.

Josephine, however, could think of little else as she crossed the terrace and, hurrying down the steps and across the lawn, came to the gate that led into the Rose Garden. On the far side of the garden, she recalled, was another gate, which opened into the deer park and the path that led to the falls. There had been a track, as well, that led away from the cliffs, a track that had been sufficiently wide for a light carriage.

Hardly knowing what she would do should she come across the runaways, Josephine picked up her skirts and began to run. Perhaps at the very least, she could force Lawrence to take her with him. With her along to play gooseberry, there was every possibility she could save both Clarissa's honor and her reputation. She refused to think of the more dire possibility that Lawrence might simply knock her alongside the head and make off alone with his coveted heiress.

She never saw the thing lying across the path. One moment she was hurrying through the darkness, and the next she was sprawled face down on the ground. Stunned, it was a moment before she could drag herself to her knees. Only, then, in horror, did she realize that what she had stumbled over was a man's body. A wave of relief washed over her as she found, not the buttons and cords of a regimental uniform, but the satin and lace of a dandy. Lawrence! Thank heavens, too, that he was alive, she breathed, going nearly weak with the discovery of a steady pulse at the wrist.

Her first thought was that Timothy must, indeed, have followed Clarissa. No doubt there had been a struggle in which Timothy rendered Lawrence unconscious. The question was, where were Timothy and Clarissa now? Surely, had Timothy taken the girl back to the manor, Josephine would have met them on the path. Unless, of course, someone else had seen fit to land the dandy a facer, in which case, who could have done it and why?

An answer to at least one of those puzzling questions came far sooner than she could possibly have anticipated. Hardly had she climbed painfully to her feet, than she heard a step behind her. Ravenaugh! she thought with a wild leap of joy and started to turn.

The next instant, a cloth, sopping wet and reeking in fumes was clamped over her mouth and nose. Fighting for air, she beat feebly against a masculine chest. Then darkness closed in on her, and that was the last that she knew.

"I am not angry, *enfant,*" Ravenaugh said with a steely calm. "I am simply trying to discover where Miss Powell has gone. Unfortunately, this note is the only clue I have."

"But I never went to the garden, I swear it, Papa," declared Clarissa, clinging to Timothy's hand. "I-I confess I considered it, but only because I was stupidly angry with Ti—with Captain Powell. I'm afraid I was quite beside myself."

"It was all my fault, my lord," broke in Timothy soberly. "That last day in Harrogate, I behaved like a boor. It is true, however, that Lady Clarissa never kept that assignation. She courageously came to me and confessed the whole. We were just coming to tell you about it, when Ridings found us. Are you certain, sir, that my sister is nowhere to be found in the house? She still tires rather easily. Has anyone thought to check her room?"

Ravenaugh, grim-faced, crushed the incriminating note in his fist.

They were gathered in the earl's study—Ravenaugh,

Clarissa, and the anxious Powells, and they were all looking to the Lord of Ravenscliff to resolve the mystery of Josephine's disappearance. Ravenaugh swung away to the fire in the fireplace to hide the bleak look in his eyes. "Lady Josephine is not in her chambers. At present, the servants are searching every room in the house. It would seem our best hope, however, is Lawrence. Unfortunately, he would seem to have suffered a concussion. It is not at all certain when he will come around."

"Might I suggest, then, my lord," spoke up Bancroft gravely, "that we institute an immediate search of the grounds. I understand your reluctance to alert the other guests that my daughter is missing. However, if some evil has befallen her, the last thing that should concern us is the possibility of scandal. We must find Josephine at once."

"If anything has happened to Josephine, it is all my fault." All eyes were drawn instantly to Regina, wringing her hands in distraction. "I should never have agreed to keep silent," Regina continued, "not when I knew she was in deadly peril. I should have insisted she inform you, my lord. But she would have me wait until after the ball."

Ravenaugh's hard gaze softened on the distraught spinster. "Inform me of what, Miss Morseby?" he asked quietly.

"Why, that she had proof your cousin was the one who poisoned her. She sent Wiggens to the Old Chemist Shop in Knaresborough, my lord. The very day she fell ill, Saint-Clair purchased devil's trumpet, a poisonous plant native to India. It is used in ritual murders and human sacrifice and has been associated with witchcraft for simply ages. I should have recognized the symptoms and put two and two together myself, but I was that worried about Jo that I simply never made the connection."

"But how should you, Regina?" said Lady Emmaline, clasping her sister's hands. "You had enough on your mind, surely. You must not blame yourself for what has happened.''

''But I do blame myself. Josephine thought it all out. Saint-Clair had my tea drugged with a sleeping potion to make sure I should not stay awake. I daresay it was a simple matter to bribe a servant at the inn to do it for him. Then he let himself in through the secret panel in Josephine's room and dosed her barley-water with poison. I have yet to determine to what use he put the opium. It could not have been to render me harmless. I should have recognized immediately the narcotic odor and bitter taste of the drug. And I daresay he did not give it to Josephine. After all, the devil's trumpet should have been sufficient to his ends.''

''I don't understand. Are you saying Cousin Adam poisoned Josephine?'' Clarissa demanded incredulously. ''But he could not have done. Tell them, Papa. Cousin Adam would never do such a thing.''

Ravenaugh stood at the center of the room, his eyes glittery hard. No, Saint-Clair had not dropped the poison in the glass, but he had poisoned Josephine nonetheless. What a fool he was to think that Clarissa, even in one of her queer spells, could have pulled the thing off. Clearly, his fear for Josephine and his desire to protect his daughter had clouded his thinking. But no more. He must find Josephine before Saint-Clair finished what he had started.

''*Papa?*''

Clarissa's impassioned cry was like a knife thrust to the heart. Clarissa! he thought. She was a victim as much as was Josephine. ''You are overwrought, Clarissa.'' Ravenaugh remained with his back to her. ''I suggest you retire. We shall discuss this in the morning.''

Clarissa bridled with indignation. ''I am not a child, Papa. If Jo is in trouble, I wish to stay and do what I can to help.''

At that, Ravenaugh did come around. "Then you will do as I *say.*" His face assumed a chiseled hardness. *"Now,* Clarissa."

Clarissa stared at him, her eyes wide with hurt and shocked disbelief. Then with a muffled sob, she spun on her heel and fled from the room.

Timothy, glancing hard at Ravenaugh, started after her. He was stopped by Ravenaugh's hand on his arm. "Yes, do follow her, Captain. Stay with her. See that she does not leave the house."

Timothy's look of baffled anger faded before the earl's steady regard. "You may be certain of it, my lord," he said at last, firmly. Then, turning on his heel, he went in pursuit of Clarissa.

Ravenaugh strode to the door and opened it. "I have asked Phelps to question the servants. Perhaps one of them saw something. In the meantime I must ask you to excuse me."

"My lord," said Thomas Powell, who had remained noticeably quiet throughout. "What of this cousin of yours—Saint-Clair? Do you know where he is to be found?"

"As it happens, I do not make it a habit to monitor my cousin's movements." Ravenaugh's steely glance met Thomas's. "You may be sure, however, that I intend to find him."

Ravenaugh left them with that chilling assurance. Moments later, he let himself out of the house by way of the servants' entrance. Grimly, he retraced his earlier steps through the garden. Without pausing, he strode past the place where he had discovered Lawrence lying unconscious. Then letting himself through the second gate, he struck grimly across the deer park.

If Adam had Josephine, there would be only one place he could have taken her.

* * *

Josephine's first dawning awareness was of a dull, throbbing headache and the feeling that her mouth had been stuffed with cotton. Her next was that she was lying on an exceedingly hard surface of rock. There was a rushing in her ears, too, that she recognized but could not immediately place.

The devil, she thought, memory coming back to her. She shuddered, recalling the clamp of a hand with a wet, reeking cloth over her mouth. Someone had deliberately rendered her unconscious and brought her—where? With a groan, she pushed herself up into a sitting position and looked around her.

Even in the darkness lit only by a quarter moon, she recognized the bare outcropping of rock and the plunge of water off the cliffs. He had brought her to the falls. Why?

"So you are awake at last are you? I thought perhaps you would not be coming back. One can never be certain how a patient will react to the effects of sacred datura. I have seen victims of Indian thugs drop like flies, while others go quite insane for several days at a time. You, my dear, would appear to be a deal stronger than you look. I fully expected you to die in Knaresborough."

"No doubt I am sorry to disappoint you, Doctor Saint-Clair," Josephine said thickly, her mouth dry from the effects of the drug. "I daresay I owe my survival to my aunt's herbal remedies."

"It is doubtful that your aunt's folk remedies had anything to do with it," scoffed Saint-Clair, who was sitting cross-legged in the manner of an Indian snake charmer across from Josephine. "The truth is, I had to be very careful to keep the doses small. The cumulative effect would eventually have done the job quite nicely. Unfortunately, my cousin with the help of your aunt came to the realization that your illness was not of an organic nature. I should no doubt have been caught administering the fatal dose had I not run into Clarissa that very day.''

"Clarissa told you Ravenaugh and my brother were standing guard in my room?" exclaimed Josephine, considerably enlightened.

"The naive little fool was always of a confiding nature, and so splendidly vulnerable to suggestion. I found her as a child to be an ideal candidate for my experiments in animal magnetism. She responded beautifully to my every instruction. I came home to discover my influence over her was not in the least diminished, especially with the help of a little opium. She was easily induced to administer the final dose of poison to your barley-water with her father as a convenient witness. Amusing, don't you think? I'm sure poor Devon is now wholly convinced his daughter is the victim of homicidal madness.''

Josephine, who did not see anything the least amusing in that particular revelation, nevertheless could not but find a great many things were suddenly clear to her.

"And Lady Ravenaugh. Was she one of your subjects for experimentation, too, Doctor? Did you induce her to leap from the falls while in a state of somnambulism?''

Saint-Clair smiled in cold amusement. "Hardly, my dear. I'm afraid Eugenie was far more difficult. You see, she actually loved my cousin. When I tried to seduce her and failed, I was compelled to force my attentions on her. The little fool threatened to go to Devon with what I had done. I really could not allow that, now could I. It would have ruined all my plans.''

"Your plans?" echoed Josephine, staring in horrified fascination at Saint-Clair.

"Revenge, Miss Powell. Retribution. My father left me with money sufficient to my needs, but Devon had everything that I wanted, everything that should have been mine. All the things my father could not give me. Devon was the bloody usurper. Why should he be happy, while I was cursed to be a nobody, a by-blow, a man without a name or an identity? I determined early on I should be better off as Doctor Adam Saint-Clair in India than as the late Earl of Ravenaugh's bastard son in England. And I did it, too. I was accepted by princes and potentates for my brilliance as a healer. Before I left Ravenscliff, however, I made sure everything Devon had was turned bitter to the taste.''

"And so you made him think you and Lady Ravenaugh were lovers, and you threatened harm to Clarissa if the countess told Ravenaugh the truth. But even that was not enough. You turned his daughter against him, too. You fed her lies about him. You manipulated her. You made sure everything in Ravenaugh's life was turned to dross. But then what happened? Did you find out it was not enough? You killed Lady Ravenaugh. Why?''

"Because she was going to tell him the truth. I knew the deception could not last forever. That night he came to her in a rage over my carefully planted lies. Devon, who could never be broken no matter what my father did to him—the humiliation, the loathing, the punishments. He took it all like the bloody stoic that he was. He broke that night, however. He left in a rage, swearing he would kill the man who had dishonored his wife. She ran after him, intending, no doubt, to stop him. I was waiting for her. I had my plans all laid. I had passage booked to India. All that remained was to destroy the last shred of faith between Devon and his beloved Eugenie. I took her and I pushed her off the falls, just as I am going to do with you.''

Rising, he crossed to stand over her. "A pity you had to meddle in things that did not concern you. Clarissa was meant to be the one they found at the bottom of the cliff in the morning. But you will do as well. Better, perhaps. Poor Devon. As if it were not enough that his only daughter is mad and a murderer, but he must lose the only two women he ever loved. First Eugenie and now you. I daresay it will drive him to madness. On your feet, girl.''

Dragging her up, Saint-Clair shoved her toward the edge of the cliff.

"You are the one who is mad," cried Josephine, backing before him. "This time there will be no question of suicide. My aunt has proof it was you who tried to poison me. Ravenaugh will come after you, and this time he will find you."

"But of course he will. Indeed, I am counting on it. I have nothing to lose. You see, I am dying, Miss Powell. A wasting sickness I contracted in India. When Devon kills me, he will be doing me a favor.'' Lunging for her, Saint-Clair caught Josephine by the wrists. "I shall go to hell, happy in the knowledge that the scaffold will soon despatch my cousin to join me."

Josephine, struggling in Saint-Clair's clasp, felt her foot slip toward the edge. A scream rose to her throat. She was going to die, just as Lady Ravenaugh had died, just as one day, so long ago it now seemed, she had envisioned Clarissa, plunging off the falls to the rocks below. In horror, she saw the leap of triumph in Saint-Clair's eyes.

"It is over." His lips curled in a grin terrible to behold. "I shall tell Devon, when I see him, that you believed in him to the end."

"I am here—now, Saint-Clair. Behind you."

The voice—Ravenaugh's voice—was a bloodless murmur that carried above the din of the falls.

Saint-Clair stiffened, the terrible smile frozen on his lips, as a hand clamped hard on his shoulder.

"Let her go, Adam."

"You may be sure that I fully intend to. And, when I do,

she will go over the cliff to her death. Wish her goodbye, Devon.''

Josephine's terrified eyes met Ravenaugh's across Saint-Clair's shoulder.

"You always were a bad actor," said the earl with pointed significance.

Josephine sustained a wild leap of joy as it came to her— the one thing she might do to help.

"Oh, you may be sure this is not an act, Cousin," Saint-Clair grinned, his intentions quite obvious.

The next instant, Josephine sagged, a dead weight in Saint-Clair's grip.

All in a flash, Saint-Clair's hold broke. Josephine dropped to her elbows and knees on the rock floor of the ledge. Ravenaugh hauled Saint-Clair back, away from the cliff, and, spinning him around, landed him a bone-crunching right to the jaw.

Crawling on hands and knees away from the cliff-edge, Josephine saw Saint-Clair land, asprawl on the ground, saw Ravenaugh turn his back on the downed man and step toward her.

It was all a terrible dream. Saint-Clair shoving himself to his feet, his eyes, burning with hatred and madness, as he gathered himself for the leap. Ravenaugh, his back to his cousin, his eyes on Josephine. A scream welled up in Josephine's throat.

"Ravenaugh, behind you!"

Ravenaugh spun about. Saint-Clair launched himself bodily at Ravenaugh. Ravenaugh, ducking beneath Saint-Clair's hurling assault, rammed a shoulder hard into Saint-Clair's midsection. In sickening horror Josephine saw Saint-Clair stagger back, saw his face contorted in loathing as he struggled to regain his balance at the edge of the precipice. Ravenaugh lunged forward, reaching in vain for his kinsman. A terrible scream, high-pitched with horrified

realization, etched itself in her memory. Then abruptly
there was the silence, filled only by the din of the falls.

Josephine, clinging to consciousness, knew when
Ravenaugh dropped to his knees beside her. How grim
was the look in his eyes as, wordlessly, he lifted her in his
arms to carry her away from that dreadful place!

"Devon, darling. Pray do not look at me like that! I am
all right, truly. It was all your cousin. Clarissa never knew
what she was doing." She laid her hand against the side
of his face. "Do you hear me, my dearest? No matter what
you witnessed in my room that night, she is neither mad
nor a murderess."

"Hush, mad little fool," Ravenaugh rumbled deep in
his throat. "What I did not hear Adam confess, I had
already figured out for myself. It is over now, finished."

"Not quite, my lord. You still do not know about your
wife. It was never a suicide. Saint-Clair pushed her over
the falls. She loved you. She meant to tell you everything.
Saint-Clair wanted you to carry the blame for what was to
appear a suicide. He wanted you to go your whole life
believing you drove your wife to her death."

Ravenaugh, coming to a halt in the shelter of the trees,
held her with one arm while he allowed her feet to slip to
the earth. His eyes in the pale glow of moonlight brought
an ache to her throat.

"No doubt I should have done just that, had it not been
for you and your aunt. I was prepared to accept exile with
Clarissa to rid myself of Ravenscliff's legacy of malicious-
ness and hate. Then you dropped into my life—an indomitable angel of light amid all the darkness." His lips twisting
in a mirthless smile, he brushed a smudge of dirt from the
tip of her nose. "Impossible child. You cannot know what
you have put me through with your stubborn insistence
that we should suit, no matter that I am twice your age."

Josephine felt a melting pang in her midsection at the

tender light in the look he bent upon her then. Poor, dear Ravenaugh. He really must get over the absurd notion that he was too old for her. "But next year, my darling," she did not hesitate to instruct him as, daringly, she lifted her arms about the back of his neck, "you will be less than twice my age, and every year after that the difference will decrease practically exponentially until one day, when we are both old and grey, there will be hardly any difference at all. Now, don't you think you have waited long enough to kiss me? And pray do not try and tell me that you do not wish to. In case you have forgotten, I am gifted with a keen insight into people. I can see very well that you do."

"Little devil," growled Ravenaugh, who, still suffering an unbearable pressure in his chest occasioned by the sight of Josephine struggling with Saint-Clair at the edge of the precipice, tightened his arms around her. "Thanks to you and your propensity for flirting with death, I am a deal closer to being old and grey than I was before your coach nearly collided with my curricle."

Josephine, far from being in the least intimidated at the possibility of having the breath crushed from her, tenderly brushed a disheveled lock from Ravenaugh's forehead. "Then all the more reason to marry me—now, my lord, *before* you grow any older. For, if you must know, I have decided that what Ravenscliff requires is a whole parcel of boisterous Roths to make it a real home. You may begin by kissing me, my darling, and then we shall see about obtaining a special license. I do not intend to wait a day longer than is necessary to see you legshackled. Life, I have discovered, is far too short to waste even a minute of it arguing over things that do not signify in the least."

"Jade," rumbled Ravenaugh, feeling himself growing younger by the moment. "I have yet to ask you to marry me."

"Oh, but you are going to," said Josephine, taking advantage of what she perceived to be the weakening of his defenses to brazenly press her lips to the silver over his temple. "Or if you cannot bring yourself to come up to scratch, I shall be happy to ask you instead, my dearest lord. After all, between two kindred spirits, a proposal is only a rather silly formality. We have both been aware almost from that first moment of sublime illumination that our marriage was practically an inevitability."

"Impertinent brat." Ravenaugh, pushed beyond even the limits of his formidable powers of self-control, gave vent to a groan and covered her lips ruthlessly with his own. Only then, as the last bastions of his resolve tumbled before Josephine's sweet, unbridled response, did he feel the cold grip of horror loosen its hold on his vitals. Adam was dead, and the darkness that had weighed upon Ravenaugh's soul for all the interminable years was to be dispelled at last by a small slip of a girl whose gentle, but enduring spirit was greater than all of his bleak memories of Ravenscliff and whose understanding was surpassed only by her unlimited capacity for love.

Josephine, who had been waiting a seeming eternity for Ravenaugh's capitulation, was amply rewarded for her perseverance and patience. Indeed, she felt shaken to the core by her dearest lord's unbridled passion. Never had she known such need or such aching tenderness as she sensed then in Ravenaugh. And when at last he released her to kiss her eyes, her cheeks, and her lips again, she knew even without his low, anguished words of love that she had found her Greensward and that it was real and lasting, unlike the wisp of a dream that vanishes before the dawning of reality.

Epilogue

It was a late afternoon in September, and Greensward, sparkling like a gem in the midst of the green, rolling fields, reverberated with the shrieks and gurgles of children at play on the lawn, while their mamas, seated in lawn chairs beneath an awning, talked and watched over them.

"Lawrence," Josephine was saying to her sisters, "confessed that Saint-Clair bribed him to pursue Clarissa, even going so far as to have Lawrence slip her the note setting up the tryst in the rose garden at Ravenscliff. It seems, however, that when Lawrence realized what Saint-Clair intended, he balked at becoming involved in a kidnapping."

"I see. Carrying an heiress off to Gretna Green to force her into marriage falls in a different category from abducting one for purely nefarious purposes," Lucy, the Duchess of Lathrop, humorously extrapolated.

"It would seem so, at least where Mr. Lawrence was concerned," Josephine laughed. "There was an argument, and Saint-Clair bludgeoned Lawrence."

"Upon which, you came along and stumbled over him," speculated Francie, the Countess of Ransome, reaching down to lift her eighteen-month-old daughter, Olivia, into her lap. "I daresay you saved Lawrence's life, Jo. Surely, Saint-Clair never intended to leave Lawrence alive to be a witness against him."

"But what about Lady Clarissa?" demanded Florence, the Marchioness of Leighton. "If she saw Saint-Clair throw her mama over the cliff, why did he leave her alive? He surely could not have known she would remember none of it."

"Perhaps she did not actually see him push her mama off the falls," Josephine theorized. "When she followed Lady Ravenaugh out of the house and through the deer park, perhaps she only heard her mama scream and caught merely a glimpse of her hurtling off the cliff. Then, after-wards, it is possible Saint-Clair came upon Clarissa and made sure she remembered none of it by putting her into a sonambulistic state through the power of suggestion. No doubt he told her it was all only a dream. Very likely he would suggest that, when she awakened, she would not remember any of it."

"Which, one must presume," Lucy interjected, "is why she could remember slipping down to the Music Room to overhear her mama and papa arguing, but nothing of what came after. Oh, Patrick, dear," she called to the seven-year-old heir of Lathrop, who, having chased Snippet under a bush, was attempting to drag the kitten out by the tail. "Play nicely with the cat. You would not want someone to pull you by the tail."

"I haven't a tail, Mama," observed the slender youngster with hair the color of ravens' wings and eyes the grey-green of the mist on the moors.

"No, but if you did have one, you may be sure you would take exception to having it pulled," his mama persisted.

She watched as the boy released his hold, and, crawling under the bush, retrieved the kitten in a rather more humane manner.

"Well, *I* think it must have been the shock of what she had seen more than any power of suggestion that caused Lady Clarissa to forget," Francie postulated with a puckish frown. Dropping a kiss on the top of her squirming daughter's head, she set the little girl down and watched her toddle away to plop down beside her two-year-old cousin, Lord Montescue, who was the heir apparent to the Marquess of Leighton. "I find it difficult to believe one could forget something like that because of a suggestion."

"Oh, but it is apparently scientifically sound," Josephine countered. "In spite of the fact that Franz Mesmer's theories of animal magnetism have fallen into disrepute of recent years, artificially induced somnambulistic states have been documented. It seems, furthermore, that Clarissa, was beginning to remember more and more of what happened. Things kept popping up in her dreams. I believe she was unwittingly playing out one of those fantasies the day she lured me to the falls. In retrospect, I realize that it was all a desperate plea for help."

"Well, I find the entire subject of flinging people off cliffs perfectly dreadful," Florence said with a shudder. "I should much rather talk about weddings and babies. Who would ever have thought our Jo would be the one to elope, or that, apparently inspired by Josephine's example, Aunt Reggie is even now on her way to London to marry Colonel Bickerstaff."

"I always knew you would have a grand, glorious adventure one day, Jo," professed Francie, beaming at the youngest of the Powell sisters. "I never thought you would turn out to be a matchmaker, however, and one on such a grand scale. Here we are gathered to celebrate Tom's engagement to Lady Juliana, and, if Lady Clarissa does not drive

Timothy to distraction, I daresay there will be another wedding announcement no later than next June."

"Which leaves only one Powell yet to be induced into Parson's Mousetrap," Lucy pointed out. "Will."

Instantly Josephine's face lit up. "We shall all have to put our heads together, just as we were used to do whenever the boys tried to gang up on us."

"But of course," instantly agreed Florence, who was already mentally checking off a list of marriageable females. "I daresay among the four of us, we can come up with a suitable candidate for Will."

Francie exchanged a conspiratorial glance with each of her sisters. "Will is almost seven-and-twenty," she said. "We simply cannot allow the heir to turn into a confirmed bachelor."

"Heavens, no," exclaimed Josephine, thinking of the bourne teeming with fish waiting to be caught and the stables populated with horses waiting to be ridden and the attic room filled with memories waiting to be added to. "Greensward would not be Greensward without at least the promise that there will be a whole brood of boisterous Powells to take up where we left off. Mama and Papa simply would not know what do with themselves here, alone."

Emmaline, strolling arm and arm with Bancroft out of the house and across the lawn, gave a startled gurgle of laughter as the earl pulled her without warning into the entrance of the evergreen maze and, pinning her in his arms, held her a willing captive.

"It occurs to me my dearest Emmaline that it has been nearly twenty-eight years since you and I were truly alone together. It seems to me I remember a time when you and I talked about seeing something of the world."

"As I recall," Emmaline said, smiling with the recollection, "we were on the point of purchasing a yacht with the intention of sailing around the world rather in the manner of sea gypsies. Only I discovered I was increasing, and six months later we had Lucy."

"Exactly my point. It is time we did something for ourselves. Just the two of us, my love. Now that the children are all grown, what could there possibly be to stop us from taking off for the south of France, say, for a second honeymoon? Or a walking tour in the Alps, perhaps. Or anywhere your heart desires. You have only to name it, and it is done."

Emmaline gave a startled laugh. "This is all so sudden, William. I hardly know what to say. There is Thomas's wedding in November. After that is Christmas. We shall naturally wish to be home for the Yule Tide. All the children are planning to come. And then in March, Josephine is to have her lying in. Our eighth grandchild, William, and it is Josephine's. You cannot wish me to miss that. And then there is—"

What it was that was to come after the birth of Josephine's first child, Emmaline was not allowed to say. Bancroft covered her lips with his, a method of silencing her that Emmaline did not find in the least objectionable.

"My dearest Emmaline," Bancroft murmured some moments later, nibbling at an exposed earlobe, "do you not think it is time we let go? They are all adults now. We are perfectly free to live our own lives."

"I was not aware that we were not living our own lives, William," replied Emmaline, tilting her head to one side to allow him greater leeway in his delectable explorations. "The past thirty years have been everything I should have hoped for, and more."

"Have they, my dearest?" queried Bancroft, cradling her face between his palms. "No man could have been happier than I. I have wondered at times, however, if you did not regret our life in the country. You were used to be quite fond of the theatre and the opera, not to mention the museums and all the other things the City has to offer."

Emmaline gazed, smiling, up into his eyes, lit with an inner fire for her alone. "Then you may cease to wonder. I have not regretted a single moment. How could I? We have always shared everything, William. How many women can claim that sort of intimacy with their husbands?"

"Then you do not mind that we shall be alone now at Greensward?" he said, folding her to him in his arms.

"Alone?" Emmaline echoed, thinking of all the golden years before them which they could fill in any manner they chose to do. "We are never alone, surely, my dearest. Not so long as we have each other."

ABOUT THE AUTHOR

Sara Blayne lives with her family in Portales, New Mexico. She is the author of eight Zebra Regency romances. Sara loves hearing from her readers and you may write to her c/o Zebra Books. Please include a self-addressed stamped envelope if you wish a response.